Richard asked her to dance.

'Why did you not tell your aunt and sister you had met me when I am so obviously a subject for their tattle?' he demanded as the opening bars of the music signalled that he should execute a sweeping bow.

Georgiana looked up into his dark eyes and felt them searing into her, just as they had done once before, and she found herself growing weak. How dared he make her feel like that, as if she hadn't a bone in her body? Thankfully the dance separated them, but he returned to the subject as soon as they came together again. 'What have you to hide?'

Born in Singapore, **Mary Nichols** came to England when she was three, and has spent most of her life in different parts of East Anglia. She has been a radiographer, school secretary, information officer and industrial editor, as well as a writer. She has three grown-up children and four grandchildren.

TO WIN
THE LADY

Mary Nichols

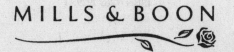

All the characters in this book have no existence outside the imagination of the author, and have no relation whatsoever to anyone bearing the same name or names. They are not even distantly inspired by any individual known or unknown to the author, and all the incidents are pure invention.

MILLS & BOON, the Rose Device and LEGACY OF LOVE are trademarks of the publisher.
Harlequin Mills & Boon Limited,
Eton House, 18–24 Paradise Road, Richmond, Surrey TW9 1SR
This edition published by arrangement with
Harlequin Enterprises B.V.

© Mary Nichols 1995

ISBN 0 263 79295 1

Set in 10 on 12 pt Linotron Times
04-9509-82995

Typeset in Great Britain by CentraCet, Cambridge
Printed in Great Britain by
BPC Paperbacks Ltd

AUTHOR'S NOTE

IN 1831 Squire George Osbaldestone, reputedly the finest athlete in the early part of the nineteenth century, completed a historic two-hundred mile ride round the four-mile long Newmarket Round Course in 8 hours 42 minutes 40 seconds, using twenty-eight horses. I assume this ride was inspired by Dick Turpin's legendary ride from London to York a century before, which is also two hundred miles.

In 1993, the jockey Peter Scudamore attempted to beat that long-standing record on the same course, using fifty horses. He succeeded by a mere 4 minutes 49 seconds.

My story, set in 1815, a few years earlier than Osbaldestone's ride, has been inspired by these rides, although I have made it more difficult for my hero by having the ride take place on the road, which is how Dick Turpin would have done it.

CHAPTER ONE

MRS BERTRAM was decidedly miffed. It was not so much that there had been no one to greet her, for she was not expected and it was late in the afternoon, but to be told by a servant that she would like as not find Miss Paget in the stable was the outside of enough! What was the world coming to when a visitor was expected to go in search of her hostess?

'Can she not be fetched?'

'There's no one to fetch her,' the housekeeper said. 'If you don't care to go to the stables, ma'am, you could wait for Miss Felicity in the drawing-room.'

'And, pray, where is she?'

'I believe she walked to the village.'

'And how long is she likely to be?'

'I am afraid I can't say, ma'am. She's visiting Mrs Wardle.'

Mrs Bertram decided she would have something to say about the rag-mannered way she had been received when she came face to face with her nieces, but for now there was nothing to do but wait until one or other of them put in an appearance. Drawing herself up to her full height, which was nothing to speak of, for she was as round as she was tall, she allowed herself to be conducted to the drawing-room.

It was a large rambling house, full of solid furniture that had been there a half a century or more, and though that in itself did not signify she was appalled by the general air of neglect. Although the carpets could not be said to be threadbare, they had certainly lost their colour and the paint on the doors was beginning to peel. It smacked of genteel decay. Added to that, the drawing-room into which she was conducted was cluttered to say the least and there was a film of dust on the polished surfaces. A fringed silk shawl had been flung carelessly across a sofa; there was an open book on a low table and a couple of wolfhounds were sprawled across the hearth. A cat rose from a chair and stretched itself lazily before jumping down and padding out of the room.

Bidding her to be seated, the housekeepr excused herself on the grounds that she had a bran-mash on the boil and must attend to it. Bran-mash! In the kitchen! Had they run mad?

Mrs Bertram looked about her for somewhere to sit and, deciding not to risk getting her plum-coloured silk covered in animal hairs, turned about and left the house to go in search of her niece. She walked round the side of the house and, holding her skirts clear of the cobbles, crossed the yard to the stable block. In contrast to the house, the stables exhibited every sign of being well-maintained. The paintwork was good, the ground swept clean and the horses, looking out of their loose boxes, were well-groomed and alert. There were grooms and stable-boys busy about the yard and she asked one, who was raking straw out of one of the stables, for the whereabouts of Miss Paget.

'In the foaling box, ma'am,' he said, nodding towards the end of the row of boxes. 'Though I shouldn't. . .' But the lady had gone, striding off towards the box he had indicated, and he shrugged and went on with his task.

'Georgiana?' Mrs Bertram peered short-sightedly into the gloom of the box. 'Georgiana, is that you?'

At the sound of her name, the young woman kneeling in the straw beside the mare looked up with a slightly puzzled expression. She had been so engrossed in the task of wiping the mucous from the damp coat of the new-born filly, she had paid scant attention to the sound of a carriage drawing up, knowing her sister would deal with any callers. But her visitor had obviously eluded Felicity. Georgie did not immediately recognise her, but there was something familiar about the plump figure who stood on the threshold, silhouetted against the light. She had a round pink face and corkscrew grey locks which were half concealed by a huge mauve bonnet sporting a sweeping green feather.

'You will forgive me for not rising, I know,' Georgie said. 'This little one needs all my attention at the moment.' And with that she turned to concentrate on the important task of looking after the filly, which was trying to get to its feet, all spindly legs on a body seemingly too big for it. It had a good head, though, an Arabian head with wide nostrils and brown eyes which hinted at the intelligence she hoped it had inherited from its sire, Grecian Warrior, son of Bucephalus, the stallion her father had bred for the Prince of Wales before he had become the Prince Regent. Bucephalus had been a prince among stallions and Warrior was almost as good. Georgie had high hopes for all Warrior's progeny and this one looked most promising. It had a dark chestnut coat, a white flash on its nose and white socks. Georgie smiled as it tottered towards its mother, already on her feet and whinnying to it. 'Warrior Princess,' she said aloud.

'I beg your pardon?' The figure in the door moved slightly, allowing the sunlight which flooded the yard to penetrate the dimness of the stable.

'Oh, I am so sorry.' Georgie scrambled to her feet, revealing herself to be clad in a man's breeches and shirt. 'It's the filly's name. Warrior Princess, sired by Grecian Warrior. That,' she added, pointing to the mare, 'is Royal Lady. Foals are nearly all born during the night, did you know that? The Arabs considered it unlucky for one to be born in the daytime and would often destroy it. Thank goodness we are not so barbaric, for this one is a little beauty.' She laid a hand gently on Royal Lady's nose. 'You let me have my sleep, didn't you, Lady?'

'It *is* Georgiana, isn't it?' Mrs Bertram enquired again, as if she could hardly believe the dreadful apparition which confronted her.

'Yes, I am Georgiana Paget.' No one had called her Georgiana since her father died six months before and he had only used her full name to express his displeasure at something she had done or left undone and that in itself had been rare. To her sister, Felicity, and close friends she was Georgie and to the servants Miss Paget. 'But I'm afraid. . .'

'Don't you know me. I am your aunt Harriet. Your housekeeper said I might find you here, and that was bad enough in all conscience, but I hardly expected. . .'

Georgie stroked a lock of hair from her face and managed to daub her cheeks with dirt. 'Aunt Harriet! I am so sorry, I did not know you. It's been years. . .'

'Indeed it has—eight at least. I should have come

sooner. . .' She stopped to survey her sister's elder daughter from her brown riding boots, up over the breeches stuck here and there with straw, and the voluminous shirt with the sleeves rolled up, to her smudged face and crop of auburn curls. They were cut in what, had she been a man, might have been called the wind-swept style but which was really the result of Georgie having taken the scissors to them herself to keep her hair out of her eyes when she was working with the horses. It was convenience, not fashion which dictated her looks and that much was painfully obvious to her aunt. 'I knew Henry had some very strange ideas about raising children, but I never thought to see the day when his daughter took to being a stable-lad.'

Georgie looked down and tried unsuccessfully to brush the straw from her breeches. 'Petticoats are hardly practical for acting midwife to a horse,' she said, giving her aunt a rueful smile. 'Let us go back indoors and I will bath and change.'

'Let us do that,' Harriet said crisply. 'And when you are fit to be seen we will talk.'

'Yes, Aunt, of course.' She turned to the stable-master who had been hovering in the shadows. 'Look after them, Dawson,' she said, indicating the mare and her foal. 'And get someone to see to Mrs Bertram's carriage and horses.' With a last wistful look at the filly, now sucking strongly at one of the mare's teats, she led the way across the cobbles of the stableyard and into the house by a side-door.

'Do sit down, Aunt,' Georgie said when they reached the drawing-room. 'If only you had sent word, we would have been in a better state to greet you.'

In spite of the gravity of the situation, Harriet

Bertram smiled; it would, in her opinion, have taken
an army of servants working a month to have made the
place ready to receive visitors. 'Would the mare have
postponed her lying-in for me?'

Georgie laughed. 'No, but Felicity would most
assuredly have been here to welcome you. I can't think
where she is.'

At that moment Felicity herself appeared. At eighteen she was eight years younger than her sister and
tiny by comparison, and, though there was a family
likeness if one looked closely for it, it was masked by
the elder girl's masculine attire and the younger's pale
frailty. Mrs Bertram looked from one to the other as
Felicity, in grey jaconet half-mourning, came forward
and dropped a curtsy. 'I am sorry I was not here when
you arrived, ma'am,' she said. 'I was visiting Mrs
Wardle; she is the gardener's wife and helps in the
house occasionally, but she was taken sick two days
ago.'

'And is that why this room is in such a parlous state?'
demanded Mrs Bertram, flicking a lace handkerchief
ineffectually over a chair before sitting on it.

Both girls looked round the room as if seeing it with
a stranger's eyes; it had what Georgie chose to call a
lived-in look, but she could not deny it would have
been better for the use of a broom and feather duster.
Felicity glanced at Georgie with an eyebrow raised as
it to ask who it was who had the temerity to criticise
someone else's home, even if the criticism was a little
justified.

'Felicity, this is our aunt Harriet,' Georgie explained.
'She has but lately arrived from Brussels.'

'Brussels! Oh, were you there for the battle?' The

defects in the housekeeping were of less importance to Felicity than news of the outside world. She plumped herself down on a stool beside her aunt and leaned towards her. 'How exciting that must have been. Did you see it?'

'The battle was nine miles away at Waterloo,' their aunt told them. 'And that was certainly too close for comfort. We could hear the guns from the city walls. But I did not come to talk about war, though by the looks of this room there might have been one here. Is the gardener's wife your only servant?'

'After Papa died it seemed an extravagance to have a household of servants to look after just two of us,' Georgie said. 'But there is Fanny, who is really a maid of all work, bless her, and Mrs Thorogood, whom you met and who has been in the family for years and years, and Mrs Wardle. Most of the outside staff have been kept on because they are needed to run the farm and stud.'

Mrs Bertram clucked her tongue and the plume on her hat nodded in unison as she commented drily that it was obvious where Georgiana's priorities lay, but she would say no more until her niece had washed and changed her clothes, for she did not think she could abide the smell a moment longer.

'My husband has been a cavalry officer for the best part of twenty years and he would not dream of bringing the odour of the stables into the drawing-room,' she said, wrinkling her nose. 'And as for those dogs, why are they allowed in the house?'

'Papa was always used to let them in,' Georgie said. 'He said they were company for him and they have grown accustomed to the run of the place.' She looked

down at herself and then at the animals and conceded
that her aunt had a point. She called to the hounds
and, when they went obediently to her side, gently put
them out of the low casement window, not withstand-
ing the fact that they stood outside on the terrace
looking aggrieved. 'I shall be back directly,' she said,
making for her bedroom and the hot water Fanny had
put out for her.

Half an hour later she returned to the room in a
simple grey sarcenet gown, and though the colour did
nothing for her Harriet was forced to admit that her
niece was as comely as any young woman could be who
spent half her life out of doors and was prey to the
elements.

'Now,' she said, when all three were seated once
more and Georgie was dispensing the tea. 'It seems I
have not arrived a moment too soon.'

The girls looked at one another and then back at
their aunt. Georgie's spirits sank. She knew she was in
for a scolding and though she did not know what she
could have done differently she felt guilty and ill at
ease.

'What do you mean, Aunt?' Felicity asked inno-
cently. 'We know you could not have come any sooner,
what with Uncle Edward being in the army and the war
and you travelling with him and everything. How is
Uncle Edward?'

'He is well, came through without a scratch, thank
the good Lord. I left him in Belgium, but now that pip-
squeak Napoleon has finally been defeated he will be
home in a matter of weeks. I came ahead to open up
the house in Holles Street.'

'Did you know that Papa. . .?' Georgie gulped and

made herself speak evenly. 'Did you know Papa had died?'

'I received your letter telling me of it, long after the funeral, of course, for it followed me all over the Continent. I came as soon as I could to be with you. Now, tell me all about it.'

'He died as he lived,' Georgie said. 'In the saddle.'

'A fall?'

'No, Warrior would not unseat him. He had a heart seizure and though Dr Penreddy came almost at once there was nothing he could do.' She paused, remembering that dreadful day and her own despair when she'd realised that the one person she had loved and depended on above all other was no more and that she, being the elder, must stifle her own misery to comfort and care for her sister. 'I think Papa would have approved of his end.'

'What provision did he make for you girls? Where are you to live?'

'Live?' queried Georgiana. 'Why, here, of course. It is our home.'

'Alone? It is out of the question.'

'We are not alone. We have servants. And it was Papa's wish.'

The reading of the will had taken only a few minutes and had shocked even Georgie, who was used to her father's idiosyncrasies. All Sir Henry's assets were tied up in the stud farm and he had left them solely to his elder daughter, just as if she had been a son, and adjured her to take care of her sister, who was left only a small annuity. Old Benson, who had been her father's lawyer since time began, had been embarrassed and unhappy, but Georgie had cheerfully told him she would manage. And manage she had, but it was still a struggle. No one wanted to buy horses from a woman and by continuing to live alone the girls had put themselves beyond the pale as far as social visits were concerned.

'He must have been queer in the attic,' Mrs Bertram said crisply. 'How can you expect to find husbands tucked away in the country with no one to bring you out?'

'Aunt, I am six and twenty—well past the age when I need bringing out,' Georgie said. 'And as for Felicity, I shall bring her out myself, just as soon as I can come about.'

'Come about? What do you mean by that? Have you not been well provided for?'

'Yes, Aunt,' Georgiana said, determined to remain calm. 'Papa left the house and the farm and all the horses to me. It is up to me to make a living for both of us from it. I am saving hard to give Felicity a Season and a dowry, but when everyone thought the war had ended last year the demand for horses fell. Not that I liked the thought of any of our horses getting killed, but—'

'Child! You are surely not trying to run a commercial undertaking?' There was horror and disbelief in her voice.

'Of course I am. How else can we live? Papa taught me how. Ever since I was big enough to totter to the stables and sit in a saddle, he had me by his side and talked to me about what he was doing. He has made me into a good judge of horseflesh. Felicity manages the house and I look after everything out of doors. We have been doing it for twelve months now.'

'Good heavens!' was all Mrs Bertram could manage, and again, after a pause, 'Good heavens!'

'I am going to breed racehorses,' Georgie said. 'With the end of the war and so many of the officers coming home, they will be looking for recreation, and as most are very fond of a wager I think racing will take an upturn. Papa thought so, for he was far-seeing enough to keep Grecian Warrior instead of selling him when he could easily have done so and he bought a couple of good brood mares several years ago. You met Royal Lady, didn't you? Warrior Princess is her fifth foal.'

Mrs Bertram seemed to be beyond words. She sat and stared at her niece as if she had gone mad.

'We are managing very well,' Felicity said in defence of her sister. 'Georgie knows what she is doing.'

'Give me leave to doubt that,' Mrs Bertram said. 'She cannot know that she is condemning you both to a reputation for being eccentric or she would not countenance such a life. Eccentric women do not make good marriages—in fact they rarely marry at all unless it be to someone equally touched in the attic. I should have thought that you, Georgie, were old enough and sensible enough to realise that.'

'What else could we do?' Georgie asked.

'Sell up. Buy an annuity and live in gentility. . .'

'Sell Rowan Park?' Georgie exclaimed. 'We could not do that. Papa would turn in his grave. . .'

'It is a pity my brother could not see he had a couple of females on his hands and not boys,' Mrs Bertram said with some asperity. 'He always did treat you more like a son than a daughter, Georgiana. I warned him years ago but he would not listen. He said you would go on very well and there was sure to be a sensible, well set up young fellow who would appreciate your abilities.'

She paused but did not give either girl an opportunity to reply before going on. 'He was as blinkered as one of his precious horses over the pair of you. Now we must do something about it. You will put yourself in my hands.' She sighed heavily and made room on the cluttered side-table for her cup and saucer. 'I shall do what I can for you, though I think it may be too late for you, Georgiana.'

'No, it isn't,' Felicity cried. 'Georgie is a wonderful sister to me, so capable and caring, and she will make a admirable wife for someone.'

'We'll see,' their aunt said, though there was doubt in her tone. 'If you wish to keep Rowan Park, Georgie, we shall have to find some gentleman interested enough to take that as a dowry. A more mature gentleman, obviously.'

'Some old bufflehead!' exclaimed Georgie. 'I would as lief remain single.'

'And how much longer do you think you can go on before the whole place goes to rack and ruin?'

'It won't,' Georgie said stubbornly.

'Oh? You have buyers and sellers beating a path to your door?'

'No, not exactly, but there have been a few. We have to give them time to become used to the idea. . .'

'That a woman can run a business? Never! Anyone who did arrive could only be coming to gape or gull you into bad bargains. You are not so lacking in wit that you cannot see that, surely?'

'Then they will have their come-uppance, for I know a good horse from a bad one, so you need have no fear

I shall be gulled,' Georgie said, and though it was no less than the truth it did not stop her from recognising the accuracy of her aunt's assurance that men would not do business with a female. Those that had put in an appearance had come out of curiosity or to try and cheat her, but when they'd found they could not they'd gone away empty-handed. It might have given her a sense of satisfaction, if it had not also meant that business was lost.

'Late in the Season as it is, you will come back to London with me, the pair of you, and I will endeavour to introduce you to all the eligibles,' her aunt said. 'Henry has been gone a year now and you have mourned long enough.'

'I cannot be spared from here,' Georgie told her, though she recognised that her aunt was right. Tucked away on the borders of Hertfordshire and Cambridgeshire, seeing no company but each other, she and her sister were becoming almost bucolic, and though she did not mind that for herself it was wrong for Felicity. She had been mothering her sister ever since their mother died many years before and she was determined, now that Papa had also passed away, that she would be a father to her too. And that meant giving her a Season and doing her best to find her a husband. She had decided on that before their aunt's arrival; all Mrs Bertram had done was to bring the decision forward. 'But of course Felicity must go, if she would like to. I am very grateful to you for offering to sponsor her, for I could not have done it before next year at the earliest. Neither do I have your contacts; you can open doors I never could.'

'I should like that above everything,' Felicity said,

trying to keep the eagerness from her voice for her sister's sake. 'But I do not want to leave you here alone.'

'I shan't be alone. There are servants and outside staff and more than enough to keep me occupied. And there is the new filly. . .'

'A filly?' Felicity asked eagerly. 'Oh, how wonderful! Did you have any trouble?'

'None at all; it came away as sweet as a nut.'

'Georgiana!' cried Mrs Bertram, shocked to the core. 'How can you mention such. . .such delicate matters in the withdrawing-room?'

Georgie laughed. 'It is hardly a delicate matter, Aunt, which is why I wear old clothes for it.' She turned to Felicity. 'She is a little beauty. I'm going to call her Warrior Princess.'

Felicity clapped her hands and nothing else would do but that she must go immediately to the stables and behold the paragon so their aunt temporarily gave up trying to talk sense into them. She returned to the subject at dinner, by which time she had been shown to her room by Fanny, changed her gown, inspected the house and viewed the grounds from an upstairs window.

Beyond an extensive stable-block, whose roof was almost immediately below her window, there were two or three large paddocks in which upwards of thirty horses grazed and beyond that a few farm fields, in one of which the haymakers were busy with their scythes. In the other direction, alongside a copse of trees, was a private gallop, where she could see a couple of stable-lads exercising horses. She had not realised until today how large her brother's stud was, nor how much there

was to do in the managing of it, and she was filled with
admiration for her elder niece. Not that it made any
difference to her disapproval or her determination to
do something about both girls. It was her duty and
Harriet Bertram had never been one to shirk her duty.

'I must return to London as soon as maybe,' she told
the girls over the fish, which was surprisingly well-
cooked, though Harriet found herself wondering how
close it had been to the bran-mash. 'Your uncle
Edward will be home soon and I must make sure
everything is as it should be before he arrives, so I
suggest you pack your bags and we will go tomorrow.'

'Tomorrow! I cannot possibly leave so soon,'
Georgie said. 'You had best go without me and I will
follow when the haymaking is done and I am assured
Warrior Princess is doing well.'

No amount of arguing would budge her and their
aunt gave in. Felicity and Mrs Bertram would post to
London, in the lady's carriage, and Georgie would
follow a week later in Sir Henry's travelling coach, with
a groom driving and Fanny as maid and chaperon. It
was not, in Harriet's opinion, an ideal solution but it
was the only one Georgiana would agree to, and that
young lady was far too self-willed for her own good.
Harriet blamed Henry, who, while acknowledging that
he could not produce a living son—there had been two
stillbirths between Georgie and Felicity, both boys—
would not deny himself the pleasure of bringing one
up, and Georgie had been turned into a hoyden as a
result. A very capable hoyden, but a hoyden none the
less.

'I will undertake to fit you both up with clothes,'
their aunt said. 'And I'll give a ball. The Season is half

over so it will have to be at the end, and by then you
will perhaps have made your mark on Society, if I can
prevail upon Lady Hereward to invite you to her ball
next week and Mrs Sopwithy to include you in one of
her routs. Then there is Almack's and perhaps, if you
are lucky, a drawing-room. It is fortunate that so many
young men are returning from the Continent for I
declare every eligible in town must already have been
spoken for long ago.'

She murmured on in like vein throughout the remove
of mutton and braised sweetmeats and the fruit flan
that followed them, and Georgie, who was made to
feel that their deficiencies were all her fault, was glad
to escape and return to the stables, once more clad in
boots and breeches, leaving Felicity to complete the
arrangements with their aunt over the teacups.

Georgie loved horses with a passion which could
only be matched by her father's and had often sat up
all night with a sick animal or a mare that was foaling.
She had watched stallions at stud and cared for mares
in foal right through until the time of the birth, a fact
which horrified her aunt. She could break and train a
new horse and was an excellent rider, liking nothing
better than to feel the wind in her hair as she put a
horse through its paces on the gallops. Dawson, the
stable-master, and the other outside staff were used to
her and would have died for her right to continue her
father's work; they cared little for convention and knew
nothing of the ways of London Society. If the Rowan
Park stud was sunk then so were they and none fancied
being among the ranks of the unemployed, swollen by
returning soldiers.

Today Georgie had helped a new filly enter the

world and she was as proud as if it had been a daughter of her own. She acknowledged, with a wry smile, that horses were likely to be the only children she would have; at twenty-six she was already firmly on the shelf. No man would look twice at her. For a start, her complexion lacked the pale fragility that was fashionable and she was too tall, overtopping her sister by a head. She was also the equal of any male when it came to horsemanship and there were few who excelled her; it was enough to deter any man from offering for her.

She sighed as she knelt to fondle the new filly, drawing a neigh of protest from its mother. If she could not have a husband and family of her own, then she would make sure of being a success in her chosen sphere. She would be the best horse-breeder in England. And she would make sure that Felicity wanted for nothing. A husband for her sister before the year was out would be her goal.

Felicity herself did not disagree. She loved Georgie and was no more selfish than any other young lady who had been cosseted since birth and it never occurred to her that her sister might not be entirely happy with the way their lives were shaping, for she never complained. As far as Felicity was concerned, Georgie preferred horses to people and liked nothing better than mucking out a stable dressed in breeches. Her sister did not, as far as Felicity knew, hanker for a husband and a family of her own. Having explained this to her horrified aunt, she gave herself up to the enjoyment of planning her wardrobe and looking forward eagerly to all the social occasions Mrs Bertram could devise for her.

'There are some exceedingly handsome officers in my husband's regiment,' Mrs Bertram told her as they journeyed towards the capital the following day. 'Some I am well-acquainted with, for they have been close to my husband, the colonel; others I do not know so well but I shall contrive to learn all I can about them. They will need to be well up in the stirrups, of course; that goes without saying.'

'It doesn't matter about being rich, Aunt,' Felicity said. 'So long as I love him.'

'Love him!' exclaimed her aunt. 'What foolishness is this? We will find someone suitable, from a good family with an independent income and a title if possible, and if all goes well and he offers and you accept, then you can think about love. Ten to one that will not come until after the wedding, so you may set your mind at rest on that score.'

'Did you love Uncle Edward when you married him?'

'No, of course not, but he was agreeable and kind and we came to depend on each other. I would not change him for the world.'

'And Mama and Papa?'

'The same.'

'Oh. Do you suppose Georgie knows that?'

'Of course she does; your sister is not a ninnyhammer, for all her cork-brained ways.'

'Could you not find someone for her too? I should not like to think she was left to be an ape-leader; she is not like that at all, you know. She pretends to be hard because she doesn't like anyone to know how soft she really is, but I have seen her cry over an injured horse and when old Bucephalus had to be put down she mourned for weeks.'

'Horses!' expostulated Mrs Bertram. 'Horses are not people.'

Felicity, who had often been constrained to say the same thing, made no comment on that. Instead she continued to extol her sister's virtues. 'She is very pretty, you know, when she takes the trouble to dress and arrange her hair.'

'Then why she did not make the effort long before this I cannot conceive.' Mrs Bertram sighed heavily. 'I blame my brother-in-law. . .'

'I don't suppose Papa even noticed how she looked.'

'No, I do not suppose he did.' Mrs Bertram sighed again. 'If only I had not been out of the country. . .'

'Aunt, I doubt it would have made any difference; Papa did not take kindly to criticism.'

Her aunt laughed. 'Of that I am persuaded. Now, let us talk about you. . .'

Felicity was only too happy to comply and the remainder of the journey passed pleasantly, and the following afternoon, after an overnight stay in St Albans, they arrived at Mrs Bertram's modest villa in Holles Street.

London was celebrating the defeat of Napoleon and there were flags and bunting everywhere and everyone laughing and joyous. Ballad-sellers were doing a roaring trade and returning troops were clapped on the shoulders and told what valiant men they were, though the soldiers themselves, deprived of their livelihood, if so dangerous a calling could be so named, were not so happy. Glad enough to have returned alive, though many were missing limbs, they had to find civilian jobs or resort to thieving or begging and already many were

on the streets with their hats in their hands. Most of
the officers who had returned had gone back to their
homes to be received into loving families; some might
be low in the stirrups, but they would find other
occupations, or service in other theatres of war. It was
different for them.

All the same, Major the Honourable Richard
Baverstock, son of Viscount Dullingham, had not yet
returned home to Cambridgeshire. Before he faced his
father, he intended to have a little fun; in fact he
intended to have a lot of fun. And he was doing it in
the company of his friend, Captain John Melford. They
had only just rrived in England, being among the first
to return on account of slight wounds, but already they
were amusing themselves sparring at the Fives Court
in Martin Street, mixing with the noisy crowds who
frequented the Cockpit Royal and laying bets on a
couple of fighting cocks.

They had been to Astley's Amphitheatre to watch a
troop of wire-walkers and a dancing bear and had
danced the night away at Ranelagh Gardens where the
aristocracy rubbed shoulders with the proletariat and
where they had enjoyed the company of a couple of
delightful bits of muslin. Both handsome and well set
up, they had soon learned how to deport themselves
and dress in the latest mode and were, as a consequence, greatly in demand among mamas organising
social occasions for their daughters. They had been
taking full advantage of the fact, flirting with the young
ladies but never losing their hearts.

Sometimes Richard wondered if he still had a heart
to lose. He had seen some gruesome sights in the eight
years he had been a solider; he had seen good friends

killed and maimed, and priceless treasures looted. He had seen barbarity and compassion, bravery and cowardice in equal measure and he had watched Maria bleed to death in his arms and wept for her and his own inadequacy. Determined to put it all from his mind, he was, a few days after Felicity's arrival in the capital, out on Hampstead Heath cheering on his jockey in a private race.

It was a foolish wager and he would not have made it if John had not bet so heavily on that card game at Watier's. His friend had been somewhat disguised at the time and the more he'd lost, the more reckless he'd become. Richard, who had pulled out long before, had tried unsuccessfully to lever him away, but he would have none of it. 'My luck will change,' he'd kept saying. In the end he'd lost everything of value on his person and the heap of paper vowels beside Lord Barber's elbow had borne witness to the fact that his luck had not changed and if he continued he would have nothing left at his bank either. He'd been writing yet another voucher when Lord Barbour had put a hand over it. 'No more vowels.'

'I have no more money or valuables on me,' the young man said. 'You must allow me to continue. These will be honoured.' He turned to Richard, who stood behind his chair. 'You'll vouch for that, won't you, old friend?'

Richard agreed, for what else could he do? But it meant that he might be called upon to make up any deficit.

'No more vowels,' his lordship insisted.

'My hunter, then. It's a prime animal.'

'That old nag against this?' He indicated the heap of

money, the rings, pins, fobs and the scraps of paper and laughed. 'Do you take me for a fool?' It was then that he looked up at Richard. 'I'll take your stallion, though.'

It was Richard's turn to laugh. 'Lose the best horse I ever had on a hand of cards? No, my lord, I am not such a sousecrown.'

'Then the captain will be known for a welsher.'

John, suddenly very sober, looked at him in anguish. 'Richard, play my hand for me. . .'

'No.' He had never been very good at cards; now, horse-riding that was another matter. He turned to Lord Barbour. 'I'll race Victor over a measured mile against the best in your stables, my lord. If I win, my friend's debts are cancelled. If I lose, you take the horse.'

Richard had played the only hand he knew. Lord Barbour's stables were among the best in the country except for one thing. They lacked a really great stallion such as Richard owned. The young man had a vague feeling that his lordship had manoeuvred the whole situation, but there was nothing he could do about it, short of abandoning his friend to his fate. As soon as it became known that John had been unable to pay his gambling debts, every tradesman in town would be dunning him and he would be left without a feather to fly with.

John tried to dissuade him and was still trying to do so the next day, when, with a pounding head and sick to his stomach, he called on Richard to go to Hampstead Heath. 'I can't let you do this,' he said, mopping his face with a handkerchief soaked in lavender water. 'Leave me to my fate. . .'

'No. I can no more go back on a wager than you can. It's done now.'

'You know Barbour is down on his luck,' John said. 'I heard he was mortgaged to the hilt at Baverstock's bank and he ain't known for his generosity. Old Ten-in-the-hundred, they call him.'

'My cousin,' Richard said thoughtfully.

'Oh, I had forgot; sorry, Richard, but I'll wager Lord Barbour will refuse to hand over my vouchers even if you win.'

'Not even he would renege on a debt of honour.'

'No, but there are other ways of avoiding payment.'

'Cheat, you mean? He wouldn't dare.'

'Not exactly. I had heard his lordship intends to put his fourteen-year-old son in the saddle and the boy is only half your weight.'

'Is that so?' There was nothing in the rules of the wager which said either protagonist had to ride himself, though Richard had assumed they would and so was glad of the information. 'Then I shall have to employ a jockey, shan't I?'

The jockey weighed less than seven stones; Victor, who was used to Richard, who weighed double that in uniform with all his accoutrements, hardly knew he had a rider on his back, except for the sharp little spurs and the whip, something he was not at all accustomed to. He flew over the heath like the wind. The race was so close that the two horses were neck and neck; first Salamanca drew ahead, then Victor. Lord Barbour, on the sidelines near the finish, yelled at his son, 'Unseat him! Unseat him!' The boy, half a head behind, pulled his horse alongside Victor and flayed his whip at Richard's jockey, causing a spurt of blood to appear on his face. The injured man veered away from another blow and Victor, confused by conflicting messages on the reins, stumbled and almost unseated him. Both recovered quickly but the set-back was enough to lose them the race.

Richard, his face dark with fury, strode over to Lord Barbour, who was embracing his son. 'If you imagine, my lord, that I will hand over my horse to you after that demonstration of cheating, you may think again.' He turned to his jockey whose face poured with blood. 'I'm sorry, Daniels. Get off to the physician and have that cut seen to. Have the bill sent to me. You will be paid as if you had won, which you would have done if the race had been fair.'

'All's fair in love and horse-racing, don't you know that?' Lord Barbour said, with a self-satisfied smile. 'I'll have your mount, if you please.'

'You will not. The wager is void and you must know that.'

'I can only suppose you have been soldiering so long, you have forgotten what a debt of honour is.'

Richard was about to vouchsafe his opinion that his lordship did not know the meaning of the word, when John tugged at his sleeve. 'Don't, I beg of you, provoke him.'

'You expect me to hand Victor over when he so flagrantly cheated?'

'Yes,' John advised him. 'You cannot prove the boy did it on purpose.'

'We both saw it.'

'Who will believe us? Two rakes, home from the wars, against a respected pillar of society with a great deal of influence?'

'You would do well to listen to your friend, sir,' Lord Barbour said. 'He may not be the best card-player in the world, but he speaks a great deal of sense.'

'I will have satisfaction.'

Lord Barbour smiled. 'Name the day and the conditions. I will accommodate you.'

'No,' John said, horrified. 'My friend did not mean to duel with you.'

'Did I not?' Richard said through gritted teeth. 'I am persuaded nothing would please me more than to make him eat grass before breakfast.'

'You can't do that,' John insisted, pulling him to one side. 'The contest would be so uneven it would be denounced by the whole world. Look at him. He's so fat and out of condition you could hardly miss, either with pistol or rapier, and he's nearly old enough to be your father.'

It was the thought of his father that decided Richard. He had been in enough trouble before he left home to wish to add to it now. Reluctantly he unsaddled the horse, threw a blanket over it and handed the reins to his adversary. 'Consider he is on loan, for I shall have him back. I claim a return match.'

'Any time,' his lordship said complacently. 'Any time.'

'Mind you treat him well while he is in your care,' Richard added. 'For if I hear anything to the contrary, blood will be spilled.' He patted the horse's neck and walked swiftly away, carrying the saddle. Not for anything would he let anyone see how down he was. The horse had been with him through many a battle; he was full of courage, steadfast and loyal as any

human comrade and Richard felt as though he had
betrayed him. He turned to John who had hurried after
him. 'If you are going to start apologising again, you
may save your breath.'

John knew better than to argue, though he felt every
bit as blue-devilled as his friend. 'No, I was going to
suggest you ride behind me to the nearest tavern where
we can drown our sorrows in a bottle or two.'

'That will do for a start.'

Two hours later, after two bottles of the landlord's
best claret had been consumed, Richard was still cold
sober and the loss of his mount was still foremost in his
mind. 'If that blackguard Barbour thinks he has done
me over,' he said, 'he will soon learn different. I mean
to get Victor back.'

'How?'

'I don't know yet, but I will think of something.
What will you do? It might be prudent to take a
repairing lease in the country until the fuss dies down.'

'No. My mother is lately come to town and I mean
to stay with her. She may be persuaded to keep the
duns off my back. But as to Victor, if I can do
anything. . .'

'My mount is my affair,' Richard said brusquely. 'I'll
call at Rowan Park on my way to Dullingham House
and see what Sir Henry has to offer. He served me well
before; Victor was one of his.'

'You are going home?'

'Yes, it has to be faced.'

'You can hardly blame Lord Dullingham for being
vexed,' John said. 'It ain't done for the heir of an estate
like yours to go off to war, especially when there is no
second son to take your place. But considering you

served with distinction I'll wager he is very proud of you and now you are back safe and sound all will come about.'

'Perhaps, but his last words to me were if I was such a codshead as to stand in the line of fire I should deserve to be hit and he would not mourn my demise. . .'

'I'll wager you said something equally hot-headed to him.'

Richard laughed. 'Maybe I did.'

'Why did you join? You've never said.'

'Pride, I suppose. I was barely twenty and something of a scapegrace. I needed to sow a few wild oats.'

It was not exactly the truth but as he had never told anyone why he had left it was all the answer he intended to give. He had been nineteen when his father married for a second time and the shock of it had stunned him. He could not understand how his father could have so far forgotten the love he bore his first wife as to marry Honoré Montellion, a French *émigrée* as grasping and vicious as a hawk.

From the very first she'd set out to marry stepson to daughter, a whey-faced, over-indulged girl of fifteen; if her own children could not inherit because Richard was the heir, then she was determined that the next generation would through a union between Richard and Lucille. But when Richard had declined to fall in with her wishes she had made his life a misery, finding fault with everything he did, sending him on futile errands and alienating him from his father, who could see no wrong in her and had encouraged her in the matchmaking. Unable to stay and fight her without filling the whole house with discord and upsetting his father, he had left home and enlisted.

He looked at his friend across the empty bottles and glasses on the table and smiled ruefully. 'If my father had carried out his threat to disown me and make my cousin William his heir. . .'

'Is the estate not entailed?'

'Not so he can't get out of it.'

'He was bamming you.'

Richard was not at all sure of that. His parting with his father had been acrimonious, to say the least, and it had been with him all the years he had been in the army. They had corresponded, to be sure, but neither had felt able to put his true feelings on to paper and the letters had been stilted, full of battles and army matters on Richard's part, and politics and estate affairs on his father's.

But Honoré had died in childbirth several years before and the war was over, which meant there was no longer any excuse for staying away. And, if Richard was honest with himself, he was more than a little homesick. It had grown worse since Maria died; he saw his homecoming as a way of coming to terms with that, of accepting that she was part of another life, another world which those who had been left behind in England could never comprehend. He wanted to lock it away and begin again.

It was what he was thinking about as he descended from the coach at The Barley Mow inn on the Great North Road just north of Baldock, instructing Heacham, his man, to continue on to the next stage with his luggage, from where he would easily be able to hire a conveyance to take him to Dullingham House.

The inn was quiet and a few minutes later, having bespoken a bed for the night and left his cloak-bag, he took his saddle, which he had obstinately brought with him, and went out to the yard to hire a hack to take him to Rowan Park. It was a poor beast and the fine saddle looked incongruous on it, but Richard set out cheerfully enough. It was a new beginning and the day was set fair for new beginnings.

CHAPTER TWO

IT WAS a cloudless summer's afternoon with a gentle warmth quite unlike the searing heat of Spain; a slight breeze caressed Richard's cheek and lifted his hair from his neck. A couple of kestrels hovered over Royston Heath, bees droned on the purple heather and the clop, clop of the mare's hooves almost lulled him to sleep.

A few minutes after he had turned down the lane which led to the stud farm he was suddenly alerted by the sound of hooves thundering towards him and only just had time to pull the mare to one side before a shadow loomed over the hedge beside him and a horse and rider flew over it and galloped on towards the heath, leaving him swearing fluently and once more in solitary possession of the lane. It had either been a completely irresponsible act of someone ignorant of the consequences or the rider was a supremely confident horseman to take a hedge like that, but then he was in Paget country where reckless riding was normal.

He rode on down the hill towards the house and outbuildings of Rowan Park. If the horse came from there, then he would speak to Sir Henry about it; horse and rider should not be risked in that fashion.

Dawson came out to meet him as he rode into the stable-yard and dismounted. 'Can I be of assistance, sir?'

'I have just been almost run down by a maniac on a black stallion, which I assume came from here. Have you no control over your lads at all?'

'The lads are all sensible riders, sir.'

'This one wasn't. Six foot, that hedge was. Six foot and the rider so slight, I wonder you dare put him up. I had thought Sir Henry had more in his cockloft that to allow such a thing.'

'Sir Henry died a year ago, sir. Had you not heard?'

Richard's seething anger subsided. 'No, I am sorry to learn of it; Sir Henry was the best judge of horseflesh I ever knew.'

'Yes, sir, he was that.'

'But that is no excuse for ramshackle behaviour. Are the stables still in business? I collect Sir Henry had no son.'

'The stables are in perfect working order, sir.'

'Then where is the new owner? I would have a word with him.'

'Coming now.' Dawson, barely able to suppress the grin which creased his rugged features, nodded in the direction of the lane along which Richard had himself arrived. He turned as the horse and rider he had seen earlier walked calmly into the yard. In spite of his annoyance, he found himself admiring the way the young horseman controlled the restive stallion and brought it to a halt a few yards from him.

'You are a sapskull, bratling,' he said. 'A veritable thatchgallows. It is a good thing that, unlike you, I am a careful rider, otherwise my horse might have bolted with me. Don't you know better than to jump blind?'

'I wasn't blind. I saw you clearly enough even if you

did not see me and I have taken that hedge any number of times.'

He was alerted by the voice into looking more closely into the rider's face and found himself gazing into a pair of dancing green eyes, which thoroughly unnerved him. His surprise must have shown for she laughed aloud. 'Have you never seen a woman on a horse before?'

He was tempted to tell her what he thought of women in breeches who galloped about the countryside without benefit of groom or chaperon, but decided against it. It was probably not her fault if she was a daughter of Sir Henry, and she looked oddly vulnerable, in spite of the easy way she handled the horse. 'Not riding an animal like that,' he said, appraising her mount appreciatively. 'And most assuredly not one so foolhardy. You were lucky your horse did not bolt at the sight of me.'

'Why sir,' she said, throwing a breeches-clad leg over the saddle and sliding to the ground, 'I did not think your appearance so very out of the ordinary. If you had two heads, then Warrior could be forgiven for taking fright, but an ordinary man on a very ordinary horse—what is that to fly into the tree-tops about?' She was aware as she spoke that he was not in the least ordinary. For a start, he was a very big man, tall and broad-shouldered, and his features had a ruggedness which in no way detracted from his good looks; his jaw was clear-cut and his mouth firm. 'Did you ride down here especially to ring a peal over me? For I can tell you the lane is private property. . .'

'I would not have wasted my time on such a fruitless

exercise, ma'am,' he retorted stiffly, 'had I not needed to come on business.'

'Oh.' She handed Warrior's reins to Dawson who had been listening to the exchange with something like glee. 'Have him rubbed down and when he's cooled you can give him a good dinner; he's earned it.' She cast a cursory glance at Richard's hired hack before turning to face him, aware that he was much taller than she was and she was tilting her head up towards him— a most unusual occurrence. 'I am sorry, sir, we seem to have begun on the wrong foot. I'm Georgiana Paget. What can I do for you?'

He grasped the hand, though he was unsure whether to shake it or convey it to his lips. 'Miss Paget, your obedient servant. Am I to understand that you are the new owner of Rowan Park?'

'Yes,' she said, unable to avert her gaze from his dark eyes which seemed to be looking into hers as if they could perceive the uncertainty there.

'I need a good hunter,' he said, releasing her hand and breaking a spell which had lasted only seconds but which, to Georgie, had seemed like minutes. 'The one on which you nearly rode me down would be just the thing.'

She was about to protest that she had come nowhere near riding him down, but stopped herself with a laugh which sounded empty to her own ears. 'Mayhap it would, but Warrior is not for sale, and certainly he would not do for you.'

'How do you know that?'

'Simply by looking at the animal you are riding. I never saw such an apology for a horse in my life; it is definitely dishing. And you are far too heavy for it.'

He turned to look at it and grinned ruefully; she was right but he would not give her the satisfaction of telling her so. 'That is no excuse for terrifying him and me along with him. And you must allow me to be the judge of what will do for me, madam. Pray ask whoever is in charge of this establishment to show me what there is on offer.'

'I am persuaded it would take more than that to terrify you, sir,' she said, watching his face for his reaction, ready to fly into the boughs the minute he exhibited any reluctance to deal with her. 'I will show you what we have if you tell me what you have in mind.'

'Another like Victor,' he said, deciding to humour her. When she found herself out of her depth, she would have to call her guardian or manager or whoever now looked after her affairs. He admired her spirit, though what she hoped to gain by this delaying tactic he did not know.

'Victor? You mean Bucephalus's colt out of Winning Streak? I collect he was bought by a cavalry officer. Viscount Dullingham's son, I believe.'

He grinned and gave a mock-bow. 'Major Richard Baverstock at your service, ma'am. You have a good memory.'

'I know the lineage of all our horses, Major, and where they went. What happened to Victor?'

'He has been acquired by Lord Cedric Barbour and I need a replacement.'

Georgiana felt unaccountably angry with the young man for parting with Warrior's half-brother but glad that the brave horse had not died in battle as so many others had done. Perhaps, as a returning soldier, his pockets were to let and he had been forced to part with him but, in that case, he could hardly afford to replace the stallion with anything like the same quality.

'Come with me,' she told him, and led him past the main stable-block to the paddock, where several horses grazed. 'Take your pick,' she said. 'They are all prime animals.'

'I said a replacement for Victor, not a mount for a gentle hack in the country,' he said, hardly sparing them a glance. 'It is obvious you do not know the difference and I would do better to take my custom to someone who can appreciate my requirements.'

'That, sir, is your prerogative,' she said, then, remembering that pride did not put money into the household coffers and would not pay for Felicity's come-out, relented. 'I am sorry, Major Baverstock; I had thought the best might be above your touch. Please come with me and I will endeavour to find something that will suit.'

She led the way across the yard and into another enclosure which was surrounded on three sides by loose boxes. Horses looked out over open doors and he was forced to admit that they seemed alert and interested in what was going on about them. On the fourth side was a small parade ring where a young groom was patiently lunging a strawberry roan on a very long rein, round and round, getting the young colt used to obeying the pressure on its mouth. Richard noted that the commands to go left or right were gentle and that the animal did not seem distressed, before turning his attention back to Miss Paget who was leading a stallion from the first of the boxes.

'This is Paget's Pegasus,' she said. 'Sired by a half-brother of Bucephalus. His dam was one of Eclipse's granddaughters.'

It was a beautiful grey, nearly seventeen hands, not quite up to Victor or the horse she had been riding, but it was well-proportioned, with good sloping shoulders, a shortish back, powerful hindquarters and a good depth in the girth. He observed it from a little distance before approaching it quietly and walking slowly round it, feeling the tendons in its legs and looking into its eyes and mouth. Its good breeding was obvious and it looked well-groomed, but only a horse trained, fed and exercised properly would have the speed and stamina he required. With Sir Henry gone, had the stables kept up to the mark?

'Four-year-old?' he queried, patting the horse's neck.

'Yes, not quite in his prime, but on the way to becoming a good goer. My father bought him as a two-year-old and brought him on to ride himself. He turned down several offers for him.'

He was aware of a wistful note in her voice and found himself suddenly feeling sorry for her—and that would not do at all. He thought he could guess at her character well enough to know that she would hate that. 'As good a recommendation as any,' he said. 'Sir Henry would ride only the best. But why sell him? Do you not want him to. . .?' He stopped suddenly, remembering that for all her male garb she was a lady and he ought not to offend her sensibilities by speaking of breeding.

'Put him to stud?' she queried, laughing.

'Yes. Why not?'

'I have. He sires good solid workaday horses, but they are not outstanding, in spite of his pedigree.'

'Surely it is good solid workaday horses which are the bread and butter of the stable? The outstanding ones provide the cake.'

'Do you want to buy him or not?' she asked, made uncomfortable by his questions. It would not do for it to become known how low in funds she was. The only way to keep the stables going was to sell some of her stock, but even that was not easy when so few customers came to Rowan Park since her father died. She had sent one or two horses to Tattersalls but she hated doing that because, apart from the fact that he took a percentage—which he had every right to do—it made people wonder why she was obliged to do it. And selling stock was not the long-term answer or she would have nothing left. And, looking up at this big handsome man, she knew he could read her thoughts as if they were written on her forehead and she did not like the feeling at all.

'I should like to ride him out. May I?'

'Of course. You will find him a little frisky: he hasn't been out today.'

His saddle was transferred from the hired hack while Georgie ordered a fresh mount to be saddled for her and they set off for the gallops at a smart trot which soon became a canter as the horses warmed up. She was right—Pegasus was spirited and anxious to have his head, but Richard held him in check for a couple of miles before he allowed him to gallop, and when he did let him go the stallion moved freely and had an easy, ground-covering stride. Half an hour later, they drew up at the boundary fence at the limit of the estate.

'Well?' Georgie asked, pushing back a tendril of hair from her cheek. 'What do you think?'

'Not Victor, of course, but a sweet goer and well up on the wind.' They turned and walked the horses side by side towards the distant buildings of Rowan Park. 'Are you sure you will not sell Grecian Warrior instead?'

'Yes.'

'Then Pegasus will do me very well. Let us go back and you can take me to your man of business.'

She laughed. 'There is no such creature. I strike the bargains at Rowan Stud, Major Baverstock.'

He turned to look at her. Her cheeks were pink, her hair wind-blown and the hands that held the reins so easily were brown and work-worn. What in God's name had her father been thinking of to allow her to become such a hoyden? If he had any sense he would not encourage her by doing business with her, but he doubted he would find a better mount and no doubt she was in need of the money. But if she were not very careful she would soon lose the whole farm. He wondered idly if it would go piecemeal or as one lot and then found himself wishing she might succeed in spite of everything.

'Very well,' he said. 'Name your price.'

Before another hour had passed, Richard was forced to admit that Georgiana Paget knew more than most men about horses and she was also a hard-headed business woman. When he left he had paid top price for his hunter, had agreed to give her exclusive stud rights for the next five years and, besides that, had acquired, at an astronomical price, a superb two-year-old filly called Bright Star, with which he had an idea

that he might be able to revenge himself on Lord
Barbour. Leading his hired hack, he rode away on the
grey, leaving the filly with Miss Paget. He did not want
to take delivery of it and advertise its presence in the
Baverstock stables until he was ready, and against his
better judgement he had allowed her to persuade him
to let her train it.

He didn't know how that had happened; he was not
usually swayed by female guile. But in truth there had
been no guile; she had simply stated that she knew
what she was about and he had believed her! What a
flat he had been! He all but turned round and went
back, but knew that would make him feel even more
foolish. He might as well give her a chance; her man,
Dawson, whom he knew to be very knowledgeable,
would keep her on the right track and he would go
back in a couple of weeks and take the filly to a
reputable trainer. He would race it against Barbour's
best and this time he would not lose.

But he reckoned without Miss Georgiana Paget.

She was elated. Dawson, who had been witness to the
transaction, was grinning from ear to ear.

'Well done, Miss Paget,' he said as soon as the man
and horses had disappeared. 'You are your father's
daughter and no error. But do you know what you
have taken on with that filly?'

Did she? It was one thing to watch her father at
work and listen to his theorising, quite another to put
it into practice, but the opportunity had been too good
to miss. Not that she hadn't nearly sunk it at the start.
Fancy assuming that just because a man rode a hired
hack he knew nothing! She should have taken note of

his buckskin breeches and well-tailored riding coat, not to mention the top-boots! Only an experienced servant could have put the shine on those. And the hack had sported a beautiful military saddle.

But she had seen none of that at the time because she had been overwhelmed by the man himself, like a silly miss at her first coming-out ball. Anyone would think she had never beheld a man before. And that was patently untrue because there were always men visiting the stables—or had been when her father was alive. All manner of men, too—old and young, fat and thin, greedy men, easygoing men who thought nothing of losing a thousand guineas on a wager, desperate men selling their horses to pay their debts, cits and mushrooms, farmers and aristocrats and, in the old days, royalty.

When she was small they had patted her head patronisingly and said what a knowing little miss she was, but when she had grown tall, taller than most of them, they had treated her with polite indifference. And since her father's death all but a few had stopped coming. She knew it was because she was a woman, and women were certainly not considered capable of horse-trading, not even in workaday farm animals and carriage horses and certainly not in hunters and race-horses, which were the main stock-in-trade of the farm. And as for training a racehorse, that was lunacy. She had to prove she could do it and Major Baverstock had given her the chance. Did he know what a gamble he was taking? she wondered.

'I certainly mean to give it a try,' she told Dawson. 'But I shall need all the help you can give me. Will you do it?'

'Of course, Miss Paget; you do not have to ask. And that goes for everyone else in the yard. But. . .' He paused.

'You have doubts?' And when he hesitated she added, 'Come, Dawson, you can speak freely.'

'I was thinking of Mrs Bertram, miss. She gave me a fair old dressing-down when she first arrived for allowing you into the stable during a foaling. She would not approve. . .'

Her laughter pealed out. 'No, she wouldn't, would she? But you must leave me to deal with my aunt. At the moment she is fully occupied with looking after my sister. And as I have promised to join them for a few days we will postpone discussion of how we will bring Bright Star along until I get back.'

Dawson had been at Rowan Park, man and boy, for almost half a century and he knew Sir Henry's methods as well as anyone. If anyone had the training of Bright Star it would be him, but he knew his place, and besides, Miss Paget was a brave, resourceful girl and he would do all he could for her, as he had done for Sir Henry. 'Miss Paget, Mrs Bertram said I was to drive you to London.'

'So she did. I had forgot. I'll drive myself.'

'Miss Paget, begging your pardon, that won't rightly do and you know it.'

'Oh, very well,' she conceded. 'Tom can drive me.'

Tom was his son, a strapping boy of eighteen who had been working at Rowan Park almost since he could walk.

'Very well, Miss Paget. I'll give him his instructions.'

'You know what to do about Bright Star while I am gone?'

'Yes, Miss Paget—gently does it for a week or two,' he said with a smile. If, while she was away, she were to find a nice, easy-stepping husband, with a well-lined pocket and a liking for horses, then no one would be more pleased than Bert Dawson.

But it was not prospective husband which filled Georgie's mind as she journeyed to London the following day, but impatience to keep her promise to her aunt and return as soon as possible to making Bright Star famous and vindicating herself.

She arrived late in the afternoon to find her aunt and sister in her well-furnished though by no means opulent drawing-room taking tea with Lady Hereward and Mrs Melford. They were busily engaged in discussing the age-old subject of husbands and the getting of them. And Felicity, clad in newly purchased sprigged muslin, was listening silently with something like awe.

'If only you had come earlier,' Lady Hereward said, addressing Felicity. 'Such loveliness would have taken the *ton* by storm a month ago. Now those young blades already betrothed will be cursing their haste.' She smiled encouragingly. 'But let us not give up, for I am sure we can contrive to find a handful who are not already spoken for. I will go over my invitation list again and see whom we may present to you.'

'Oh, I wish you would not,' Felicity said, squirming uncomfortably. 'I would not like to be thought forward. . .'

'Nonsense, my dear,' her aunt said. 'It is the way it is done. Has no one instructed you on how to go on?'

'No,' Georgie put in. 'For there was never anyone to do it.'

'Oh, you poor dears!' exclaimed Lady Herward. She

was a very tall, angular woman, made to seem taller by the high feather which swept up from the crown of her bonnet. 'Harriet, you never told me. We must remedy the situation at once.' She looked from Georgie to Felicity and then back again and Georgie almost laughed aloud because it was obvious that she did not think anything could be done for her.

Georgie was dressed in a double-breasted caraco jacket, trimmed with braid, over a simple dove-grey carriage dress, and though it was not the height of fashion she would certainly not have described it as dowdy. It had hung in her closet unworn since her father's death, when all visiting had ceased in the light of her mourning and the need to keep at work. She was, she knew, becoming something of a workhorse herself, and a few days in London, shopping and paying calls, would have brightened her life, if only she could have spared the time. She returned Lady Hereward's smile, surprising that good lady into realising that the girl was very far from plain.

'Do not think of me, my lady; I must return to Rowan Park almost immediately——'

'Oh, no, you do not,' interrupted her aunt. 'You must stay at least until after Lady Herward's ball. It would be churlish to refuse. And besides, it is your duty to your sister. I have a young man in mind for her and you must meet him, seeing as your bufflehead of a father stipulated that you must approve of the man your sister marries.'

'Oh, please stay,' Felicity pleaded. 'I really do need you, for I am nervous as a kitten.'

Georgie stilled her conscience over Bright Star by telling herself that Dawson knew what to do and once she returned to Rowan Park there would be no release; she must work and work, with no time for anything else, and a few days of enjoyment would set her up for that. 'Very well,' she said. 'I'll bear you company for a sennight.'

Felicity clapped her hands delightedly. 'Oh, we shall have such fun! I have been learning to watlz, you know. Apparently it is permitted since Lady Jersey allowed it at Almack's. You will have the waltz, Lady Hereward, won't you?'

'Of course; all the young men expect it, though there are some dowagers who disapprove of a young man putting his hand about a lady's waist.'

'Oh, I think it does no harm as long as the couple stay a good foot apart,' Mrs Melford put in. 'John dances it very well.'

'Is John looking for a wife, Melissa?' Mrs Bertram enquired. 'I collect he is a good-looking boy.'

'And that is all he is,' his mother said sharply. 'A boy. He needs another year at least before he settles down. And then we have expectations that he will offer for Juliette.' She smiled at Lady Hereward as she spoke; Juliette was Lady Hereward's daughter. 'It has been understood since they were children.'

'And what does John say about that?' Mrs Bertram demanded.

'He adores Juliette, has done since they were both in leading-strings.' She paused. 'But Baverstock! Now there is a young man who needs a wife.'

Georgie, with a swiftly beating heart, found herself listening intently as the three women began discussing Richard Baverstock just as if he were a yearling in one of her father's sales. She felt suddenly angry, but she could not for the life of her have said why.

'He is Viscount Dullingham's only son,' Mrs Melford said, addressing Lady Hereward, knowing that Mrs Bertram was already aware of the young man's history because he was one of her husband's officers. 'It is said he quarrelled with his father years ago, which is why he bought into the regiment. He is a major now.'

'Has his father cut him off?'

'It was rumoured so, though I cannot believe he really did it, but the Major is already nine and twenty and still unmarried. What father of any note would allow such a situation to continue? You may take my word for it, he is in want of a wife.'

'He is a very handsome man,' Harriet put in. 'A trifle large, but he carries it well. He distinguished himself in the Peninsula and was mentioned in Wellington's dispatches.'

'Ah, but does he know how to go on in Society? Some of these young officers are a little wild, you know.'

'He will settle down,' Mrs Bertram said complacently. 'He is a gentleman and it goes without saying that he knows how to behave.'

Georgie looked from her aunt to her sister. Felicity's face was alight with anticipation; she could just imagine her falling for the gallant major. She did not know why she did not tell them she had already met the gentleman, but somehow she thought it might put a damper on Felicity's pleasure, and besides, her sister must make up her own mind and not be swayed by anything she had to say about him. Once she knew Georgie had met him, she would bombard her with questions, and, however carefully she considered them, her replies were bound to colour Felicity's own opinion when she met the young man. Suddenly Georgie felt very blue-devilled and could not have explained why.

'I will invite him to my ball,' Lady Hereward said. 'Do you have his direction?'

'I believe he has gone home to Cambridgeshire,' Mrs Melford said. 'I do not know if he can be prevailed upon to return. Lord Dullingham will perhaps want to keep him by his side after so long an absence.'

All the ladies became silent at this news for it was a considerable stumbling-block and, except for Georgie, all had set their hearts on making the match. Georgie did not know why she had reservations.

'I will send the invitation anyway,' Lady Hereward decided. 'There is plenty of time for it to reach him. And if I also add a note that I shall be mortally offended if he refuses, it might bring him back.'

Georgie, during the rush of shopping and visiting that ensued in the next few days, almost managed to forget Rowan Park and Richard Baverstock and horses and everything else that had occupied her mind before coming to town. Mrs Bertram had already bespoken a wardrobe for Felicity, which set Georgie fretting about how she was going to pay for it all, for she could not let her aunt stand the whole expense, and now the good lady was determined to do the same for her. In vain did Georgie protest.

'I am not having a niece of mine going about like a frump,' Mrs Bertram said. 'What will my friends think of me, if I did that? And how you can expect to find a husband if you do not make the lease push I do not know. . .'

'Aunt, you are backing the wrong horse in me,' Georgie said on one particularly trying morning when her aunt insisted on taking her to the best modiste in town to purchase a ballgown. 'I shall never have occasion to wear it again after Lady Hereward's ball. . .'

'I should hope not!' exclaimed her aunt. 'One should never wear the same gown twice. And I wish you would not use those stable expressions.'

'Stable expressions, Aunt?' Georgie queried with a smile, wondering if her aunt had ever heard a true stable expression, in spite of being a cavalry officer's wife.

'You know what I mean. Now, look at this silk; is that not a green to set off your colouring?'

'Yes, Aunt, but——'

'Oh, it is perfect,' Felicity said. 'I find green does not suit me, but for you. . .' She held the material up against her sister and looked at her with her head on one side. 'Oh, do have it, Georgie.'

The pattern she chose was an open one, very simply trimmed at the hem and neck with matching ruched ribbon and oversleeves of lace, and was not too high-waisted, which, though fashionable, would have made her look taller than ever. 'That's settled,' her aunt said, allowing Georgie no time to demur. 'Now for the accessories. A pea-green taffeta underskirt, I think, white stockings and green silk slippers, of course, a shawl and fan and a beaded reticule.' She paused to look carefully at her niece as all this finery was added to the pile being boxed up for delivery. 'Though what we can do about your hair I cannot think. I will send for Michel just as soon as we return to the house.'

If Georgie thought that meant her shopping was done and they were returning to Holles Street, she was to be disappointed. They did not arrive there until well after noon, by which time they had been to the Pantheon Bazaar and several other establishments and her purchases included two or three gowns for morning calls, a dimity undress gown for wearing on the rare occasions when she would be at home, a carriage dress and jacket for excursions in her aunt's barouche and—if she was lucky enough to be invited—rides in the phaetons and curricles of those gentlemen whose attention she had engaged, a new riding habit in peacock-blue, for her aunt declared the one she had was worn to a thread, shoes, boots, petticoats, shawls, a pelisse and a domino of green velvet with a satin-lined hood. These, together with Felicity's earlier purchases, which had been even more extravagant, had taken every penny she had from the sale of Paget's Pegasus and Bright Star. While she was left wondering how soon she could expect another transaction quite as good, her aunt was sending out for the hairdresser Mrs Melford had recommended to her.

Monsieur Michel arrived soon after they had taken a light luncheon and his reaction to being instructed to do something about Miss Paget's hair was to throw up his hands in horror and declare, '*C'est impossible*! It eez. . .'ow you say?. . .a bush.'

'Then she must wear a wig,' Mrs Bertram said.

'A wig!' shrieked Felicity. 'Oh, Aunt, wigs went out years ago. Georgie will look a veritable antidote.'

'A leetle one, like 'er own 'air, perhaps,' Monsieur

suggested. 'I show you.' And he delved into his bag of brushes, combs and powders, and brought out a switch of hair, which he fastened under Georgie's own hair with a comb and let it fall on either side of her face in loose ringlets. The result was striking; it made her face seem wider and softer, though the false hair was much darker than her own.

'It doesn't match,' she said, unwilling to admit that it was an improvement.

'No,' he agreed, looking at her shorn locks; one minute they seemed a rich brown chestnut, the next, auburn, and, when caught by the light, a real ruby-red. Never had he seen such colouring; if only there had been more of it to work with. . . He sighed. 'You must dye your 'air, *mam'selle*.'

'No, I will not. Find a match.'

He sighed. 'It will be *difficile*, *mam'selle*. The *couleur*, it is not ordinary.'

She laughed. 'Then I shall start a new fashion for short hair.'

She did not know how he did it, but on the evening of the ball, when she was being helped into the green gown by Fanny, Monsieur Michel arrived with a hairpiece which was as near a match as made no difference and she sat with a powder cloak about her shoulders and watched in the mirror as he transformed her.

She hardly knew herself when he had finished. With a topknot of her own hair hiding the ends of the false ringlets so that they blended perfectly, a touch of pearl powder on her cheeks and with the garnets which had belonged to her mother about her throat, she had to own that the boyish look had gone and in its place was a lady of fashion, as feminine as anyone could wish, except for her height. Nothing could be done about that but she carried it well and it made her look stately, almost regal. Fanny laid a gossamer shawl about her shoulders and handed her the cotton gloves which would hide her hands and told her fervently that she would be the belle of the ball and if someone did not offer for her, then they needed their cocklofts looking into. Georgie, slipping her feet into the delicate satin pumps, thanked her with a smile and went in search of her sister.

Felicity, petite and tiny-waisted, with her golden ringlets and peach-bloom complexion, was dressed in light blue net laced with silver and looked like a beautiful doll. There could not have been a greater contrast than the two sisters as they went downstairs to join their aunt who waited impatiently in the drawing-room, tapping her fan against her ample bosom. Both were striking in their way and Harriet found herself more optimistic than she had been for days that she might find a match for them both.

'Come, my dears,' she said briskly. 'The barouche is outside the door and we must be off or we will be lost in the crush.'

Neither girl understood what she meant until they found themselves at a standstill at least a quarter of a mile from their destination. Little by little the carriage inched forward as those in front deposited their passengers and drove away and the next vehicle moved up in the line. It took half an hour to reach the door of Lady Hereward's town house in Bedford Square and another fifteen minutes before the three ladies found themselves at the head of the stairs and being greeted by their host and hostess and Juliette, for whom the ball was being given.

'He's not here yet,' Lady Hereward whispered to Harriet after the girls had been presented to her husband. 'I do hope he means to come. You'll find Melissa and John in the alcove by the potted palm, endeavouring to keep seats for you. It is a fearful crush; I am sure I did not invite all these people. . . .'

'Indeed you did,' her husband put in. He was a very small man with gingery whiskers and a red face. His twinkling blue eyes, which showed a wry humour, were his saving grave for he would otherwise had been nothing out of the ordinary. 'You invited the whole *ton*—you know you did.'

'Not quite all, Basil,' she said, smiling fondly at him. 'But I'll allow I asked extra to account for refusals.'

'There haven't been any,' he said.

'I should hope not!' she retorted, making him roar with laughter.

A country dance had just finished and the couples were strolling back to their places. Mrs Bertram guided her charges across the floor to where Mrs Melford sat, with John standing at her elbow. He bowed to Mrs Bertram and made an elegant leg to Felicity before being presented to Georgie. 'Miss Paget, your obedient,' he said, sweeping her a bow, but it was obvious that his eyes were only for her sister as he arranged chairs for them all and offered to fetch cordial or ratafia.

He hurried away on his errand and the two girls sat looking about them at the glittering scene. The myriad chandeliers alone would have been enough to make the eyes ache, but added to that there was the sparkle

of jewels and shimmer of silks and satins and so many
flowers and so much greenery that one could have been
forgiven for thinking the garden had been brought
indoors, not to mention the hum of chatter and the
music of the orchestra; it was an assault on the senses
which both astonished and perplexed them. Surely
their aunt was not proposing to equal this extravanga
for them?

'The Major has not come?' Harriet queried of Mrs
Melford, settling herself in a chair beside her friend
and lifting her quizzing-glass to see who was present.

'Not yet. John thinks he may not.'

'No matter. He is not the only one; there is quite a
gaggle of young blades in that corner. It is a pity no
one has instructed them how to go on. They must be
winkled out.'

As soon as John returned with a waiter carrying a
tray of full glasses, she insisted that he go over to the
young men and suggest that some might like to be
presented to the Misses Paget.

Georgie watched as he interrupted some uproarious
joke that one was telling, saw him speak and nod in
their direction, saw them lift quizzing-glasses and then
frowned as they all came clamouring over demanding
to mark the girls' cards. In no time at all Felicity had
no dances left and was scolded by her aunt for not
leaving at least one free, in case the elusive Major
Baverstock should arrive. And even Georgie had few
spaces left on hers.

She was quite sure the Major would not appear, for
he had told her he was going to his home and had no
plans to return to London. She didn't know how she
felt about that; she would have to see him again, and

more than once, if their business relationship was to develop, but did she really want to dance with him?

Yes, yes, her traitorous heart told her, while her head insisted that business should not be mixed with pleasure, lest both should suffer. And if their aunt had set her mind on capturing the Major for Felicity, who was she to object if that was also what Felicity wanted? She had no idea how such a thing could be brought about; it all sounded so contrived, so calculated. Sitting beside her aunt, watching Felicity dancing a gavotte with John, she was reminded of how her father bred horses, mixing the best characteristics of stallion and mare—looks, speed, stamina—and she found herself smiling. Was it any less cold-blooded for humans?

'Miss Paget, may I present Lord Barbour to you?'

Georgie looked up, startled out of her reverie, and found Lady Hereward standing in front of her with a man in his late forties. He was heavily built and, she suspected, tightly corseted—his complexion was florid and his grey eyes slightly watery—but she could easily see that he might have been handsome in his youth. He was dressed in old-fashioned knee breeches and white stockings with a long coat of ochre satin trimmed with pearl buttons, a shirt whose collar-points reached his cheeks and below which a diamond pin gleamed in the folds of a cravat of immense proportions. His dark hair was cut short and curled forward over his ears. He gave her a sweeping bow and held out his hand. 'Do me the inestimable honour, Miss Paget, of taking a turn round the floor?'

Nudged into action by a sharp dig from her aunt's elbow, she rose and accompanied his lordship on to the

floor for a minuet. They were the same height and she
found she could not avoid those watery eyes.

'Liked the cut of your jib as soon as I clapped eyes
on you,' he said as the music began and they bowed
and curtsied. 'Asked our hostess who you might be.
Old Henry Paget's daughter, so she told me. Isn't to
be wondered at. Knew a good bit of horseflesh, that
one. Same for me. What happened to his horses when
he stuck his spoon in the wall? Sell up, did you?'

'No,' she said, not at all sure that she liked to be
compared to a horse. 'Rowan Park still deals in horses.'

'That so?'

'Yes.'

'Got a brother or cousin to run things for you?'

'No.'

He was certainly out of condition and his questions
had been asked breathlessly, but now he paused suddenly, making the following couple collide with them.
'Beg pardon,' he said, turning to make them a bow.
'Talking too much. Come, Miss Paget, let us peram-
bulate.' And, without waiting for her to reply, he
offered her his arm and led her to the side of the
ballroom, where they circulated round the perimeter in
stately fashion.

'No one to run things?' he asked. 'How do you go
on?'

'Very well, my lord. I manage everything myself.'

Her answer seemed to amuse him but she would not
let it fluster her. If she wanted to breed and sell horses,
she must be prepared to answer questions, and she had
nothing to hide. But when the questions became a little
too personal she was not so sure.

'Left you well up in the stirrups, did he, old Henry?'

'Well enough,' she said.

'Good dowry?'

'Lord Barbour, that is hardly a question I care to answer.'

'Have to answer if you want to wed, m'dear.'

'Naturally, I shall answer such questions when the time comes. . .'

'Had no offers, then?'

'That, too, is a question I do not care to answer.'

He smiled easily, not in the least offended. 'Just wanted to know the odds. Ain't one to waste my time.'

She was so astonished, she could only turn and gape at him, but he did not elaborate; instead he said, 'In the market for a horse. I've a mind to look over what you've got.'

'Of course,' she said as they reached her aunt's position. 'I shall be returning to Rowan Park next week.'

'I shall look forward to that but I hope I may further our acquaintance before that. Call on you tomorrow. Your servant, ma'am.' He bowed to both ladies with a flourish which set his corsets creaking and strolled away.

Georgie collapsed into the seat beside her aunt. 'Who was that?'

'Lord Cedric Barbour—surely you were introduced?'

'Yes, of course. I meant what manner of man is he?'

'He was widowed a little over a year ago and one must surmise is looking for a wife and a mother for his children. Two of them, I believe. Let me see. . . The boy must be about thirteen or fourteen and the girl a year or two younger. He is very well up in Society and has influence at court, so I am told, and he is prodigious rich. What's more he keeps a good stable. You could do worse, my dear.'

Georgie, thoroughly taken aback, swung round to face her aunt. 'You can't mean that he and I. . .?'

'If he chooses to drop the handkerchief, why not pick it up? It could be the answer to your dilemma.'

'What dilemma, Aunt?'

'Why, becoming respectable. You must, you know, not only for your own sake but for Felicity's. Who would want an eccentric for a sister-in-law? If you persist in that ramshackle life you have been living, you will both be the talk of the *ton* for a Season and then forgotten. You may not mind it, but I am persuaded your sister would hate it. Oh, she is loyal to you now and sees no wrong in it, but later, what then? When you are both ape-leaders, will she blame you for not making a push to put matters to rights?'

Georgie could find nothing to say in her own defence and did not answer, but deep in her heart she knew her aunt was right. But Lord Barbour!

She was so engrossed in that horrible prospect, she was not aware of anyone approaching until a shadow loomed over her. She lifted startled green eyes to see Major Baverstock, splendid in dark blue regimentals with silver-laced crimson facings and silver-tasselled epaulettes, bowing to her aunt. 'Your servant, ma'am.'

CHAPTER THREE

'LA, MAJOR, we had almost given you up,' Mrs Bertram said. 'Never mind, you are here now. Let me present you to my niece, Miss Paget.'

'Miss Paget?' Richard turned to Georgie and the expression of surprise on his face made her smile, for it was obvious that he had only then realised who she was.

She found herself laughing. 'Oh, Major, have you never seen a foolhardy woman before?'

'Only one in your mould,' he said, making a swift recovery. She looked beautiful, not at all like the mannish woman he had met at the stables. And her hair was magnificent. He was tempted to ask how she had achieved it but decided that would be asking for a put-down and her aunt was looking from one to the other in a very disapproving way. He bowed. 'Your servant, Miss Paget.'

'And this is my other niece, Miss Felicity Paget,' Mrs Bertram put in as Felicity was returned to her on the arm of her latest partner. 'Felicity, my dear, this is Major Baverstock.'

He turned to bow to her and Felicity coloured prettily as she dropped a curtsy. 'I am pleased to meet you, Major Baverstock,' she said. 'I have heard a great deal about you.'

'From your sister?'

Felicity glanced at Georgie in surprise. 'Why, no,

63

sir; how can Georgie have spoken of you? I meant from my aunt and Mrs Melford.'

'Take her off and dance with her,' Harriet said, suddenly aware of a tension in the atmosphere which she was anxious to dispel. 'You have this waltz free, Felicity, do you not?'

'Mr Melford. . .' she began tentatively.

'Oh, he will not mind, will he, Major? Besides, he has not come to claim it. Now run along; I wish to have words with Georgiana.'

They glided away just as John returned. 'You are too late, Captain,' Mrs Bertram told him. 'Besides, you have danced twice with Miss Felicity already.'

'Then perhaps Miss Paget?' he asked, chagrined.

'No,' Mrs Bertram spoke for her. 'Miss Paget is fatigued and sitting this one out. I have not yet seen you doing a turn with Miss Davenport. I perceive her sitting beside her mama over there and looking quite doleful.'

He could not ignore so blatant a dismissal and as soon as he had gone Harriet turned on her elder niece. 'Such familiarity! Were you off your head? "Fool-hardy", you said. Yes, you are indeed that. When did you meet him and where? And why did you say nothing?'

It was the first time that question was asked but it was not the last. When Felicity returned at the end of the waltz, she asked it too, and Georgie was faced with it again half an hour later when Richard asked her to dance a Chaîne Anglaise with him.

'Why did you not tell your aunt and sister you had met me when I am so obviously a subject for their tattle?' he demanded as the opening bars of the music signalled that he should execute a sweeping bow.

'That isn't fair!' she exclaimed, dropping into a deep curtsy. 'Just because my aunt and Mrs Melford mention your name it does not make Felicity a gossip. She is a sweet, kind girl, and very biddable.'

'I am sure she is,' he said laconically as the first movement began.

She looked up into his dark eyes and felt them searing into her, just as they had once before, and she found herself growing weak. How dared he make her feel like that, as if she hadn't a bone in her body? Thankfully the dance separated them, but he returned to the subject as soon as they came together again to execute a *tour de main*. 'You did not answer my question. What have you to hide?'

'I have nothing to conceal, Major,' she said, forcing herself to sound cool. 'I simply thought it would be better if Felicity made up her own mind about you.'

He threw back his head and laughed. 'Oh, I see; the matchmakers are at it again, are they? I've no doubt they told you I was in want of a wife.'

'Are you?' she demanded, disconcerting him. His father's ultimatum was fresh in his ears. 'Find yourself a wife,' he had said. 'Give me a grandchild. Do you really wish to see William take over when I'm gone? I don't like the thatchgallows above half, but if he is obedient, and you ain't, what choice have I?'

He had returned again and again to the same topic during the three days Richard had been at home, until Richard was ready to explode, and when William himself had arrived from nearby Borton where he had a small estate it was the last straw. The man was a toad-eater of the first water; he had married Lucille, Honoré's daughter, the young lady Richard had rejected, and produced a family of five in no time at all.

Richard could not stand by and watch him unctuously doing his utmost to put himself in a good light and the son of the house in a bad one; it had been done before by his stepmother and resulted in Richard's self-imposed exile. He would be damned if he would allow it to happen again.

He had slammed out of the front door, mounted Paget's Pegasus and ridden to town, racking up overnight at the Swan in Stevenage, smouldering every step of the way. His ire had not been helped by the knowledge that he had not been the best of sons and he would do well to try and make amends, not only because of the inheritance, but in order to please his father. He would find a wife and one his lordship would approve of.

'Well, are you?' Georgie demanded, breaking in on his reverie.

'Am I what?'

'Looking for a wife.'

'Perhaps.'

'Then I am persuaded you should look no further.'

He looked down at her in astonishment; that she was outspoken and lacking in reserve he already knew, but to be so blunt about it was past comprehension and he was at a loss to know how to answer her. 'You? Why, Miss Paget, you flatter me. . .'

'Not me,' she snapped, disconcerted by her *faux pas* and anxious to rid him of the idea that she was putting herself forward. 'I was referring to my sister. Though, on reflection, perhaps you would not do, for you are far too conceited. And if you were to make her unhappy I think I should kill you.'

'Oh, dear, that has me quaking my boots.'

'And it is excessively uncivil of you to make fun of me.'

'I am sorry,' he said contritely. 'You are evidently very fond of your sister.'

'Of course I am. I want her to be happy. My aunt has pointed out my duty very plainly and I must do my utmost to help Felicity to the best possible match.'

'And you?' he asked softly. 'What about you?'

'Oh, I have my horses,' she said airily, giving herself no time to wonder why he had asked the question. 'They are enough for me.'

'And, of course, you never jump a hedge blind,' he murmured, leaving her pondering on what he meant. But there was no time to ask him for the dance had ended and he tucked her hand in the crook of his arm to return her to her aunt.

The rest of the evening passed in a blur as far as Georgie was concerned. Afterwards, she thought she had danced once or twice and gone in to supper, though what she ate of the hundreds of dishes put on the long tables in the dining-room she had no idea. Returning to Holles Street just before dawn, she told herself it was because she was not used to town hours. At Rowan Park she retired early so as to be up betimes for her work in the stables and she had had no time to become acclimatised to the change. That was possibly true, but she knew it was also because she had realised how she had allowed herself to slide so that she had become the antidote of all antidotes. 'Eccentric', her

aunt had said. How right she had been! And she had
made a fool of herself with Major Baverstock; it made
her cheeks burn even to think of it.

'And what did you think of Major Baverstock, my
dear?' Mrs Bertram asked Felicity, who had been
chattering on about what a wonderful time she had
had. 'He is a handsome man, is he not?'

'Yes, indeed, Aunt, and he has engaged to call on us
tomorrow. I think he means to ask me to go for a
carriage ride in the park.'

'Good.' Mrs Bertram leaned back on the squabs with
a sigh of satisfaction. 'Georgiana will chaperon you,
for I declare I was never so exhausted. I doubt I shall
rise before noon and I have undertaken to visit Caro
Sopwithy in the afternoon.'

Georgie opened her mouth to protest, but shut it
again. After all, what possible reason could she have
for refusing? Major Baverstock made an ideal suitor;
he was polished and wealthy and would one day be a
viscount. And her sister found him attractive. It was
her duty to go. It was a pity that doing one's duty was
sometimes such a mixture of pleasure and pain.

'Of course, Aunt Harriet,' she said as the coach drew
up at the door and all three were admitted by a footman
who had been dozing in a chair by the door, waiting
for their return. She followed her aunt and sister up
the stairs to their respective rooms where their maids
were waiting to help them to bed. After a good night's
sleep, Georgie told herself as she climbed into bed, she
would feel more the thing, but the ormolu carriage
clock on the mantelpiece reminded her that it was four
in the morning and in less than twelve hours she must
face the Major again. Why did she dread that so much?

She plumped up her pillow, shut her eyes firmly and told herself he was only a very ordinary man and she would not give him the satisfaction of making her feel foolish.

Most of the young men who had danced with the sisters at the ball arrived to pay their respects at some time during the following afternoon, many bearing flowers or sweetmeats, anxious to forward their suit with the younger Miss Paget. She was flattered, there was no denying it, and accepted several invitations, but it was obvious that she was not paying as much attention as she should and was listening anxiously for the arrival of one of their number who had not yet put in an appearance. After staying a few minutes, they left, one by one.

'He is not coming,' Felicity said when the two girls were alone once more.

'There is time. Be patient.'

'There's a carriage now.' She ran to the window and peeped from behind the folds of the curtain. 'Oh, it is Major Baverstock!'

'Come away from the window, do,' Georgie admonished her. Her own heart was beating unaccountably fast and she did not notice the drop in her sister's voice. 'It is not done to appear too eager, you know.'

Her sister had barely left the window and arranged herself prettily in a chair when Major Baverstock was announced. He strode into the salon where they had been receiving their callers and bowed to both ladies. He was obviously ready for their outing, for he wore a well-cut coat of Bath cloth, biscuit pantaloons and highly polished hessians.

'Your servant, Miss Paget, Miss Felicity,' he said,

tucking his curly-brimmed hat beneath his arm and sweeping them a bow. 'I trust I find you both well?'

Somehow the pleasantries sound affected coming from him, as if he was repeating something he had learned by rote and did not really comprehend. Georgie smiled. 'We are very well, Major, and looking forward to our ride, aren't we, Felicity?'

'I beg pardon? Oh, yes, of course. . . .'

Felicity seemed to be in a world of her own and having trouble concentrating; Georgie surmised that she was nervous and overawed by the attentions of the Major and decided she would have to speak to her about it. 'We will go and put on our bonnets and coats,' she said. 'It will not do to keep the horses waiting.'

She took Felicity's arm and propelled her from the room and up the stairs, notwithstanding the fact that her sister seemed reluctant to go. 'What are you thinking of, Felicity? You must not be so missish. He does not expect you to go into vapours at the sight of him; you should have smiled and welcomed him and made some conversation. Do pull yourself together, dearest, or he will be quite put off.'

'If he is so easily discouraged, I would as lief not entertain him at all,' Felicity said with more than usual spirit. 'I should like him to have a little more resolution than to be deterred because I am a little distracted.'

'Why are you distracted?'

They had reached the door of Felicity's room and she turned to go inside, saying, 'Oh, I am tired. After the quiet of the country, London is all rush and tear. I shall be in fine fettle directly.'

Georgie went to her own room and five minutes later, having donned a light silk shawl and a plain straw bonnet, which was all that was needed for the weather was very warm, she went downstairs again to find Felicity already there in a light pelisse and ribbon-trimmed bonnet, chattering nineteen to the dozen to the Major. 'Oh, here is my sister. Now we can go,' she said brightly. 'Come, Georgie, it was you who said the horses must not be kept waiting.' She turned to Richard as they left the house together. 'That is all my sister thinks of, Major. Horses are her only interest. She would sleep in the stables if she could. It is all Papa's fault, of course. He would have liked a son. . .'

'Felicity, I am sure the Major does not want to know about me,' Georgie put in, noticing the twitch at the corner of Richard's mouth.

'On the contrary,' he said politely as he handed them both into the phaeton which stood at the door. 'It is pleasing to hear sisters so loyal to each other. I am persuaded that is not often the case.'

'Have you sisters, Major?' Georgie asked.

'I fear not. I am my parents' only child.'

'I think that must be sad for you,' Felicity said. 'But no doubt you and your father are very close.' And before he could reply to this impertinence she added, 'We have lost our dear papa, you know.'

'Yes. I was sorry to learn of it.' He climbed in to sit facing them and commanded his driver to proceed. 'It must have been very difficult for you, especially with no man about the place.'

'Indeed it was,' she said, while Georgie sat mute. She had scolded her sister for having no conversation and now she was displaying the same tendency. 'But Georgie looks after everything so well. She was deter-mined I should have my come-out and when Aunt

Harriet arrived back from the war the opportunity seemed too good to miss. . .'

'Then I am doubly fortunate to have arrived back in town at the same time. It is the merest chance, for I had determined to stay in the country.'

'Oh, but Lady Hereward said she was sure you would return for her ball. She said——'

'You served with Wellington, did you not?' Georgie put in to cover her sister's ingenuousness. 'Do tell us about the great man. They say he can be rather short-tempered on occasion.'

He smiled. 'Yes, but he has every right to be angry if he is let down. He accords praise where it is due and apportions blame in no small measure if he thinks it is deserved. I am proud to have served under him.'

'Were you at Waterloo?'

'Yes, and in Spain before that.'

'And now the war is over what will you do?' Felicity asked. 'I believe Captain Melford means to return to his regiment. Will you do that?'

'No, Miss Paget, my soldiering days are done. I must leave the colours and be a dutiful son.' He paused to smile down at her. 'My father tells me it is time I settled down.'

The remark brought floods of colour to her cheeks for it seemed to confirm that he was indeed looking for a wife, but she was saved from having to reply for they were entering Hyde Park and taking their place in the long procession of other carriages—barouches, landau-lets, phaetons, curricles—which were filling the carriageway, all proceeding at a pace which was hardly faster than a man could walk. It seemed as if half of fashionable London was out to see and be seen in that one small corner of the capital.

All thought of sustained conversation was abandoned as they found themselves greeting and being greeted by everyone they had met in the last week. Georgie was astonished at the number and could not remember half their names, though Felicity seemed to have no difficulty and was enjoying herself hugely. She looked remarkably pretty in her face-framing bonnet with its ribbon bow securing it under her chin; her cheeks were flushed and her eyes sparkled so that the young blades found themselves eaten with envy for the handsome man who escorted her. Georgie was forced to admit that her sister had made a hit.

They were just leaving the park on their way home, when they were hailed by a man on horseback who had been riding along the Row.

'Oh, it is Captain Melford,' Felicity cried. 'Do let us stop and speak to him.'

Richard called to the driver to pull up close to the rails which divided the Row from the carriageway and John reined in to greet them. 'Your servant, ladies,' he said, calming his horse with an outstretched hand on its neck, for it was not pleased to have its exercise so abruptly halted. 'I trust I find you in good spirits? Good afternoon, Richard. I perceive you could not stay away from town, after all.'

Richard smiled. 'Do you blame me when I have two such beautiful ladies to escort?'

'No, though I don't think it was very sporting of you to cut me out.' He turned to the girls. 'I called at Holles Street earlier but you had left.'

'Did you?' Felicity asked, colouring prettily. 'We are sorry we missed you, are we not, Georgie?'

'Yes, of course,' Georgie said.

'I went to ask if you would care to ride with me,' he explained. 'But this dog got there first.' He grinned at Richard. 'No matter, there is always another day.'

'It will have to be soon,' Felicity told him. 'Georgie is going back to Rowan Park soon and, though Aunt Harriet will quite happily chaperon me in a carriage, I do not think she will want to ride.'

'Then let us all four go,' John said enthusiastically. 'How about it, Richard? Shall we all ride in Green Park tomorrow?'

'If the ladies are agreeable,' Richard said, smiling at Georgie with eyes that seemed to be teasing her. 'But I fear Miss Paget will find riding in town a sad disappointment after the Rowan Park gallops. I doubt there are suitable hedges.'

'Hedges?' queried Georgie, determined not to let him have the upper hand. 'We are not going hunting, Major. A simple hack is what is intended, is it not, Mr Melford?'

John, who did not understand the crackling tension between his friend and the elder Miss Paget, laughed uneasily. 'Of course. But if you prefer something a little more strenuous, then Hampstead Heath or perhaps Richmond. . .'

'Oh, no,' Felicity put in quickly. 'That sounds a little too boisterous and I am not the rider my sister is. The park will do me very well.'

'I think the gentlemen are teasing us, my dear,' Georgie said. 'And I think it is very uncivil of them. I have a good mind not to ride at all.'

'Oh, but you must!' Felicity cried. 'If you do not go I cannot and I should like it very much.'

'Very well.' Georgie, who could not deny her sister anything it was in her power to give, relented. 'But we shall have to hire mounts; Aunt Harriet has only carriage horses.'

'Leave that to me,' John said. 'I will undertake to bring mounts to your door, if you state the time.'

'For me, you may call as early as you like,' Georgie said. 'But I think we must observe the proprieties and not set out before the streets are aired. Shall we say ten?'

'Ten it shall be,' he agreed. 'I would offer to accompany you home, but I am engaged to call on Lady Hereward with my mama in half an hour.' He touched the brim of his riding hat and rode away, leaving Richard to accompany the girls back to Holles Street.

It took only a few minutes and for the first five of those he seemed to be too engrossed in watching Heacham negotiate the press of traffic to have much conversation, but as soon as they were out of the park he turned to Felicity and enquired about her preferences for a mount, gently drawing from her the information that although she could ride quite well—any daughter of Sir Henry Paget would be required to learn at an early age—she had not her sister's skill and would prefer not to have too spirited an animal. Georgie, watching him from under the brim of her bonnet, saw him relax, as if the news that the younger girl was not also a madcap rider was a relief.

'Georgie rides like a man,' Felicity went on, then, because she was suddenly afraid that she had said

something disparaging, added quickly, 'Not that she is
the least like a man really.'

He turned and gave Georgie a wry grin. 'So I had
observed.'

Georgie, who was not sure if he meant that he had
observed the way she rode or the fact that she was not
like a man, could find no reply to this, even if one was
expected, and she was glad they were drawing up at
her aunt's door. By the time he had jumped down and
handed them both our, instructed Heacham to walk
the horses up and down until he returned and accompanied them to the door, a reply was not necessary.

Tibbet, an old campaigner who had been engaged as
a footman by Colonel Bertram when he became too
old for soldiering, admitted them to the cool hall. A
bowl of sweet peas stood on a table and filled the air
with perfume. 'Mrs Bertram is in the blue salon with
Lord Barbour, Miss Paget,' he said.

Georgie ignored Richard's sharp intake of breath as
she took off her shawl and hat and handed them to the
servant. 'He came to see my aunt?'

'No, miss, I formed the opinion it was you he wished
to see.'

'Oh, you have made a hit!' Felicity cried. 'And you
did not say a word of it to me.'

'Didn't I? It must have slipped my mind.'

Richard gave a loud grunt which made them both
turn towards him and he quickly changed it to a cough.
Of all the men in London who could have attached
themselves to Miss Paget, it had to be Barbour. 'Your
pardon, ladies, but I must take my leave,' he said. He
could not face the man in Mrs Bertram's drawing-room

where the rules of etiquette obliged him to be polite. 'A pressing engagement.'

'Will you not stay and meet Georgie's admirer?' Felicity asked him. 'I must admit I am excessively curious.'

'Felicity!' Georgie cried. 'How can you be so rag-mannered?' She turned to Richard, her face flaming. 'I must apologise for my sister, Major. She is sometimes less than tactful.'

'Not at all; I find her candour delightfully refreshing.'

'Then you will stay?' Felicity asked.

'I am already acquainted with the gentleman,' he said, endeavouring to keep the frigidity from his voice but aware that the elder Miss Paget was not easy to deceive. 'I will call tomorrow as planned, unless. . .' he looked directly at Georgie, making her squirm uncomfortably '. . .unless Miss Paget would like to change her mind?'

'Of course I haven't changed my mind,' she said quickly. 'Felicity wishes to ride with you and I shall chaperon her. There is no more to be said.'

She watched him as he bowed himself out and then, with a sigh, went to join her aunt, followed by her sister. Lord Barbour, who had been ensconced in an armchair by the hearth, rose ponderously to his feet and hurried forward to bow over Georgie's hand.

'So sorry to miss you, my dear Miss Paget,' he said. 'Said I would call, if you remember. . .'

'So you did,' she said lightly. 'I forgot. May I present my sister Felicity?' She turned and quelled her sibling's inclination to giggle with a furious look. 'Felicity, this is Lord Cedric Barbour.'

He inclined his head towards her. 'Your obedient, Miss Felicity.'

'His lordship has been here this past half-hour,' their aunt said, trying not to sound as if she was complaining, though it had been excessively tiring trying to follow the gist of his lordship's staccato conversation, laced as it was with horsey allusions; he was worse than her brother-in-law and Henry had been bad enough. 'We have had a most interesting prose, have we not, my lord?'

'Indeed?' said Georgie, with a sinking feelng; that she had been a subject of their discourse she did not doubt. 'I am sorry I missed it.'

'Oh, you will be apprised of it, do not fear,' his lordship said. 'Your aunt has given me permission to invite you to ride with me. Got a new mount, you know. Black stallion. Not tried his paces yet. Told you're a bruising rider y'self.'

'I cannot think who told you that,' Georgie said, giving her aunt a meaningful look. 'I do not care for the term; it smacks of cruelty.'

'No, wrong thing to say,' he corrected himself. 'Meant capable. Capable, that's the word. What do you say? Will you ride with me tomorrow? Bring your sister if you want.'

'Oh, but we are going riding tomorrow in Green Park,' Felicity said before her sister could stop her. 'With——'

'I am sure Lord Barbour does not want the details dearest,' Georgie interrupted her. She turned to their visitor and gave him the benefit of a sugar-sweet smile. 'I am sorry, my lord, but I am already engaged for tomorrow.'

'Later, perhaps—a carriage drive?'

'We are taking tea with Mrs Melford. I am sorry, my lord; you seem to be out of luck.'

'The next day, then? You do not go back to Rowan Park before the week is out, do you?'

'No, but. . .'

'Georgiana will be pleased to ride with you the day after tomorrow,' Mrs Bertram said, frowning at her niece. 'Tom Dawson will accompany her.'

'I have no mount.' Her excuses were wearing thin, she knew it, and she knew she was exasperating her aunt, but she really did not see why she should be thrown at this unattractive man. If she had to marry, then why could it not be someone a shade younger and with a little more countenance?

Her aunt told her the answer to that in less than flattering terms when his lordship had taken his leave, after promising to provide her with a suitable mount and to call for her two days hence. 'It is no good you playing hard to get, my girl,' she said as soon as Felicity had left them to go to her room to change. 'He does not strike me as a patient man and you may lose him.'

'I wish that I might.'

'How can you say that? You are fortunate that he is interested. You are not in the first flush of youth, you know, and you have no call to turn your nose up at him. He is wealthy and generous to a fault. Why, he told me that he has a mare he thinks you will like. He hinted he would make you a present of it, if you pleased him.'

'I am to be bribed, is that it?'

'Not at all,' Mrs Bertram said, realising she had made a grave error. 'You will not be coerced into marrying someone you take in aversion, I promise you, but do give him a chance. You will not be committing yourself if you agree to ride with him. And even if he were impatient enough to offer for you so soon, which I doubt, for he is a man of breeding and knows how to go on, you do not have to answer him straight away. Give yourself a chance to become better acquainted with him.'

'And if after that I say we shall not suit?'

'Then no more will be said.' Her aunt sighed melodramatically. 'Though where else you will find another opportunity like it I declare I do not know. And you really ought to be married before your sister. . .'

'Why?'

'Because you are the elder, and besides, once she is married it will be the end of any interest in you. You will be put out to pasture. Is that not the term you horse-lovers would use?'

Georgie laughed, though she was far from amused. 'Then I shall become fat and contented like an old horse.'

'No, you will not. The stables will become run-down for want of business, the staff will have to be stood off and the house will go to rack and ruin without a family to fill it. You will not grow fat, for you will not have two grigs to rub together and certainly you will not be content because you will be lonely, banging around in that great barn of a place like a pea in a rattle. Is that what you want?'

The picture she painted was certainly not an enticing one. 'No, of course not.'

'Then consider it carefully, my dear. You may think me hard and unfeeling, but someone has to point out

the pitfalls of what you are doing. For your sister's
sake, I beg you not to turn Lord Barbour down out of
hand.'

'Very well, I shall ride with him, but if I do not find
him agreeable I beg leave not to encourage him.'

She really was not in a position to dictate terms, she
realised. She did not consider herself beautiful—striking perhaps but not beautiful—and she should have
come out eight years ago. Eight years! Where had they
all gone? She had been so content at her father's side,
looking after the horses, learning the day-to-day routine of a busy stables, breaking, exercising and grooming the horses, watching Papa haggling over prices,
putting a horse through its paces for a potential buyer,
sitting up all night with a sick animal. Oh, there had
been a great deal to do, especially when the army
needed so many horses. The seasons had followed one
upon the other, each busier than the last, and her small
sister had grown into a lovely young lady without her
even noticing the transformation. She didn't think Papa
had noticed either. And then he had died and everything had fallen on her shoulders.

Sometimes the burden seemed too much to carry.
Sometimes she wished desperately that she did have a
cousin or a brother to take charge. Sometimes she
longed for a little fun. But never, never would she
abrogate her responsibilities. She might argue with her
aunt and resist pressure simply because it was pressure,
like a young colt testing its will against its trainer, but,
like the colt, she would become docile in the end.

She tried telling herself that living with Lord Barbour
would not be so bad. He was interested in horses and
kept an extensive stable; combining their interests

could be beneficial to them both. He had been married before and had a family already and it was unlikely that he would make unnecessary physical demands on her. None of her arguments carried any weight beside the overwhelming one that she did not even like him.

If only someone young and handsome would come along and sweep her off her feet, someone who would carry on the stables in Sir Henry's tradition—someone like Major Baverstock. The thought, coming to her so suddenly, brought her up short. Why had he come to her mind? Unless. . .

She must not think along those lines, not for a single moment. Major Richard Baverstock was not for her. He had made it abundantly clear that he did not like mannish women and that was what she had become, and besides, Aunt Harriet had set her heart on marrying him off to Felicity and it seemed to her that both parties were more than agreeable. She followed her sister up the stairs to take off her outdoor clothes and wished, with all her heart, that she had never come to London.

Richard had ordered Heacham to take the phaeton back to the mews behind his father's town house in Portland Square and gone on foot to Bond Street where he proceeded to work out his ill temper at Gentleman Jackson's boxing establishment, though if he had been asked he would have strongly denied that his irritability had anything to do with Lord Barbour being at Holles Street. Mrs Bertram could entertain whom she pleased; so, for that matter, could Miss Paget. But Barbour! What was he up to?

When sparring failed in its purpose, he took himself

off to Watier's where he polished off a bottle of wine and sat down to play a hand of cards with Lord Hereward and a couple of his cronies. But he could not concentrate on the game and when John appeared soon after midnight he was glad enough to throw in his hand and repair to the smoking-room.

'Are you playing deep?' John demanded, looking at his friend's dishevelled appearance.

'No, just dabbling. Nothing better to do.'

'You don't look quite the thing, old fellow. Been given the rightabout by Miss Paget, have you?'

'Not at all,' Richard said morosely, lighting a cigarillo. 'It seems I have found favour.'

'Then you're a lucky fellow, that's all I can say.'

'I only hope my irascible parent may think the same.'

'Why should he not? Miss Paget is lovely, and well-bred, and though I ain't so sure about the dowry it don't much signify, does it, you having plump pockets anyhow?'

'I shan't have if my father leaves everything to my cousin William.'

'He ain't still on that tack, is he? I thought you went home to set that to rights. . .'

'Easier said than done, old fellow. William is still toadying round him, bringing those odious brats of his. They seem to take it for granted that they may have the run of the place in expectation of it becoming theirs. Noise and sticky fingermarks everywhere and the dogs teased until I wonder they do not turn round and bite. I am persuaded William positively encourages them to misbehave in order to infuriate me.'

'Don't you like children?'

'How should I know? Never had any.' He paused

and smiled. 'With the right wife, I suppose I might become the doting papa.'

John laughed. 'I cannot see you as a family man.'

'It seems my father can. I'm to find a wife as soon as maybe.'

'What's so hard about that? You ain't still thinking of Maria, are you?'

'No, that's all over with, but damn me, John, I just do not like being pushed.'

John laughed. 'No and nor don't I. I've just spent the more boring hour of my life in the company of Juliette Hereward and our respective mamas.'

'Matchmaking, are they?'

'I wouldn't mind so much but the chit is hardly out of the schoolroom.'

'There speaks an old, old man,' Richard said, with a laugh.

'I'll be twenty-one in a few months. I may be young but I've had plenty of time to grow up in the last three years, wouldn't you say?'

'I can't deny it. Battle certainly hardens a man.'

In his mind's eye Richard saw again the smoke and flames, the blood of men and horses mingling on the baked earth; heard the guns, the clash of sabres and the cries of the wounded. Every battle was the same, though he wondered if anyone ever became truly hardened to it. But in time it had a numbing effect; you pretended indifference, convinced yourself that you were invulnerable and sometimes it worked; he had come through with only a slight shoulder wound which only troubled him when the weather was damp or if he had to put undue strain on it.

But Maria, who had no business near the fighting,

had died. She had died because some clunch of a trooper had told her that her lover had been wounded and she had hurried to his aid, as so many of the wives and other camp followers had. Making his way back to the hospital wagon on foot, he had seen her coming and shouted to her to go back. She had heard his voice but, unsure of its direction, had stopped to listen and the shell had landed right beside her. It had been his fault; if he had not shouted, she would have kept moving. The day had been won but he could find no joy in the victory. Now the war was over and he had to try and forget.

'Juliette doesn't seem to have matured by as much as a day.' John's voice invaded his memories and brought him back with a jolt.

'Protected as she is, she has no reason to grow up too soon, has she?' he said. 'Have patience, my friend.'

'Thank God there's no hurry and I don't have to offer for her before I come of age. And by then who knows. . .?' He laughed in an embarrassed way and got to his feet. 'Do not forget we have an engagement to go riding tomorrow at the ungodly hour of ten o'clock, so I am away to my bed.' He beckoned to a waiter who was passing with a tray of glasses and bade him fetch a hackney, before turning back to Richard. 'Do you want a lift?'

Richard, befuddled by the smoky atmosphere and the wine he had consumed, needed fresh air to clear his head and said he preferred to walk. By the time he arrived back in Portland Square dawn was just coming up over the chimney-pots and the milkmaids were leading their charges out of the parks and taking them to the kitchen doors of the big houses to dispense their milk. He was greeted at the door by Heacham, still fully clothed.

'Why are you still up, man?' he asked in surprise. Unlike many, he did not expect his servant to wait up for him.

'I thought you'd like to know the Viscount has arrived,' the valet said, helping him off with his coat.

'My father?'

'Yes, Major.'

'Damn!'

Heacham thought it tactful not to hear that remark. 'Before his lordship went to bed, Major, he bade me tell you he will take breakfast with you. I told him you would be up and out by half-past nine but he did not seem to take exception to that. I heard him order his man to wake him at half after eight.'

Richard had barely set his head on the pillow—or so he thought—before Heacham was shaking him into wakefulness again. He had pulled back the curtains and the sun was streaming in at the window, hurting his eyes. 'Time to rise, Major. I left you as long as I dare.'

Richard grunted and took the cup of coffee his servant held out to him, swallowing it scalding hot and demanded another while he hauled himself out of bed, washed and dressed in soft buckskin riding breeches and a linen shirt. He swallowed the second cup of coffee before carefully tying his cravat. His third was consumed after he had pulled on his tasselled riding boots and Heacham had helped him into a jacket of Bath cloth with velvet facings. By the time he went down to the small family dining-room he was feeling more himself. He was not in the least surprised to find his father, in a quilted dressing-gown, already at breakfast.

'Good morning, sir,' he said, pretending a brightness he did not feel. 'Heacham told me you had arrived. What brings you here?'

'I can come to my own house, can't I?' his lordship said irritably. His gout was more than usually troublesome today, probably because he had sat up waiting for his son the night before and drunk too much claret. 'You bolted without so much as a by your leave. Dashed bad manners, don't you know?'

'I'm sorry, Father. I thought we had said all there was to say. . .'

'Well, we did not. At any rate, I had not. Seems to me if I want to have a conversation with you I must uproot myself from a comfortable home and chase after you. You know I don't like town above half; the fog gets into m'lungs.'

Richard forbore to point out that it was the middle of summer and there was no fog. 'I'm sorry to have put you to that inconvenience, sir.'

'The devil you are! Where did you get to last night?'

'Watier's. If I had known you were coming. . .'

'Watier's! You'll not find a bride there, my boy. I begin to wonder if you are making any push at all. Good thing I did come, if you ask me. . .'

Richard's heart sank. 'What's the haste? You are in plump currant, aren't you?'

'If you mean by that am I about to wind up my accounts, then the answer is not if I can help it. Another reason I had for coming to town was to see my physician.'

'Then you are ill.' Richard was beset by feelings of guilt. 'I am sorry to hear that, Father.'

'You'll be even sorrier if I stick my spoon in the wall before I can change my will. . .'

'Change it?'

His lordship favoured his son with a wry grin. 'When you ran off to war, I disowned you, made a will in favour of William; thought you knew that. . .'

'You threatened it. I didn't know you had done it.'

'Don't threaten what I don't mean to do,' he asserted. 'I was angry and too hasty, perhaps, but I shan't reverse it unless you come up to the mark.'

'You must do as you wish, of course,' Richard said stiffly.

'I wish to be succeeded by my son and his sons, that's what I wish. I have told William so.'

'He must have been very disappointed,' Richard said pithily. No wonder William was so constantly at Dullingham House!

'No doubt, but I would rather he were disappointed than I.' His lordship's voice softened and he reached out a thin veined hand to touch Richard's sleeve. 'It's up to you.'

The fact that his father was employing a not so subtle blackmail did little to make Richard feel any better. He had been a poor sort of son and if his lordship was really ill, perhaps dying, it behoved him to make amends. . .

There was no time for further discussion, for Heacham came to say that Captain Melford had arrived. 'He says he won't come in,' the servant said. 'He is mounted and is leading two park hacks with ladies' saddles.'

'Is that so?' his lordship said, grinning at his son. 'It seems I did you an injustice, m'boy. Who is she?'

'Sir Henry Paget's daughter.'

'That so? I liked old Henry, you could do worse, though I hope it isn't the elder. I've heard she's become a sad case. Tries to play the man. Can't have you leg-shackled to a horse-face.'

Richard smiled, thinking of Miss Georgiana Paget; whatever she was, it was certainly not horse-faced. In her own way she was stunningly beautiful; she had character and fire, but she was also maddeningly independent. Anyone foolish enough to marry her, even if he could break down the barrier she had put up around herself, would undoubtedly have a daily battle on his hands. On the other hand, his father would definitely approve of Miss Felicity Paget, and what more could a man ask for in a wife? Sweet and kind and biddable, wasn't that what Georgiana had said? After nine years of war he was tired of fighting; he would settle for biddable. 'No, sir, she is chaperon to her sister.'

'Then be off with you. You mustn't keep the ladies waiting.'

Richard, feeling himself sinking deeper and deeper into a quagmire of his own making, took his leave and, fetching Pegasus from the stable, joined his friend, taking one of the park hacks in hand, to call on the Misses Paget.

CHAPTER FOUR

BOTH ladies were ready when the young men arrived; Felicity wore a burgundy riding jacket, frogged in silver, and a riding hat whose sweeping feather brushed her cheek, and Georgie was in peacock-blue, frogged and braided. A high-crowned beaver hat with a stiff brim around which a gossamer scarf had been tied was perched on her auburn curls.

Georgie half expected some comment about the side-saddle as Richard threw her up, but he had evidently decided that antagonising the chaperon was not a way to win the lady and remained silent. In fact, he seemed a little vague, as if he had something else on his mind, which was hardly flattering, but as Felicity and Mr Melford seemed to have no difficulty in maintaining the conversation it hardly mattered and by the time they turned in at the gate of the park he had recovered sufficiently to make an effort at small talk.

Georgie longed to let her horse go and gallop, but, deciding that was hardly the behaviour to be expected of a chaperon, rode sedately beside her sister, who had the gentlemen vying for position on the other side of her. Surprisingly, John seemed to win that particular manoeuvre and Georgie found herself with Richard on her other side.

'How do you find Pegasus, Major?' she asked, looking at the stallion a little wistfully.

Richard leaned forward to pat the grey's neck. 'Oh,

we are dealing together very well, aren't we, Peg, old fellow?'

'Why did you bring him to London?'

'Why not? I wished to test his stamina.'

'I hope that does not mean you rode him hard all the way. I should not have let you have him if I thought you would do that.'

'And I am not flattered that you think me such a mopstraw as to ruin a good horse, Miss Paget. I am no Dick Turpin.'

'Dick Turpin?'

'He was a high toby of a hundred years ago; have you not heard of him?'

'Of course I have. He was supposed to have ridden from London to York in a day, or a night—I forget which. It's all a hum, of course; it can't be done.'

'You don't thinks so.'

'Not on a single horse; I believe it is all of two hundred miles.'

'Yes, but supposing you had any number of horses?' He was smiling, as if he had discovered some secret he was half inclined to share with her.

'How many?'

'I don't know—twenty, shall we say?'

'That's one every ten miles. You can't gallop a horse for ten miles, Major, not without ruining it.'

'More, then—shall we say thirty?'

'You may say what you please; it is purely conjecture.'

'I think I should like to put it to the test,' he said slowly, as an idea began to form in his mind which excited him. 'Yes, I think that might serve.'

'Major, I am persuaded you are bamming me as

usual. Even if you had a hundred horses, you would still need to be in the saddle twelve hours at least.'

'Nine.'

She turned her head to survey him from beneath the brim of her hat, but he was looking straight ahead with a faint smile on his lips. 'Why nine?'

'Supper in London, breakfast in York.'

'It can't be done.'

He turned towards her, smiling. 'Now, would you care to put money on that, Miss Paget?'

'Certainly not!' she said. 'I never gamble. And I am surprised at you. I had thought you a man of sense. I wish now I had not sold Pegasus to you, if that is the kind of thing you do.'

He laughed and turned back to John who was riding just behind him. 'Would you back me, John?'

'Oh, yes, old fellow, every time,' his friend said complacently.

'You cannot have heard our conversation, Captain, and do not even know what Major Baverstock has proposed,' Georgie said sharply.

'What? Has he proposed?' Felicity asked, coming up a little behind John. 'Am I to offer felicitations, then?'

'No!' Georgie's retort was sharp and all three looked at her in surprise. 'No, of course not; you mistake the meaning, my dear. Major Baverstock was proposing a wager, not. . .' She stopped, embarrassed.

'A wager? Oh, forgive me. How silly of me. To think——Oh, dear. . .' She was clearly mortified.

Georgie came to the rescue, as much to save herself as her sister. 'The Major was saying he can ride from London to York without stopping,' she said.

'In nine hours,' Richard added.

'We've had some pretty long spells in the saddle in the last few years,' John said. 'And in the heat of a Spanish summer, but never that far. No mount would stand up to it.'

'Oh, I wasn't intending to do it with a single horse,' Richard told him. 'Thirty horses, posted along the way. It would be an endurance test for the man more than the animals.'

'Then I supose it could be done, but I'll tell you I wouldn't attempt it.'

'It's all gammon,' Georgie said. 'And all because I said I wondered at him bringing Pegasus to London. It would have been quicker by coach.'

'But nothing like as enjoyable and I would not have had a mount while I was here.'

'I doubt Pegasus finds parading in the park to his liking, Major. I am sure he would rather gallop.'

He grinned. 'Would you?'

There was a wide expanse of green sward ahead of them where a herd of cows usually grazed, but they had congregated to one small area near the Bath Gate and were showing not the least interest in the riders. She turned to look at Felicity and John who had resumed their place a little behind them and were deep in conversation. Dared she leave them, just for a few minutes? It wasn't as if they would go out of sight. . . .

'Race you to that big oak,' she cried and, without waiting for him to reply, dug her heel into her hack's flank and set off across the grass.

It was only a couple of hundred yards and her mount was not Warrior or anything like him and riding side-saddle was uncomfortable at speed, but it was good to feel the horse respond and for a little while she forgot she was supposed to be a staid chaperon, forgot that it was not done for a lady to gallop, forgot that the man who soon came up alongside her disapproved of such hoydenish behaviour. She was in her element on a horse's back.

They reached the tree together and pulled up, laughing.

'You cheated,' he said. 'Setting off ahead of me like that.'

'It is strange how some people cannot stand to be beaten,' said a languid voice. 'They must forever accuse the victor of cheating.'

Georgie turned in astonishment to find a horseman she had barely noticed before sitting on his mount under the tree watching them. It was Lord Barbour, mounted on a beautiful chestnut.

Richard, who had become aware of the other man's identity at precisely the moment Georgie had issued her challenge, had been obliged to follow her, but that did not mean he had to listen to insults. 'I do not recall Miss Paget speaking to you, sir,' he said.

'Only because she did not see me.' His lordship turned to Georgie, smiling confidently. 'Is that not so, Miss Paget?'

'Why, yes,' she said, bewildered by the hostility between the two men; it fairly crackled. 'Do you know each other? Oh, but of course you do; Major Baverstock told me so only yesterday.'

'Did he now?' His lordship appeared amused. 'Did he also tell you in what connection we came to know each other?'

'No, but I recall him saying you had bought his hunter.'

His lordship laughed. 'Bought it, did I? Well, he would say that. But I should beware of striking bargains with him, Miss Paget. He will renege, to be sure.'

Richard's face was a picture of fury and Georgie thought for one dreadful minute that he would strike the man with his crop, but he seemed to make a monumental effort to hold himself in check and the raised hand dropped to his side. 'If there were not ladies present. . .'

'I see you have bought a new mount,' Lord Barbour went on, looking at Pegasus with a keen eye. 'Not bad, but not up to Victor, is he?' He leaned forward and ruffled the chestnut's ear. 'Thought you wanted him back.'

'And I will have him, too.'

'Then all you have to do is name the time and place.'

Georgie looked from one to the other, thoroughly perplexed, but they were interrupted as John and Felicity rode up.

'Oh, good morning, my lord,' Felicity greeted him. 'So, you found us, then. I thought that you might. Shall you ride back with us?'

There was a malicious gleam in Lord Barbour's eye, as if he was tempted to accept, but one glance at Richard told him not to push his luck. He made his excuses, doffing his tall riding hat to the ladies and reminding Georgie that she had promised to ride with him the next day and that he would call for her, and then he cantered away, leaving the four young people to ride back to Holles Street in almost complete silence.

The incident had put a damper on the outing and as soon as they had paid their respects to Mrs Bertram the young men rode away, taking the hacks with them.

'Did you tell Lord Barbour where we were to be found?' Georgie turned on her sister as soon as they were alone.

'No, indeed I did not. But I don't see why you are so up in the boughs over it.'

'I am not, but it was plain as a pikestaff there is no love lost between his lordship and the Major.'

'Captain Melford said it had something to do with a wager. The Major lost his hunter. . .'

'Victor?' It was extraordinary how disappointed in Richard Baverstock Georgie felt over that. She knew young gentlemen gambled on almost anything and thought nothing of it, but to put up a horse as special as Victor was nothing short of criminal. For the second time she wished she had not sold Pegasus to him.

'As to that, I don't know,' Felicity said. 'You'll have to ask Lord Barbour tomorrow.'

His lordship duly arrived the following morning, riding Victor and leading a beautiful Arab mare for Georgie to ride. 'She's yours whenever you ride with me,' he said, smiling because she could not hide her pleasure. 'And I would wish it to be every day.'

'Thank you, my lord,' she said as Tom Dawson, who was to ride discreetly behind them, held out his hands for her to mount. 'But I am sure you have other demands on your time than riding in the park with me.'

'None which gives me greater pleasure.'

He was behaving perfectly properly and there was nothing in his behaviour to give offence, but she could not like him. She could not say exactly why. Perhaps it was his smile, which she could only describe as oily, perhaps it was his eyes, small, pale and watchful, or perhaps it was the way he jerked on the reins when the spirited horse shied away from the traffic. Once they were in the park, the stallion seemed a little easier, but Georgie didn't think he liked his rider any better than she did.

'You have only just acquired Victor, I believe,' she said.

'Yes, from that young rake Baverstock.'

'As the result of a wager, I am told.'

He gave a snort of a laugh. 'Yes, and not even his. He was standing buff for that young pup of a friend of his who played too deep.'

'Captain Melford?'

'Yes.'

She didn't know if she admired the Major more or less because of this piece of information; that he had stood by his friend was certainly in his favour, but the horse had still been gambled away. 'Why don't you like Major Baverstock, my lord?'

'Did I say I did not like him? I do not like a bad loser calling me a cheat, that is what I do not like.' He sighed and smiled across at her. 'But let us not talk of him. What do you think of Silver Moon?'

She could understand the Major not liking to part with his stallion but it was his own fault for gambling. Even so, she could not imagine him being a bad loser. Calling someone a cheat usually meant that you had to substantiate your accusation or be called out. She remembered his lordship saying 'name the time and place'; did that mean there was to be a duel? It would be a most uneven match, unless his lordship had hidden talents. She looked across at him; he was smiling at her with that hard mouth of his, waiting for her answer.

She reached forward and fondled the ears of the Arab.
'Is that her name? She is beautiful.'

'Her dam was one of Sir Henry's.'

'Then she is bound to be good.'

'She could be yours.'

Startled, she looked at him. 'My lord?'

'As a gift.'

'My lord, I have horses in plenty at Rowan Park.'

'But for how long? You cannot continue to run the
stables yourself, can you?'

'I do not see why not.'

'Oh, I see,' he said, his smile widening. 'You have
had no offers.'

His assumption annoyed her. 'Do you mean for me
or for the business?' she asked mischievously.

'Why, my dear,' he said, with an attempt at gallantry
which set her teeth on edge but which she acknowledged she had asked for, 'I have no doubt someone as
comely as you has had offers a-plenty, but I meant for
the stud-farm.'

'Some, but I have refused them all.'

'Why? Because the offers were too low or because
the horses are your dowry?'

'Because they are my life, my lord. I wish for no
other.'

'Come, come, that cannot be. Every young lady
wishes to marry, but in your case you should choose
carefully. You need someone who understands horses,
who will improve the stock with his own, someone who
will allow you a certain amount of liberty. . .'

She looked at him sharply. 'What do you mean?'

'Yours is a free spirit, Miss Paget; it should not be
caged in a drawing-room. I understand that.'

'My lord, I do not think you do,' she said. 'I am as good a horse-breeder as you will find anywhere and neither Rowan Park nor the horses are for sale.' She laughed suddenly. 'Nor, indeed, am I.' And with that she urged Silver Moon into a canter to put an end to the conversation. He followed and a few minutes later they turned to go back without another word being said.

She did not like him any better at the end of the outing than she had at the beginning, but her aunt, when she recounted the conversation to her, urged her to give him time. 'What he said makes a great deal of sense,' she pointed out. 'The stud-farm is all you have to offer and do not forget it has to provide Felicity's portion as well as yours. A union of his stables with yours might be just the answer. His stock is good, I believe, and with his name the business would soon pick up. I will invite him to my ball and you can stand up with him. Perhaps in a different setting, with music and fine food, he will reveal himself as a man of sensibility.'

'I doubt it,' Georgie said.

'Nevertheless we must make sure you look your best; we can't have him thinking he is offering for a dowd.'

'I thought it was Felicity we were concerned with, not me.'

'Both, my dear, but I am persuaded your sister has already found a match. All we have to do is bring him to the mark.'

'Major Baverstock, you mean.'

'Of course I mean the Major—who else could it be? Now we must make plans. . .'

This constant talk of offers and dowries, husbands

and lovers, gowns and jewels was more than Georgie
could stomach and she was more determined than ever
to return to Rowan Park at the end of the week. It
would mean missing her aunt's ball and that would
cause a great argument, but she truly could not stand a
whole evening in Lord Barbour's company. But before
she could go there were several social functions to
attend and, for Felicity's sake, she was determined to
enjoy them and forward her sister's interest with the
Major.

Mrs Bertram made up a party to visit Ranelagh
Gardens one evening which included Richard and
John, Lord and Lady Hereward and their daughter,
Juliette. It proved to be very enjoyable, with fireworks
and dancing in the Rotunda, though it was a sad crush.

The outing was reciprocated by her ladyship with an
invitation to a play. Only too conscious of being the
odd one out, Georgie would rather not have gone but
her aunt insisted that she would give mortal offence if
she did not go and so she gave in. The play was
supposed to be a melodrama, but in Georgie's opinion
it was more like a farce and she was not surprised that
the audience spent most of the time hissing and booing
and laughing at the efforts of the players.

She noticed that Felicity and John seemed to be
enjoying it for their heads were together and they were
smiling. As for Richard, he seemed totally bored—or
perhaps it was jealousy which caused the frown? After
all, he was supposed to be Felicity's escort, not John.
She leaned across and spoke to him. 'You are looking
very serious, Major. Is the entertainment not to your
liking?'

He came out of his brown study to smile at her. 'What do you think of it?'

'I find the audience far more entertaining than the play,' she said, leaning over the box to look up at the noisy gallery. There was one couple arguing over whether they should throw fruit at the actors; he was standing up with his arm ready to fling an apple and she was trying to stop him. Others, complaining that they blocked the view of the stage, were entreating them to sit down and shut up unless they wanted to be thrown over the balcony into the pits. Fortunately they were saved by the dropping of the curtain for the intermission.

The Major and Captain Melford went in search of a waiter to bring refreshments for everyone and while they were gone Lord Barbour came to their box to pay his respects. He bowed to the ladies and sat in Richard's vacant seat. He was still there, still trying to engage Georgie's attention, when Richard returned. 'My dear Miss Paget,' he was saying, aware that the Major could not return to his chair until he left, 'I shall look forward with impatience to Mrs Bertram's ball; the invitation arrived this morning. I hope you will stand up with me for at least two. . .' he grinned '. . . perhaps three dances.' With that he rose ponderously and took her hand which he lifted to his lips. 'Until then, my dear Miss Paget.'

Georgie did not like his familiar way of addressing her and was half inclined to give him a put-down for supposing that she would agree to more than the two dances which etiquette decreed were proper, but, looking over his shoulder, she saw Richard watching them. He had a look of fury, as if she had no right to speak to whom she pleased, and a little devil inside her made her smile impishly. 'Pray, do not hurry away, my lord. The second act is not yet begun.'

With a smile of triumph, he sat down again, much to Mrs Bertram's delight. She called to Richard to sit between her and Felicity, which entailed a great shifting around, so that Georgie was sitting between his lordship and John, who had Juliette on his other side, and thus they settled down for the second act. It was all so contrived that it amused Georgie, who told herself she had no preference where she sat.

But as the remainder of the play was as bad as the first she found her attention wandering to the dimness of the box behind her. She had encouraged Lord Barbour simply to score a point over Major Baverstock and she was heartily ashamed of herself. Her behaviour would embolden his lordship, who sat gloating beside her and laughing too loudly at the antics of the players on the stage, and it would certainly give the Major an aversion to the whole family. Had she spoiled Felicity's chances? She glanced towards them. From what she could see, they were both engrossed in the drama on the stage and ignoring each other.

Mrs Bertram noticed it too, and it was the subject of her diatribe in the coach on the way home. 'Felicity, my child, you really must not behave so coldly towards the Major; you will not encourage him that way.'

'I didn't mean to be cold,' she said. 'But he frightens me. Every time he looks at me, I am struck dumb.'

'You seem to have no difficulty in smiling at Captain Melford and chattering like a magpie to Juliette Hereward.'

'They are more my own age.'

'Fudge! You must make more of a push. Your sister had made a great many sacrifices to give you this Season and you are unlikely to get another. . .'

'Oh, Aunt,' Georgie put in, laying a reassuring hand on her sister's arm. 'Please don't make a great thing out of that. I would not have Felicity made to feel guilty on my account. Besides, you have done most. . .'

'Oh, give me patience!' their aunt exclaimed as the carriage drew up at their door and they were admitted by a footman. 'How either of you can expect to take when you don't listen to a word I say I do not know. Do you want to go home without a single offer between you?'

'As for me, Aunt, I expect none,' Georgie said, all the more determined not to put herself in the position of having to hear a proposal from Lord Barbour. 'But Felicity is a different matter.'

Mrs Bertram turned to her younger niece. 'Well, child, are you going to take my advice or not?'

'I'll try, Aunt,' Felicity said meekly, squeezing Georgie's hand.

The next morning the Major called to escort Felicity to Bullock's Museum, and because their aunt had not yet left her room Georgie was once again pressed into service as chaperon. It was a duty she would willingly have laid down, not because she did not want to see the wonders on display, but because she found herself trembling at the thought of meeting Major Baverstock again. It was not fear which held her in its grip but shame that she had as good as cut him. If he was to be her brother-in-law, then for her sister's sake the sooner she put that right the better.

It was a pleasant morning, not too hot considering it was July, and they had decided to walk the short distance to Old Bond Street. The girls were dressed in cool muslins and carried lace-trimmed parasols and Richard was handsomely dressed for town in a double-breasted dark green tailcoat and buff pantaloons, his cravat skilfully tied and held with a diamond pin. They were three very handsome young people out on the town, though Felicity was, as usual, very quiet and Georgie's smile so stiff she thought her face would crack. Richard seemed unaware of it as he walked between them, stopping every now and again to doff his tall hat and greet acquaintances and chatting easily to both girls.

Georgie wondered if he had forgotten how badly she had treated him, or perhaps he had decided to ignore it for her sister's sake. Or perhaps he'd excused her on the grounds that she knew no better. That hurt most of all. She could not say anything to him in front of her sister but she did not see how she was ever going to be able to speak to him alone in order to apologise.

There was a crowd at the entrance to the museum for several new exhibits had lately arrived from the battlefields and Londoners, who had little idea of what a battle was really like, were agog to see torn standards and captured eagles, bloodied sabres and guns which had been at this and that siege. There were a great many soldiers begging along the lines of people waiting to go in. 'Spare a copper for an old soldier who fought for 'is country,' they said, and, when they were rebuffed, muttered among themselves, using language that made the girls' ears turn pink with embarrassment.

Three in particular stood near the door, entreating

those about to enter. They were filthy and dressed in rags; one had lost an arm and another had a blood-stained bandage round his head and covering one eye. 'This is what we fought and died for, is it?' one of them said, pushing against Felicity, who jumped back in alarm. 'So the rich can gape at rubbish from a battle-field. Why don't you put us on display, eh? We're rubbish, ain't that so? Never no mind it's 'cos of what we did you can sleep easy in yer bed o' nights.'

'Get away,' Felicity cried, putting her gloved hands to her face and backing against Richard, who gently put her into Georgie's care and turned back to the men.

'What was your regiment?' he demanded.

'Ninth, sir,' their spokesmen said, coming stiffly to attention, for he recognised an officer, even though he was in civilian dress, and old habits died hard.

'East Norfolks,' Richard said. 'Why haven't you returned home?'

'Nothing to go home for,' their leader said. 'We'd only be more mouths to feed. We'll go when we've got something worthwhile to take with us.'

Richard felt in his tail pocket for his purse and extracted a couple of guineas and some small change. 'Here, take this but use it to some purpose. If you won't go home, then go to Dullingham House in Cambridgeshire. Say Major Baverstock sent you and you'll be given work.'

'Thank you, Major. You're a real gent. We'll not forget you.' They touched their foreheads and backed away, murmuring apologies to the girls as they went.

'Do you think they will really go to Dullingham House?' Georgie asked.

He smiled wryly. 'They'll probably go to the nearest
tavern, but who can blame them? I certainly would
not. Now come; let us see what this estimable establishment has to show us.'

With the Major to tell them about the exhibits they
learned more than the general crowd who simply
walked round gaping at blood-stained uniforms and
gory paintings of men and horses. Long before they
had seen everything Felicity complained that she felt
faint and Georgie herself was glad enough to escape
into the fresh air. 'I didn't know it was going to be like
that,' Felicity said, holding on to Richard's arm with
both hands. 'I am sure it must be exaggerated.'

'Very likely,' he said laconically, but Georgie caught
the look in his eye and knew he was only trying to
comfort her sister and that, if anything, what they had
seen had been watered down. 'Stay here with Miss
Paget and I'll find a carriage to take you home.'

'Oh, dear,' Felicity said when he had gone. 'Now he
thinks me exceedingly foolish.'

'Oh, I am sure he does not,' Georgie assured her,
watching his tall figure stride into the road to hail a
passing hackney. 'He will appreciate your sensibility.'

'But you did not faint, did you?'

She smiled. 'No, but I am tough as old boots, aren't
I?' She was tough; she had to be. She had to be strong
enough to run a business and ignore criticism; she had
to keep up the pretence of not caring about anything
but her horses. For her sister's sake, she had to steel
her heart against falling in love. She might even have
to accept the odious Lord Barbour. But why was it so
hard?

Richard returned with a cab and accompanied them

back to Holles Street and still Georgie had not been able to speak to him alone. Perhaps it was best to let sleeping dogs lie, she thought. To apologise might be to draw attention to frailties in her she would rather keep hidden, especially if he had dismissed the incident as unimportant. And it was unimportant, for what was he to her or she to him? It was Felicity who mattered and she seemed to have overcome her shyness of the Major and was chatting away quite easily, saying how much she was looking forward to Lady Hereward's picnic and asking him if he would be there, to which he gallantly replied that he would not miss it for worlds.

The picnic was to be held at Richmond, a pleasant village set beside the Thames, where Lord and Lady Hereward had a villa and where they had removed to escape the heat of town, now that the Season was all but at an end. A few hardy souls remained to continue the victory celebrations which had been going on all summer and extended the Season, but even these were beginning to pall and many of the *ton* had taken themselves off to Paris, now in allied hands and once more the place to see and be seen. The picnic would be a little compensation for those left behind.

The day chosen for it was a warm one, the sky a clear forget-me-not blue; larks soared above the meadows on either side of the road as they left the town and passed through Hammersmith and Mortlake and down Richmond Hill to the park beside the river, which reflected the azure sky. Over the river hovered damselflies and kingfishers and moorhens and ducks shared the water with graceful swans. Lady Hereward had selected a spot on the grassy bank where chestnut trees cast their shade and here servants had spread out a cloth and were busy covering it with delectable things to eat and drink.

Georgie was glad she had chosen a cool primrose muslin and a large-brimmed cottager hat to keep the sun off her face and neck, but even then she was hot and sticky and felt sorry for the men, dressed as they were in coats and waistcoats, not to mention starched muslin cravats. But by the time the meal had ended many of them had discarded their coats and loosened their neckwear and were lounging easily, chatting animatedly about the news and gossip of the day.

Some of the more energetic began a game of cricket; others strolled off with young ladies, their chaperons a few paces behind. Felicity had gone off somewhere arm in arm with Juliette but as Mrs Bertram was dozing in a chair brought from the carriage Georgie assumed it was not necessary to accompany her sister and contented herself with sitting on a rug with her back to a tree, watching the antics of the cricketers.

Major Baverstock was a skilled batsman and managed twenty runs over the rough grass before being bowled out and joining John on the grass not far from where Georgie sat. She found herself observing him from beneath the brim of her hat as he sprawled on the grass talking to his friend. He reminded her of a leopard, muscular and sleek, with lazy dark eyes which could change in an instant to watchfulness. He was powerful and yet relaxed, his teeth were strong and white and his chin firm, but, unlike a leopard, he suddenly broke into unexpected laughter and his eyes sparkled as he responded to something John had said. They scrambled to their feet and wandered off together.

Gone to find Felicity and Juliette, she thought, suppressing the terrible pang of envy which suddenly beset her. If only there were two such men! But if there were, who was to say one would look twice at her? She looked down at her hands clasped in her lap. They were brown and workworn. She hid them in the folds of her gown and shut her eyes. For a few moments she allowed herself to dream, but the dream was broken when she heard a slight sound as someone sat down beside her. Her eyes flew open and she found Richard not a yard away.

'Major Baverstock!'

'I'm sorry, I startled you.'

'No, not at all. I thought. . . I thought you had gone to find Felicity.'

He smiled. 'Then I would have expected you to leap to her side as a good chaperon should and that might have spoiled her walk.'

She returned his smile, though her hands, still in the folds of her skirt, were shaking and her heart was beating uncomfortably in her throat. 'I am not very good at it, am I, Major?'

'At what?'

'Being a chaperon.'

'I do not see why you should be one at all. You are far too young.'

'Sir, you are presumptuous,' she said, proving that even with a tanned complexion it was possible to blush scarlet.

'Not at all. I was simply stating the obvious. Why do you pretend?'

'Pretend, Major?'

'Yes, pretend to be staid and very proper. You are

sitting there as stiff as a board and wishing you were anywhere but here. It is hardly flattering.'

'You would have me flatter you with empty phrases?'

'Not at all. But you forget, I have seen you as you really are, free as a bird, flying over a hedge on that great stallion. This. . .' he spread his hands to encompass their surroundings '. . . this is not the real you.'

'Do you have to remind me of something I would rather forget? I have apologised for startling you; is it not enough? Besides, it was part of my daily work to exercise Warrior.'

'There you go again, thinking of work and duty.'

'I have little time for frivolity. . .'

'Then you should make time. It would not hurt you to forget Rowan Park and enjoy yourself for once, even to flirt a little.'

'Flirting is a game I do not care to play, Major. I am persuaded it might easily end in tears.'

'Whose tears?' he asked softly, bending towards her. She thought for one breathtaking moment that he was going to kiss her and tensed herself ready to rebuff him, but he did nothing except look deeply into her eyes. 'Yours?'

'No,' she hastened to tell him. 'I was speaking generally.'

'Then let us speak of the particular. If you are not afraid of your own tears, could it be your sister's?'

She wondered how he could be so far-seeing. Was she so transparent that anyone could see into her head and read her thoughts? 'Felicity is all the close family I have,' she said slowly. 'Her happiness is important to me. But I cannot see what that has to be with——'

'With me?'

She hesitated, then said, 'No, I was going to say with me enjoying myself. . .'

'Don't you? I do. You would supress your own feminine instincts, give up your own chance of happiness in order to see your sister safely settled with a good dowry, which is something Sir Henry should have done for you both, instead of——'

'Sir, you will oblige me by not referring to my father in those terms. He was a good man; he did his best for both of us. After Mama died it was not easy for him. He loved her so much. . .' She stopped suddenly. Why was she telling him this? Why had she not ended the conversation minutes ago? 'You have no right. . .'

'Forgive me,' he said softly, reaching out and putting a hand on her arm. 'I have only added to your problems, when truly all I wanted was to alleviate them. You looked so sad. . .'

'I am not sad, Major Baverstock. Because I do not prattle all the time it does not mean I am unhappy.'

'I am pleased to hear it. But will you promise me something?'

'It depends,' she said guardedly.

'Promise me that you will do nothing rash in the next few days.'

'What could I be going to do that is rash?' she asked, genuinely puzzled.

'Do not dispose of Rowan Park. There is no need. . .'

'Major, I have no plans to dispose of it; you should know that. Felicity shall have her dowry. . .'

'It was not of your sister's dowry I was thinking,' he said angrily, 'but of you. If you should ever need help, I am at your service. . .'

'Thank you, Major, but I can manage my own affairs,' she told him, thrusting her chin into the air and looking him straight in the eye, though it was a rash thing to do because he was regarding her with an expression so filled with tender concern, it was all she could do not to burst into tears. 'And Felicity's, too.'

'Father and mother both,' he said. 'I fear the burden is too much for you, my valiant trooper.'

'Go away,' she said, choking back tears. 'Leave me alone.'

'Do you mean that?'

'Of course I do. Go and find Felicity.'

He picked up her hand and lifted it to his lips. 'Yours to command, dear lady.' His soft voice of a moment before had become light, almost frivolous. 'I will find your sister and bring her safely back to you.' With that, he got up and strolled away, leaving her shaking and spent as if she had run a mile in heavy boots.

And she had still not apologised for her behaviour at the theatre. But it did not seem to matter now, not after what had just happened. Their conversation had been so intimate, so deep, as if each had been trying to convey something of which they were only dimly aware. It had been wrong, even more wrong than the slight she had given him at the theatre; she felt as though she had betrayed her sister. And, in analysing the reason for that, she realised suddenly that she loved Richard Baverstock.

She was so shocked that she started up with a little cry, scrambled to her feet and walked quickly along the towpath, away from the sounds of merriment, away from the company, to be alone to compose herself. It could not be. He did not love her; he looked upon her as a rather inadequate chaperon, a provider for her sister. 'Staid and proper', he had called her, and, even though he had repudiated it, that was what she had to be.

Half an hour later she returned and calmly took her place in the barouche for the journey back to Holles Street. But her new composure was soon tested when Richard appeared with Felicity on his arm. He gallantly raised her hand to his lips and handed her up to sit beside Georgie, smiling as if there were no one else in the world for him. 'Goodbye, Miss Felicity. I shall look forward to calling on you tomorrow.' Then he touched his hat to Georgie, bowed to Mrs Bertram who was already in her place opposite, and stood back to allow the carriage to proceed.

Georgie found she had been holding her breath and now she let it out slowly and almost sagged in her seat, thankful to be away from those searching eyes. How glad she was that she was returning to Rowan Park at the end of the week. In the stables, among the horses, she could make herself busy and try to forget that she had loved and lost.

She was not the only one who was quiet on that journey home. Felicity had little to say, but Mrs Bertram was cheerful enough for all three. 'I do believe you have taken, child,' she said, addressing Felicity. 'The Major is definitely interested. He will offer within the week, I'll lay odds.'

'Oh, dear, do you think so, Aunt?' Felicity said. 'So soon? And what must I do?'

'He will ask permission to address you and when he does you must tell him you are honoured and will think seriously about it. Promise to give him his answer in

two or three days, when you have had an opportunity
to discuss it with your family.'

'It all seems a tarradiddle to me,' her niece said.
'We've talked of nothing else for days.'

'It is the way it is done, my dear.'

'And Georgie?' She turned to look at her sister who
was leaning back in her seat with her eyes closed as if
she were not listening. But she was, because she sat up
and pulled her hat straight. 'You must do exactly as
you wish, dearest,' she said, surprising herself for her
voice sounded so level and down-to-earth. 'Do not let
anyone browbeat you. If you like the Major. . .' She
could not go on for a lump which had suddenly
constricted her throat.

'Oh, I do. He is very handsome and very attentive,
but I cannot say I love him.'

'Love will come later,' Mrs Bertram said firmly. 'It
does not do to have passionate feelings before the
wedding; it doesn't do at all.'

'End in tears,' Georgie murmured, but she was
thinking of something else entirely.

'Quite right,' their aunt said. 'And I think you should
leave the details of the marriage contract to Colonel
Bertram. I will write to him tomorrow. Something as
important as this will surely bring him home.'

But she had no need to write to her husband for he
arrived the very next day with news that put his wife
into a fine froth.

Once he had been welcomed by his wife in the
restrained manner she used in company, he greeted the
girls cheerfully and they responded with affection,
though it was many years since they had seen him.

He was not a tall man, but he had a presence which

commanded respect. He had a squarish face, buffeted by wind and weather so that his skin looked almost leathery, but he had piercing blue eyes which seemed to take in a situation at a glance and missed nothing, which was why he was such a good commander in the field and why, in peacetime, he was a respected negotiator. When his services as a soldier were no longer required, he was pressed into service as a diplomat.

'Must go up and change,' he said, indicating a small portmanteau which his man was at that moment carrying upstairs. Then, turning to his wife, he asked, 'Coming, m'dear? I've something of import to tell you.'

She followed, leaving the two girls to amuse themselves until husband and wife returned and by then it was time for dinner.

'The Colonel will be returning almost at once,' Mrs Bertram told them over the turbot. 'He has been appointed to be an aide at the Embassy in Paris.'

'May I offer our congratulations, Sir?' Georgie said.

'Thank you. But that is not all.' He paused and sipped his wine. 'I am afraid I must take Mrs Bertram with me. I expect to do a great deal of entertaining.'

The implication of that slowly dawned on the girls; without Mrs Bertram they could not stay in London.

'Oh, do not give it another thought,' Georgie said. 'We can go back to Rowan Park. The Season is at an end now anyway.'

'But I had just got the Major up to the mark and Lord Barbour would take little persuasion to offer for you, Georgiana; he is already enamoured.' She turned to her husband. 'A week, another week, and I shall accompany you with a clear conscience.'

'Oh, do not trouble on our account, Aunt,' Georgie

said, feeling nothing but relief at the thought of going home to Rowan Park where she felt safe and at ease.

But her aunt would not hear of abandoning her mission; nor would she allow Georgie to return home without Felicity as she had originally intended. 'I'll bring my ball forward to next Thursday,' she said as soon as she had inveigled her husband into admitting that he was not expected at his new post for another week. 'I think it can be done and it will be a fitting end to the Season. All will come about, you will see.'

With a heavy heart, Georgie agreed to stay.

CHAPTER FIVE

THE next day the whole house was put into an uproar as Mrs Bertram endeavoured to bring forward all the arrangements for her ball, summoning the cook and the butler to go over what was needed in the way of food and drink, sending orders to the florists, booking musicians and setting the housemaids to cleaning and polishing the ballroom, a task which until then they had thought they had plenty of time to do. There was less than a week to accomplish everything which normally took three at least and no one thought it could be done, except the lady of the house and she would brook no argument. It was useless to tell her that her guests themselves might have other engagements on that day; she was a forceful lady and if she said the last ball of the Season would be the best and no one who was anyone would decline to attend, then they had to accept that she was right.

By afternoon, having satisfied herself that she would be ready, she prevailed upon Felicity and Georgie to help her write out new invitations and they were kept busy until well into the evening.

The last thing either girl wanted after that was to go out, but Mrs Bertram's great friend, Caro Sopwithy, had arranged a musical soirée for that very evening and they were required to attend. Georgie, who had the day before begun to pack ready to return to Rowan Park, found herself unpacking again and fetching out a blue crêpe open gown with short puff-sleeves and a high bodice caught under the bosom with a cluster of flowers and a long ribbon bow. The underslip of pale satin had become a little creased but Fanny was on hand to press it and dress her hair with the hairpiece she had worn before, so that when the time came to leave she looked serenely elegant. It was certainly not how she felt. Beneath the cool exterior there was a young lady in a state of panic.

It was too much to hope that Major Baverstock would not be present, for she was sure her aunt had made certain he would be, but she hoped fervently that she could stay far enough away not to be obliged to converse with him. If she did, she would give herself away; she would not be able to help it. She would be mortified with embarrassment and if Felicity found out she would turn him down, no matter that Richard himself was entirely indifferent to her. Her sister must never know.

Felicity was demurely dressed in white figured muslin trimmed with silk rosebuds and with more rosebuds in her coiled hair, the epitome of a young lady in her first Season, and Mrs Bertram smiled her approval. 'If not tonight, then next week at the ball, you will have your offer,' she promised her. 'Oh, it will be a fitting end to the Season and I shall leave for France content in the knowledge that I have done my duty by you.'

But strangely Felicity did not look at all elated by the prospect, though when Georgie tackled her about it when they were alone in the upper room set aside by their hostess for the ladies to leave their cloaks and repair their toilette she laughed. 'I am nervous, that's all.'

'There is no need to be. He cannot fail to love you, my dearest, and I am sure he will never do anything to hurt you. I'll wager he will become your devoted slave in no time at all and will do everything in his power to please you. You will be ordering him about and arranging Dullingham House just as you want it and no one to say you nay. There are servants in plenty so you won't have to lift a finger yourself.' She smiled. 'No more housekeeping on a shoestring as you have been trying to do at Rowan Park. And you will have lots of lovely, healthy children and be happy. . .' She could not go on. The picture she was painting of life with Richard was so desirable, she was making herself miserable.

'But what about you, Georgie? I do not like to leave you on your own. . .'

'I shall not be on my own. There is Fanny and Mrs Thorogood and Mrs Wardle and Dawson and Tom and the horses. . .'

'Horses!' Felicity laughed. 'I do believe you will be happy with nothing but horses.'

'Of course I shall.' Georgie realised what a whisker that was as soon as she uttered it. Now she knew she loved Richard Baverstock, she would never be truly happy without him.

'What about Lord Barbour? I am persuaded he would like to offer for you, if you would only give him the least bit of encouragement. Aunt Harriet seems to think he should suit. . .'

'Perhaps,' Georgie said. It would not do to let her sister know how much she disliked the man. 'But I am in no hurry. Whoever takes me on must realise I am no yearling and it is almost impossible to teach an old dog new tricks.'

Felicity rippled with laughter at the mixed metaphor her sister had employed, but she knew exactly what she meant. 'Oh, dear, I do not think I envy him,' she said, eyeing herself in the mirror to make sure all was well before they went down to the reception-room where the entertainment was to take place. 'I think you might fight.'

'Very likely,' Georgie agreed, picking up her reticule. 'But you must know I am used to having my own way over almost everything, so have no fear for me. Now let us hope the music is lively for if it is not I declare I shall fall asleep in my chair.'

Mrs Sopwithy had employed a string quartet, a soprano who was enormously fat and a tenor who was to sing the latest ballads, some of which were a little risqué, but he was all the rage and it was a triumph that she had managed to engage him at all. If the songs he sang were not for young ears, then it was up to the chaperons of the young ears to take them to the drawing-room to play fishes or something equally innocuous. At any rate the entertainment was lively enough to keep Georgie and Felicity awake, though their aunt dozed a little.

They did not encounter the Major until the intermission, when they went to the dining-room where a light supper was being served. Georgie had not seen him in the music-room and suspected he had been playing cards with Lord Hereward and Colonel Bertram, who followed him into the room and took up their places beside their respective wives, leaving him to join

Georgie and Felicity who were sitting with Juliette Hereward and John Melford, discussing the music.

'There you are!' John greeted him. 'I had almost given you up for lost.'

Richard bowed to the ladies. 'How could I absent myself from such dazzling company?'

'Do sit down, Major,' Felicity said. 'Tell us what you thought of the soprano.'

'A trifle overlarge,' he said pithily. 'But perhaps to have a big voice one needs a big frame; what do you think?'

She laughed. 'She certainly had a big voice. Did you manage to hear her in the card-room?'

'Oh, bang on target, Miss Felicity,' John laughed. One might have expected Miss Felicity Paget to be overshadowed by her tall, dominating sister, but she had a quiet humour of her own which he found delightful. She was certainly no wilting violet.

Richard smiled. 'I am penitent, Miss Felicity. Shall you be entertaining us later? I have been told you have a sweet voice.'

Georgie did not wait for her sister's reply; it was torment to sit so close, to watch the big soldier paying court to her sister when she wanted it for herself. She could almost have reached out and touched him and the thought of doing that set her body tingling. It was not to be borne.

She excused herself and wandered off alone, trying to calm the hammering of her heart and the buzzing in her head. Would it always be like this? In the months and years to come, would she learn not to mind so much? Would she ever be able to look on him as a brother and behave lightly and affectionately towards him, love her nieces and nephews and never wish they were her own?

Perhaps Felicity would reject him. But no, she would not; their aunt had schooled her too well, and besides, was that not what she, Georgiana Paget, had been scheming for all along?

Angry with herself, she brushed tears from her cheeks and sped along the corridor, paying no heed to where her feet were taking her. It was stifling and she needed air. She pulled open a door and found herself in a large conservatory, full of potted plants and clinging vines. Beyond it she could see the garden and a fountain playing. One or two people strolled about, enjoying the evening air after the heat of the house, and she hurried across the marble floor towards the open door to the terrace.

'Miss Paget, how opportune! We can take the air together.'

She did not need to turn to know who had spoken: the booming voice of Lord Barbour was unmistakable. He had been sitting on a bench just inside the conservatory, but now he hurried to her side. 'Hot indoors, ain't it?' he said, running a finger round the inside of his huge cravat. Its ends were arranged over the top of a striped brocade waistcoat stretched dangerously tightly over his portly stomach.

'Yes, it is,' she said, trying to sound normal; if he guessed she had been crying, he would make himself more objectionable than ever.

'Need to cool off,' he said, though she was not sure if he was referring to himself or asking her a question. 'But someone as fetching as you ain't any business to be out alone.'

'I'm not alone, my lord, there are other people. . .'

'Ah, to be sure, but you are not escorted.' He fell into step beside her as she crossed the lawn towards the fountain. Somehow it became her mecca; if she could reach it without betraying her misery, she might survive the encounter unscathed. 'Let me do the honourable. Escort you.'

'There is no need, my lord,' she said. 'I am quite happy in my own company.'

'Oh, come, Miss Paget, don't gammon me. No young lady likes to be alone. You just ain't willing to admit you ain't got an escort.'

Her misery turned to anger and she stopped to face him. 'My lord, I am not in the habit of telling lies.'

'No, course not,' he said, appearing chagrined. 'Ask pardon.'

'The evening air is cooler than I thought,' she remarked. 'I think I'll go back.'

'Now I've offended,' he said, following as she turned towards the house again. 'Didn't mean to. You're a fine specimen, high-stepping, strong in wind. But at your last prayers, ain't that so?'

'If by that vulgar term you mean I am desperate for a husband, then I tell you, Lord Barbour, you are way off the mark.'

'That so? No one will deal with you over horses; you must have realised that already. How will you come about, when you swallow a spider, if you ain't married?'

'I will not become bankrupt, my lord, you may depend upon it.'

'I hope you may not. Sir Henry would turn in his

grave to think his prime stock was dispersed. Must keep it together.'

'Quite so,' she said, angry that he should have penetrated her mind. 'I intend to keep it together. Might even expand a little.' She tried to sound confident but it was only empty boasting and she guessed he knew that.

They had arrived at the door of the conservatory and he followed her inside, dogging her footsteps as she crossed the floor to return to the music-room. 'Now, my lord, if you will excuse me. . .'

He opened the door for her and she passed through ahead of him into the foyer. The lights were so bright they dazzled her and she stood blinking for a moment before moving off. She was aware that he had put his hand under her elbow and to anyone who glanced in their direction it seemed that they had been out strolling together. Short of being downright rude and thereby drawing attention to herself, she could do nothing to rid herself of her escort. Jutting out her chin and walking very upright, she made her way back to the music-room with his lordship close beside her. Not until she had taken her place again beside her aunt did he bow with exaggerated courtesy and take himself off.

Richard had watched her progress with more than a little interest and seen the smile of satisfaction on Mrs Bertram's face and the smirk on Lord Barbour's. So that was how the land lay! Poor girl, she was in for a stormy life if she married that thatchgallows. But she was so self-possessed, so independent, why would she agree to such a match? Unless it was for the sake of the Rowan Park stables.

He allowed himself a wry smile; the marriage, if that was what was in the wind, would not be between a man and a woman but between two businesses. When Sir Henry was alive, Rowan Park had been his lordship's main rival; now he was taking the opportunity to swallow it whole and that without parting with a groat. Should he warn the spirited Miss Paget? No, he decided; she would take it ill and possibly accuse him of being prejudiced. And perhaps he was. But a man who could cheat to win a wager was not a man to be trusted with a lovely young woman.

He turned to scrutinise her as everyone's attention was drawn to the end of the room where the string quartet was beginning the second half of the entertainment. She was lovely. Fashion might dictate that she was a little too tall, her hair a little too red, that her complexion had been over-exposed to the elements, but he could see no defect in having a healthy glow and strong limbs and her sparkling eyes drew him like a magnet.

A sixth sense must have told her she was being watched, for she turned to face him suddenly and their glances met and held for what seemed an age before she put her nose in the air and began vigorously fanning herself. It had really only been a second or two, but it was time enough for him to see that the sparkle was caused in this instance by unshed tears; they lay on her lashes like diamonds. That the cool, self-possessed Miss Paget should be reduced to tears was something so unexpected, he found himself wanting to reach out to her, to comfort her, to tell her he would make all well with her. The strength of his feelings took him by surprise. He turned away, only to meet her sister's limpid gaze. He smiled; she smiled back at him.

He stayed in his place, pretending to listen to the music because there was little else he could do, and because sooner or later he must make a push towards marriage himself and it seemed his bride had been chosen for him, not only by Mrs Bertram and the elder Miss Paget, but by his father, whose approval of Miss Felicity he had made known. Although far from well and disliking the city as he did, his lordship had insisted on staying at Baverstock House until his son had 'come to his senses', which was his way of saying compliant. The devil in Richard rebelled, but for the life of him he did not know why. There would never be another Maria, he would not know love like that again, so why hesitate? Felicity Paget was eminently suitable and he did not doubt that they would deal well together; what more could he ask? And, judging by the smile she had given him, she thought so too.

The evening drew to a close at last and he escorted Mrs Bertram and her nieces to their carriage and saw them safely installed before setting off on foot for St James's and his club. It was too early to go home to bed, and besides, he did not feel in the least sleepy; a hand or two of faro might induce slumber. John fell into step beside him and they walked in companionable silence for several minutes until the Captain said, 'I noticed Barbour seems to have his eye on Miss Paget.'

'Hmm. More like Rowan Park.'

'Yes, I heard he was in Dun Territory. I suppose a merger of interests would put some prime cattle together without need of stud fees.'

'Quite so.'

'He'll use Victor. . .'

'Don't I know that?' Richard countered irritably.

'I'm sorry, Richard. It's my fault.'

Richard's answer was merely a grunt, which could have betokened assent or denial; either way John felt his culpability keenly.

'Are you going to challenge him to a rematch?'

'I've got nothing good enough to beat Victor and it is Victor he'll run, you may be sure.'

'What are you going to do, then? I suppose if Barbour were to marry Miss Paget he would be responsible for Miss Felicity's dowry; you could ask. . .' He stopped suddenly, unable to comprehend why his friend's expression had become so thunderous. 'What's wrong?'

Richard did not answer but lengthened his stride so that John was all but running to keep up with him. 'I'm sure I meant no harm. If you don't mean to offer for Miss Felicity. . .' There was something very akin to a hopeful note in his voice which was lost on Richard, deep in his own thoughts. 'Only, if you don't want her, I could make her an offer, get your horse back that way. I'd ask Barbour to give him to me as part of Miss Felicity's portion. He ain't to know I'd hand it over to you.'

Richard came to an abrupt halt and turned to face him. 'Zounds! That's a monstrous idea! My horse is not so important to me that I would allow you to leg-shackle yourself for it. Anyway, I thought you were pledged to Juliette Hereward.'

'No, it ain't got to that yet. I don't reckon we should suit.'

'Even so, I will not hear another word on the

subject.' He strode in at the door of Watier's, leaving John to follow or not as he pleased. But the fact that his friend could even consider so drastic a step on his behalf made him feel humble and unworthy. He could not and would not countenance such a sacrifice; his wooing of Miss Felicity Paget must have more purpose but he would make no formal offer until he had retrieved Victor himself. No one was going to say of him that he had married for a horse! His decision made, he was almost cheerful and even glad to see Lord Barbour when he arrived at the club in the early hours of the morning.

They did not play at the same table but Richard, whose mind was most definitely not on the cards in his hand, could tell that his lordship was losing heavily, and very soon he threw down his hand in a fury and left the table, passing behind Richard's chair as he went. Richard turned to smile up at him. 'Lady Luck not with you tonight, my lord?'

His lordship stopped. 'No, but you know what they say: unlucky at cards, lucky in love.' He nodded towards the pile of coins at Richard's elbow. 'I see you have not done so badly in the card stakes. What about the ladybirds?'

'Well enough,' Richard said evenly.

His lordship laughed. 'By that I am persuaded there will soon be an announcement.' He waited for Richard to make a reply but when none was forthcoming went on. 'If you are planning to win Victor back, you had best make it soon. I am beginning to think I do not want to part with him, after all. He would be a valuable asset at stud, don't you think? And with all the Rowan Park brood mares to choose from. . .'

'Oh, have you acquired Rowan Park?' Richard asked blandly.

'Not yet, but I will, very soon now.'

'I had not realised Miss Paget was selling.'

'She ain't, but there's more than one way to skin a cat. We may well become brothers-in-law.' He paused, watching Richard's efforts to control his temper with some amusement. 'So, what about this challenge? Have you got a horse to put up against Victor or haven't you?'

'I'll do better than that,' Richard said, aware that everyone in the room had stopped whatever he was doing and was paying rapt attention to the exchange. 'I'll challenge you to ride from London to York between supper and breakfast. Two hundred miles in nine hours or thereabouts. First man in wins.'

His lordship laughed. 'There ain't a nag can do that.'

'No, but a string of them could. Are you up to it, my lord? No jockeys either. *You* stay in the saddle the whole time.'

A ripple of comment went round the room, some saying it was a capital rig, others that someone as portly as Lord Barbour would never stand the strain even if his horses did. 'It'll take a deal of blunt, what with horses and ostlers and peck for both,' he said at last. 'More'n Victor's worth.'

'Then let us make it worthwhile. Loser to pay the winner's expenses and a brace of monkeys besides the horse. How does that suit?'

Lord Barbour looked thoughtful and everyone began to urge him to accept; it promised to be the best sport they'd had all year. 'Come on, Barbour,' Lord

Hereward said. 'You've got the best stables in the country; everyone knows that.'

'Bar Rowan Park,' Richard said.

'Bar none,' his lordship growled. 'Since Sir Henry died it's gone downhill; no one will deal with the new owner.' He laughed harshly. 'And I'll have both soon.'

Richard resisted the temptation to give him a leveller by neatly stacking the coins he had won, clinking them as he placed them slowly one on top of the other. 'Then what's holding you back?'

'Nothing,' his lordship said, realising he had been placed in a corner and could not retreat with honour intact. 'Fetch out the betting book and draw up the rules. If this young jack-at-warts thinks to make a flat out of me, he'll find the boot on the other foot.'

John sat at the desk near the window, fetched the betting book out from one of its drawers and dipped a quill into the ink bottle. 'Lord Cedric Barbour bets Major the Honourable Richard Baverstock that he can beat him riding from London. . .' He stopped writing and turned to the two men. 'Whereabouts in London?'

'Tyburn,' Richard said. 'We don't want to startle the inhabitants by setting off in the middle of the city.' He turned to Lord Barbour. 'Agreed?'

'Agreed.'

John returned to his writing. 'From Tyburn to. . . Where in York?'

'The Castle Gardens,' Richard said. 'We set off at ten in the evening. Thirty horses to be posted at intervals along the route. Referees too. Agreed, my lord?'

'Agreed,' his lordship said, but he was not looking particularly happy at the prospect. 'The day?'

'You may choose the day,' Richard said magnanimously.

'It will take some time to organise. Shall we say three weeks from today?'

'Done,' Richard agreed, holding out his hand.

Lord Barbour looked down at the proffered hand for several seconds before taking it to seal the wager and then he excused himself and left the room, presumably to go home to bed.

As soon as he had left there was a hubbub of chatter and several people came forward to add their own personal bets to the book, not all of them for Richard; a young cavalry officer who was probably a bruising rider, but little else, was not necessarily a safe bet. He was an unknown quantity whereas Lord Barbour, if not actually liked, was well-known and respected for his knowledge of all things equestrian. John wrote all the wagers down, heading them with his own, backing Richard to the tune of five hundred pounds.

My winnings will fetch me out of the River Tick,' he said, when Richard demurred at the amount.

'And if you lose you will drown in it,' his friend said cryptically. 'I wish you had not done it.'

'Too late; can't back out now,' John told him, complacent as ever. 'If I'd had the mint sauce, I'd have come in on the race with you.'

'Then I'm glad you have not. This is between me and Lord Barbour. Now I'm for my bed.' He rose and picked up his pile of winnings, jingling the coins in his hand as he went towards the door. 'There is much to be done so do not expect to see me for a few days.'

'What about Mrs Bertram's ball?' John called after him.

Richard stopped and turned; it was still there, still to be faced, but now he felt easier about it. 'I shall return for that, never fear.'

It seemed that Mrs Bertram was going to be right. The ball was set fair to be a glittering occasion and even some of the *ton* who had already left for the country were constrained to return for it. It was a dreadful crush in the vestibule as everyone began to arrive, taking their turn to be greeted by Colonel and Mrs Bertram and the Misses Paget, both of whom looked stunning, although the elder was really too old for bringing out. No matter, rumour was rife that Lord Barbour meant to offer for her, which was perhaps all she could expect. Widower he might be and with a brace of children, but he had a title and an estate, run-down though it was, and they did not suppose Sir Henry had left either girl high in the stirrups.

The younger, Miss Felicity Paget, was another matter; she was a plum ripe for the picking and it looked as though that scapegrace son of Viscount Dullingham would come up to the mark. There was a story that he had fallen out with his papa years before and left home to go to war. Such a ramshackle thing for an heir to a great estate to do. Now he had returned and the gabblegrinders could only suppose he had come back to claim his inheritance, for the Viscount was not in plump currant. That would put William Baverstock's nose out of joint, to be sure.

And there was that proposed ride to York. All London was talking about it and every betting book in every club, not to mention Tattersall's, was full of side-wagers, from whether the race would take place at all to whether it would finish because one or other of the riders had died of a seizure, or fallen off through fatigue. Bets were being laid on the probable finishing point, seeing as few expected either man to reach York; the time it would take in the unlikely event of one or both men finishing; the weather at the start and how many horses would survive the gruelling gallop. And anyone who had a half decent horse for sale or hire was hoping to make a good profit. It was going to be a lively couple of weeks.

Georgie was perfectly aware of the wager, for who could not be when London was on fire with it? And she knew it was Richard who had instigated it, for he had hinted that he might, but she wished it could be otherwise. Whatever the quarrel between him and Lord Barbour, she did not believe it was worth injuring either men or horses.

She stood at the head of the stairs, in dove-grey gauze embroidered with silver, receiving her aunt's guests with a smile and a polite greeting, but her thoughts were elsewhere. In her head she was back at Rowan Park, riding Grecian Warrior across the heath, feeling the saddle between her thighs and the wind stirring her hair, laughing for the sheer joy of riding.

And that jump. She had been reckless, she knew that, but oh, how marvellous it always made her feel! And how angry the Major had been. He had no right to anger; *she* would never ride a horse into the ground for the sake of a wager. She could almost hate Richard Baverstock for that. But she knew that was a lie.

Would he be too busy making plans for the race to come tonight? Did she want him to come? She glanced towards Felicity. She was looking beautiful in soft white

silk with a high bodice and a low neckline made
decorous with an infill of silk flowers. She had their
mother's pearls about her throat but wore no other
ornament. Georgie reached out and took her hand.
Felicity, who had been staring at the floor, looked up
and smiled.

'Nervous?' Georgie asked.

'Yes.' She paused and took a deep breath. 'Georgie,
I. . .' She stopped and looked into Georgie's face.
Their aunt was right; how could she disappoint the
sister who had been a mother to her for so long, and a
father too, this last year? Georgie had made so many
sacrifices for her, it would be churlish to throw it all
back in her face. Oh, how she wished Aunt Harriet
had never come to Rowan Park! She became aware
that Georgie was waiting for her to finish what she had
been saying. 'I expect I shall feel more the thing
directly.'

'Of course.' Georgie turned back to her duty as
another guest arrived and found herself looking into
the searching eyes of Major Baverstock. Once again
she was almost turned into a quivering jelly by his tall,
lithe figure, enhanced by the white breeches and blue
regimental coat he wore, and by those dark eyes, which
were even now burning into her. Her knees felt weak
and she knew her face was flooded with colour. He had
already greeted his host and hostess and was waiting
for some acknowledgement from her. She ought to
offer him her hand, but it was shaking so much that
she dared not bring it out from the folds of her dress.
And if she cursied she would surely collapse in a heap
on the floor.

'Miss Paget, your obedient,' he said, making a leg and breaking the spell.

She dipped quickly and forced herself to smile. 'Good evening, Major.' Then she turned to her sister. 'Look, dearest, here is Major Baverstock; why don't you take him into the ballroom? You do not need to stay here on display all evening.' She turned to Mrs Bertram. 'Does she, Aunt?' She was aware of the brittleness of her voice, the stiffness of her smile, but she could not help it.

'No, run along,' Mrs Bertram said. 'Enjoy yourselves. After all, this is your evening.'

Richard bowed to Felicity and offered her his arm and together they went into the ballroom, watched by a despairing Georgie.

'They make a delightful couple, don't you think?' Mrs Bertram said to her husband. 'He is handsome to a stare and well-breeched too; she is so lovely and such a good, obedient child.'

'Yes, perhaps too lovely and too obedient,' he commented.

'And what am I supposed to make of that remark?' she demanded.

'What you will, my love.'

'I am not disposed to solving your riddles,' she said, tapping his arm with her chicken-skin fan. 'I believe the Major will ask to speak to you tonight.'

'Why should he speak to me?'

'Because, husband, Felicity has no father, nor mother either; we stand in their stead and it is to you he will apply for permission to speak to her.' She turned to Georgie. 'Is that not so, my dear?'

'Yes,' she said, her voice barely more than a whisper as she contemplated the prospect.

'Not only that, but he was in your regiment,' Mrs Bertram went on, turning back to her husband. 'If he were still with the colours, he would have been obliged to ask your permission to marry, and, even though he is no longer a serving officer, courtesy demands no less than he should make you aware of his intentions.'

'You seem very sure of his intentions.'

'Of course. Women know these things, do they not, Georgiana?'

'I am afraid I have no experience of such things,' she said, wishing her aunt would not keep turning to her for confirmation of everything she said.

'We have stood here long enough, I think,' her aunt said crisply. 'I doubt there will be any more arrivals and I need to sit down and take a glass of ratafia. And you may wish to dance, Georgiana.' She lifted Georgie's hand where her dance card should have been attached to her wrist by a ribbon. 'Where is your card, child?'

Georgie did not like her aunt addressing her as 'child' but at the moment that was how she felt—young and bewildered. 'I do not wish to dance, Aunt. I am my sisters' chaperon and guardian, or had you forgot?'

'Fustian!' Mrs Bertram exclaimed. 'I am here, am I not? You do not need to sit with the antidotes tonight. Go and enjoy yourself.'

'Aunt, there is no one——'

'Oh, yes, there is,' Colonel Bertram interrupted, taking her arm and leading her into the ballroom to dance a stately minuet, and as soon as they were out of earshot he said, 'Now, me girl, you'd best tell me what's bothering you.'

'Nothing, Uncle, nothing at all. But I would not wish to behave improperly.'

He threw back his head and laughed, making several people in the vicinity turn to look at him. 'Is this the fearless Georgiana Paget I used to know? Why, as a girl, you thought nothing of riding to hounds and taking a hedge with the best; are you balking one now?'

'No, sir.'

'Jealous of your sister, eh?'

She looked up at him sharply and almost missed her step. 'I don't know what you mean.'

'Getting an offer before you. You are the elder, after all.'

She let out her breath in a sigh of relief. 'Oh, I do not think of that at all, Uncle. If Felicity is happy, it is all I ask.'

The Colonel wisely decided to say no more and when the dance finished he took her card from her reticule where she had hidden it and perambulated round the floor with her, bowing and chatting to his guests as he went, putting Georgie forward whenever he could, so that by the time they returned to Mrs Bertram, who was sitting having a comfortable coze with Lady Hereward, her card was almost full.

It was very kind of him and she appreciated his efforts, but it didn't alter the fact that Richard had not asked her to stand up with him and unless he did so very soon she would not have a dance left for him. And that was as it should be, she told herself sternly. She had no right to sigh after her sister's prospective husband.

She had hardly taken her seat beside her aunt when Lord Barbour was standing before her, in knee-breeches and satin coat, doing his best to make an elegant leg and creaking terribly in the process. She favoured him with a smile which was just a little too bright as he took her card and, seeing that there was no name beside the country dance then beginning, asked her to stand up with him. She retrieved her card, slipped it back over her wrist and stood up. This fat, conceited, not entirely sober coxcomb was to be her lot and she had better make up her mind to it, but even the feel of his clammy hand holding her fingers as they began the promenade was enough to repel her. She was glad that the strict etiquette her aunt insisted on meant that she would not have to endure more than two dances with him.

Her aunt, when Georgie was returned to her, was sitting between Mrs Sopwithy and Lady Hereward, watching Felicity circulating the room with Richard, her gloved fingers resting lightly on his sleeve. 'How good to see one's best efforts so well rewarded,' she told them as Georgie took her place beside Lady Hereward.

'Shall it be announced tonight, do you think?' her ladyship asked.

'He has yet to speak to the Colonel, but we shall see.' And Harriet smiled like a contented cat.

Another dance was beginning and Georgie's partner came to claim her, so she was not obliged to suffer any more of the conversation, for which she was utterly thankful. She danced well and when she allowed herself to forget the tall major who dominated the room with his presence and her pretty little sister, who seemed to be flirting outrageously with every young man in the room, she managed to enjoy herself—at least until after supper, when she found herself, for the first time, sitting alone. Her aunt was gossiping with a group of her cronies, her uncle had gone to see how the less energentic gentlemen were doing in the card-room and Felicity was dancing with John Melford and laughing at something he had said. She hardly had time to wonder where Major Baverstock might be when she saw him coming purposefully towards her. She began a detailed inspection of her fan because she could not watch his progress without the yearning in her eyes becoming obvious.

'Miss Paget, will you do me the honour of waltzing with me?'

Only then did she look up. 'Why, Major,' she said, pretending surprise. 'You have taken me unawares. . .'

'Do you not wish to stand up with me?'

Oh, yes, yes, more than anything, her heart cried, but her voice said, 'Major, I am supposed to be my sister's chaperon.'

'Still? I had supposed your aunt had relieved you of that duty. I have seen you on the floor several times, twice with Lord Barbour.'

'Oh,' she said, smiling up at him. 'Were you counting?'

'No, but I'll wager the tabbies were.'

'And do you suppose they have counted your dances too?'

'Undoubtedly.' He whirled her on to the floor and was even now spanning her waist with his big hand, leaning back a little and smiling down at her. She felt herself melting into him, so that they seemed fused by the music into a single body, moving as one. She was in a dream-like state that had no bearing on reality and she did not want to wake up.

'I thought you would dance well,' he said, after their first circumnavigation of the room. 'It's much like sitting a horse—a kind of union, combining movement and rhythm.'

She laughed. 'I am not at all sure that I like being compared to a horse.'

'I was not comparing you to a horse but complimenting you on your dancing.'

'Then I thank you, sir.'

'I am afraid I have been too long away from Society and feminine company, I stumble over the simplest exchange of pleasantries. Please forgive me.'

'There is nothing to forgive.' She couldn't help it; she had to know. 'But how does my sister take your compliments, Major? Does she understand them any better than I do?'

'I believe so. At least, she has not complained.'

'You go on very well together, then?'

'Yes, indeed.'

'And have you had an interview with Colonel Bertram yet?'

He looked down at her, surprised by the question. 'The Colonel?'

'Yes, Major, my uncle. He will have to be approached if you mean to speak to Felicity. . .'

He disliked the idea of being pushed into anything, even if it was what he'd intended in the first place, and he stiffened. 'Of course, but if you do not mind, Miss Paget, I will choose my own time. There are matters that require my attention first.'

'Something like a madcap wager, I collect. Well, Major Baverstock, it is interesting to know where your priorities lie.'

His face darkened and his eyes narrowed and she knew she had angered him, but she didn't care; she wanted to rouse him to something and if it could not be love then it must be anger. But oh, how her heart ached, and there was nothing for it but to endure. 'You know, of course, that under the terms of my father's will I have to approve my sister's choice of husband and arrange her dowry.'

'No, I did not. I can hardly believe someone as sensible as Sir Henry should have done such a thing. You are hoaxing me.'

'Not at all. Ask my Aunt.'

'Then do you approve?'

Oh, what a question! She smiled slowly, unable to resist the temptation to tease in spite of her swiftly beating heart, or perhaps because of it. She had to stay on top of herself or sink into despair. 'I have not yet been asked the question. Of whom am I to approve?'

'Miss Paget, I beg you not to play games with me; I have thrashed a man for less provocation than you are giving me.'

'I am not a man.'

'No, Miss Paget, but unfortunately it seems you have been cast in the role of one by your father.'

'Then man to man, are you requesting my permission to speak to my sister?'

'Dammit, no!' His voice had risen and she looked around to see who might have heard.

'I think perhaps we should leave the floor to continue this discussion,' she said in a low voice.

Together they retired to one side of the ballroom, where two vacant chairs were placed close to a huge potted plant, brought in from the conservatory, but they did not sit down. Instead they turned to face each other. 'I suppose you will say I asked for that,' she said.

'No, but I am not about to bend the knee to a slip of a miss who thinks she can dangle a carrot in front of me and I will meekly follow.'

'I do not understand.' She was genuinely puzzled.

'All this talk of approval and dowries. I find it hard to credit that it is in your hands.'

'But it is, Major, and believe me I wish it were otherwise; it is not a responsibility which sits easily on my shoulders.'

'And what has Miss Felicity to say to that?'

'She will be guided, as I have been, by wiser heads than ours. My aunt or, better still, my uncle will advise us.' She was quite serious now. 'But I will never stand in the way of my sister's happiness; you may depend on that. And she shall have whatever dowry I can afford. . .'

'No dowry is necessary,' he said, controlling his impulse to shake her. No, not shake her, he corrected himself, crush her to him, kiss her until she retired fire with fire, passion with passion. 'You may keep Rowan Park intact.'

'That I intend to do.'

'And Lord Barbour?'

'What about his lordship?'

'Are you going to marry him?'

'You are impertinent, sir.'

'I beg pardon, but give me leave to feel concerned

for you. He is not a man I can recommend.' It was as far as he dared go to warn her.

'I do not need your recommendation, Major,' she retorted, furious with him. 'Just because you have fallen out with him, it does not mean that everyone else should do so.' The waltz had come to an end and the dancing couples were leaving the floor. 'Now I suggest we return to my aunt, or we will give the tattlers something to talk about.'

Dutifully he escorted her back to her place beside her aunt, but he did not immediately seek an interview with the Colonel, as she had expected, but went over to a white-haired gentleman who sat on one side of the room, surveying everything about him with keen dark eyes. His features were so like Richard's that Georgie felt sure they were related.

'Who is that?' she asked her aunt.

'Oh, that is the Major's father, Viscount Dullingham, my dear. I invited him, of course, but I hardly expected him to honour us by coming.'

He had come to look them over, to decide if Felicity was good enough for his son, to see the hoyden who guarded her and with whom they would have to deal. Georgie did not know whether to laugh or cry.

CHAPTER SIX

'INTRODUCE me,' Lord Dullingham commanded his son.

Richard complied, taking his father over to where Mrs Bertram sat with her family about her, looking round the glittering company like a queen. Seeing him coming, she rose to her feet in a flurry of plum-coloured taffeta, knowing how much recognition by him would enhance her reputation and aware that everyone was watching. 'So very pleased to make your acquaintance, my lord,' she said as he took her hand and bowed over it. 'May I present my nieces?' She turned to Georgie. 'This is Georgiana, and this. . .' she drew Felicity forward '. . .this is Felicity.' The beam on her face clearly indicated her expectations and made him smile.

He was, Georgie noticed, a very handsome man, still quite slim and upright with a shock of white hair which appeared to have no particular style, though its untidiness suited him. The rest of him was neat in the extreme, though a little old-fashioned. But, unlike Lord Barbour, whose satin knee-breeches made him look ridiculous, the Viscount was the epitome of stately elegance. She found herself smiling, almost mischievously, when he favoured her with a close inspection, his dark eyes full of humour.

'I am told, Miss Paget, that you know horseflesh.'

'A little, my lord. I had a good teacher.'

144

'Sir Henry, yes. Capital fellow. Keeping up his good work, are you?'

'Yes, my lord.'

'I shall need new carriage horses soon; mine are getting long in the tooth—like their owner.' He smiled at his own joke. 'I'll come to see what you've got.'

'We shall look forward to that, my lord,' she said, trying to keep the eagerness from her voice. If Lord Dullingham bought horses from her, it would do her business no harm at all.

He turned his attention to Felicity and favoured her with a little conversation, but she was so much in awe of him, she could find little to say above a whispered, 'Yes, my lord,' and 'No, my lord,' which exasperated her aunt. After a few minutes' discourse with Colonel Bertram, with whom he was already acquainted, he took his leave, accompanied by his son. If Mrs Bertram was disappointed that Richard had not stayed to speak to her husband about Felicity, she hid it well, preening herself on the added consequence to her reputation as a hostess that his lordship's presence had given. Now everyone would know that Richard and Felicity would soon become betrothed. She only hoped it would be before she had to leave for Paris.

'Well, my boy,' the Viscount said as he and his son returned to Baverstock House in his lordship's carriage. 'Can't make up your mind, eh?'

'Sir?'

'Which of the Paget gels to offer for.'

Richard looked at him in astonishment. 'Father, why do you say that? I collect you telling me you hoped it would not be the elder.'

'So I did. Changed my mind. She's got a lot more about her than her sister.'

Richard did not know whether to be angry or downright miserable at this pronouncement, or whether, had he known of his father's change of heart before this, it would have made the least difference; probably not. 'Miss Felicity Paget is shy, Father. When you get to know her. . .'

'So you have offered.'

'No, sir, but I believe everyone expects it soon.'

'But you are prevaricating.'

'No.' But he did not sound at all sure and his father chuckled.

'You may not have been at home much in the last eight years but you are still my son, and I know you better than you think. I saw you dancing with them both and I'd say it was Georgiana who has caught your interest.'

'Oh.' He was silent for a moment, recognising the truth of what his father had said. 'Is it that obvious?'

'Only to me. What are you going to do about it?'

'What can I do?' Richard asked miserably. 'Mrs Bertram has made her wishes known. I am expected to offer for Felicity.'

'And what about her sister's wishes?'

'Hers too. If I thought she was in any way hanging fire, I might think again, because she has to approve, you know, being her sister's guardian, but she is pushing as hard as anyone for the match. I do not see what I can do but come to the mark. To do anything else would give the gabblegrinders a field day.'

His lordship reached out and put a hand on his son's sleeve. 'But not tonight, eh?'

'No, there are other reasons. . .'

'A wager?'

'You have heard about it?' Richard asked in surprise, knowing his father went out very little.

'Wendens is a fount of information.' Wendens was his father's valet, old and bent almost double with rheumatics, but he still managed to look after his lordship, if only slowly, and to keep him up to date with the latest *on dit*. 'But what has it to do with your betrothal?'

Richard told him as succinctly as he could, though it all sounded a little high-flown to the Viscount. That anyone could imagine his son, whose competence was more than adequate even without the Dullingham inheritance, could marry for the sake of a horse was beyond comprehension. He smiled. 'It seems to me that everyone is assuming that Miss Paget will marry Barbour before you marry her sister and you can't be sure of that.'

'She has more or less indicated that she will.'

'I'll lay odds she doesn't.'

'You would lose your money.'

'I don't think so. She is not such a ninnyhammer.'

Richard wished he had his father's faith. But even if Georgie did not marry Lord Barbour it hardly changed things as far as he was concerned. He had not finally committed himself to offering for Felicity Paget but it was as near as dammit and nothing short of a terrible scandal, which would hurt both families, could get him out of it. Oh, what a coil he had got himself into!

'He's come to speak to the Colonel,' Fanny said when she woke her mistress just before noon the following morning. 'They're together now, in the library.'

Georgie sat up and took the hot chocolate from her maid with hands that shook. So, it was all over, her aunt's scheming, the anticipation, the courtship; before the day was out Felicity would be betrothed to Richard Baverstock. She took a deep breath to compose herself. 'Does my sister know he's here?'

'Miss Felicity? No, she is still fast asleep. And why should she know before you?'

'Goodness, Fanny, you are a goose. As soon as my uncle has given his consent, the Major will want to speak to Felicity, won't he? You should be helping her to dress, making her look her best.'

'It's not the Major with the Colonel, Miss Georgie, it's Lord Barbour.'

'Lord Barbour!' Georgie only just managed to save the hot chocolate from spilling. She set the cup and saucer down on to the bedside table and looked at her maid like a bewildered child. 'Fanny, why didn't you say? Has he come to. . .?'

'I believe so. I heard him mention your name just as they were going into the library together.'

'What am I to do?'

'Why, get dressed, miss.' She went to the large wardrobe. 'What shall you wear? The blue or the pea-green?'

'Neither. I do not feel well; I think I shall remain in bed all day. You may tell that to anyone who comes for me. Last night's exertion. . .'

Fanny, who had known her since she was a tiny girl and fetched her out of many a scrape, turned from selecting clothes to smile at her. 'Who'll believe that, when they know you think nothing of staying up all night with a mare who's foaling? You are inexhaustible.'

'Then perhaps Lord Barbour will take the hint and realise I do not want to speak to him.'

'He is very persistent, that one. He won't give up that easily.'

'And I will not give in that easily. Now I am going back to sleep. You may go, Fanny.' And she lay back on the pillows and shut her eyes. She knew she would not sleep and she hated lying in bed, but anything was better than facing his lordship. And so early in the day, too.

At two o'clock Fanny brought her a light meal and the news that his lordship had been disappointed not to see her and wished her well. 'I heard he is coming back tomorrow afternoon,' her maid told her. 'So what excuse will you give then for not seeing him?'

Georgie had been nurturing the fond hope that her uncle would refuse to allow the match, but now that that was dashed she did not see how she could refuse to see his lordship. She could not marry him, she just could not. Somehow or other she must make a success of the stables. She must make people respect her as a horse-breeder and trainer and forget that she was a woman. She must put aside all womanly traits and concentrate on business affairs. Felicity must have her dowry and she must live alone at Rowan Park and to hell with her reputation. She smiled wryly; if thoughts and language like that entered her head so easily, then she was already halfway to being the man. Then why did she feel like crying: men did not cry, did they?

Although she went down to dinner, she did not see the Colonel, who had gone to a meeting with some government officials and was dining with them; it was not until breakfast next morning that she was able to talk to him about it. They were alone at the table; her aunt and sister were still in their rooms.

'Of course you must not marry the man if you hold him in aversion,' her uncle said. 'I did not know you were so against the match or I would not have agreed to let him speak to you. Mrs Bertram led me to believe you would look on his suit with favour.'

'I am afraid Aunt Harriet is too much of an optimist, sir, though I did agree to think about it. I have thought and we just would not suit.'

'Do you mind telling me why?'

'I can't. I. . .'

'Is there someone else?'

'No, of course not.' Georgie's answer was a little too quick; colour flooded her face and she could not meet his eyes. He knew he had hit the nail on the head. 'I am, and will remain, an old maid.'

He reached out and put his hand over hers. 'You are too young for that, my dear.'

'Then a hoyden. I live for my horses.'

'His lordship gave me to understand that he did not object to that—within reason. Wives of peers can get away with a little eccentric behaviour now and again which would not be tolerated in a young unmarried woman. And his name would give your stables some credence.'

'I am conscious of that, Uncle, but it doesn't make any difference. One must surely like the man one marries, even if it is a business arrangement, and I do not like him. I shall tell him so, when he calls.'

'I hope you may not be so blunt.'

Georgie laughed; it was a hollow sound, devoid of humour. 'No, I shall try and let him down lightly.'

'Do not be too hasty, Georgiana. Tell him you need more time to think about it. That would not hurt, would it?'

'It would be dishonest, Uncle. I do not need more time.'

He stood up to leave. 'It is your decision, my dear. I have already told his lordship that I will not influence it. Now, I have work to do.' And with that he took his leave.

Georgie did not feel like eating. She rose and hurried out to the stables and sent Tom to hire a hack. She wanted to ride; riding had always helped her to overcome any fit of the blue devils and today it would be even more significant because being on the back of a horse would show her just what her life would be like when that was all she had to give her fulfilment. While he was gone she went upstairs and changed into her new blue habit and set her tall feathered hat on her short curls. By the time she returned to the stables, Tom was back with the horse.

He helped her mount and as she rode out of the yard and down the drive he saddled one of the carriage horses, hoping fervently that neither the Colonel nor Mrs Bertram would want to drive out before he returned. He could not let his mistress ride alone; his father would skin him alive if he heard of it.

Georgie, only half aware that she had an escort, rode confidently through the traffic of Oxford Street and turned into Hyde Park. Here she left the usual rides to canter across the grass to an area not so frequented, making it very difficult for Tom to keep up with her. It became even more difficult when she broke into a gallop. He reined in and watched as she pushed the hack to go faster. It was not one of her high-breds but even so it didn't seem to be doing too badly. And then he gasped and dug his heels into his mount as the horse ahead stumbled and Georgie went flying over its head and into a patch of bushes.

She was unconscious when he reached her. He bent over her to make sure she was still breathing and then straightened up to look about him. He was only a stripling and did not think he could lift her; even if he managed it, he could not put her across her horse like a sack of grain, nor ride supporting her. He needed to fetch help. There were a few early riders and carriages in the Row; he remounted and rode hell for leather for the nearest.

Georgie came to her senses to find herself lying in the arms of Major Baverstock. For a moment she thought she was having a dream, and a very enjoyable, though scandalous, one it was. Not even in her waking moments had she dared to imagine what it would be like to be held in his arms; how could her subconscious betray her so? She stirred and a sharp pain at the back of her head forced her into reality. It was reality. Richard was kneeling on the ground with her head in his lap and looking down at her with such a look of concern in his eyes, it made her heart leap.

'Lie still. Your groom has gone for a carriage to take you home.'

'Home,' she murmured.

'I meant your aunt's home. Did you suppose you were at Rowan Park?'

'Yes. No. Oh, dear. . . Where am I? What are you doing here?'

'Looking after you until Tom gets back. It was fortunate that I, like you, enjoy riding out early.' He looked up as the sound of a carriage could be heard. 'Here it is. Now I am going to lift you as carefully as I can on to the seat. I am afraid it might hurt a little. But we'll soon have you home.'

It was painful, so much so that she almost lost her senses again and did not fully recover them until she was safely in her bed and a doctor was bending over her.

'No broken bones,' he said, leaning over her. 'But you've had a nasty bump on your head. Can you see me?'

'Yes.'

He smiled. 'Only one of me?'

'Yes.'

'How many fingers am I holding up?'

'Three.'

'Good. You have been lucky, Miss Paget. Now, all I prescribe is rest and, if the pain becomes too unbearable, perhaps a little laudunum.' As she tried to struggle into a sitting position he pressed her back on the pillows and added, 'No quick movements; gently does it or you will make yourself swoon.'

He turned to her aunt who was hovering anxiously. 'Please see that the patient is not disturbed or troubled by anything for the next two or three days. Time is all that's needed.'

Georgie's effort to try and sit had left her breathless and exhausted and she was glad enough to be left alone to sleep. She drifted off, smiling to herself in spite of

her throbbing head. Now she would not have to receive
Lord Barbour, not today anyway! And she had been in
Richard's arms. And he had kissed her after he had
lifted her into the carriage and sat on the floor so that
he could hold her on the seat. He had, hadn't he? She
had not dreamed it. The memory of that butterfly
touch on her cheek would have to sustain her in the
future because it was all she would ever know of love.

When she woke, she found Felicity sitting by her
bedside and Fanny busy arranging a huge basket of
flowers on the table by the window. There were more
flowers on the mantelshelf and on other tables round
the room. 'Where did they all come from?' she asked,
astonished that anyone could have heard of the accident so quickly and taken the trouble to send flowers.

'Most came from Lord Barbour. He has been almost
camping on the doorstep and anxious to know when he
can see you. Aunt Harriet has been keeping him at
bay,' Felicity told her.

'And the rest? He surely did not send them all?'

'That basket by the window came from Lady
Hereward and Juliette with their good wishes, and the
vaseful on that table from Mrs Sopwithy, and those
from Major Baverstock.' She pointed to a small posy
of marguerites almost hidden by the foliage of an
ostentatious basket of hothouse lilies. 'He brought you
home, did you know that?'

'Yes, though I was out of my senses most of the
time.'

'He said you had been galloping. I am afraid Aunt
Harriet will ring a peal over you the minute Roscow
says you are fit enough. It is just not done in town, you
know. And you were alone.'

'Tom. . .'

'He could not keep up with you. He saw you thrown and went for help. Fortunately the first person he approached was the Major, so there will not be a scandal about it.'

'I am sorry to have been so much trouble to everyone.'

'No matter. We are all prodigious relieved no lasting harm was done.'

'How long must I stay in bed?'

'Until you feel well enough to get up without becoming dizzy.'

'Then I shall remain dizzy just as long as I possibly can.'

'Goodness, Georgie, whatever for?'

'Until Lord Barbour tires of coming. I simply cannot face him.'

'Well, of course, if you do not want to, you do not have to, but he is not going to give in, you know. He has been here every day.'

'Every day?' Georgie repeated. 'How long have I been lying here?'

'Three days and three nights. The first was the worst—you were in some sort of delirium and we were very worried. Oh, you do not know how glad I am to see you restored to your senses.'

'Did I talk much?'

'Not that anyone could understand—just odd words. And you cried. Do you know, Georgie, I do not think I have ever known you cry before? You were always so strong. Is there anything amiss?'

'No, I expect my head hurt.' She struggled into a sitting position and put her hand on her sister's arm.

'You have not stayed at home to be with me, have you? You haven't given up all your social engagements?'

'Of course I have. Did you think I would go out and enjoy myself when you were lying here at death's door?' She smiled. 'Well, not quite at death's door, but you have been very ill. I could not leave you.'

'But the Major. . .'

'He quite understood. He said it was very commendable of me and he would not have it any other way.'

'Has he spoken to you? Are felicitations in order?'

'No, he has too much sensibility to broach such a subject when he could see I was so worried about you.'

'But he has spoken to Uncle?'

'Many times, but, I am persuaded, not about marriage.'

Georgie could not understand her sister's lighthearted manner. 'Are you not disappointed?'

'No, why should I be? There is plenty of time.' Then, changing the subject abruptly she asked, 'Now, what would you like for luncheon? Cook has some chicken broth, or beef tea, or perhaps something a little more substantial?'

Georgie laughed. 'I am as hungry as a hunter, but whatever you do don't let Lord Barbour know that. As far as he is concerned I am still very weak and unable to receive visitors.'

'Very well,' Felicity said, getting up to give orders for a light meal to be prepared. 'But anyone would think you fell off your horse on purpose.'

'I did not fall, I was thrown,' Georgie called after her. Her pride would not let her admit that she could not stay on a simple hack, side-saddle or astride, but she smiled as the door closed on her sister; the accident had certainly been opportune. She would have to see Lord Barbour sooner or later, but if she could manage to hold him off until just before her aunt was ready to leave for France she could get the unpleasant interview over with and then she and Felicity could return to Rowan Park. Once there, she would prepare herself for her sister's wedding in surroundings which would make it easier to bear, among her beloved horses.

She reached out and picked up the tiny vase containing the posy of marguerites and stood it on the little table beside her bed where she could see them even when she was lying down. She lay very still for a long time, gazing at them, studying each petal. Tears welled in her eyes and slowly chased each other down her cheeks, soaking her pillow, but she did not brush them away; they were washing away her weakness.

Once she had been assured that Georgie was getting well, Felicity lifted her self-imposed ban on going out, but as her sister was not there to chaperon her and their aunt was busy with preparations for shutting up the house the following week she was left very much to her own devices. Most of the time she spent with Juliette Hereward and Captain Melford, acting chaperon to her friend. When Georgie asked her if she had been on any outings with Major Baverstock, she said she had seen little of him.

'He is too busy over that silly wager, you know. John. . .' She stopped and corrected herself hurriedly. 'Captain Melford says there is a great deal to do: the route has to be gone over very carefully, extra horses have to be hired and places decided for changing them.'

'Oh, you have not quarrelled with him, then?'

'Oh, no!' Felicity cried. 'But to be honest I am becoming a little bored by all this talk of horses.'

Georgie was pleased to see her so much more relaxed and happy; she seemed to have suddenly come out of her shell and Georgie supposed the few weeks her sister had had in Society had done wonders for her self-confidence. It made it easier to leave her and return to Rowan Park, which was what she had decided to do.

Lord Barbour called every day to enquire about her health and ask when he might see her. Aunt Harriet, bless her, had kept him out of her niece's room, if not out of the house, by saying she was still not up to receiving visitors and did not want him to see her looking anything less than her best. He would have been furious if he had seen Richard Baverstock being shown, one afternoon, into Mrs Bertram's small upstairs sitting-room. where Georgie, up and dressed, was receiving him.

'You really must allow him to visit you, my dear,' her aunt had said when she had demurred. 'He brought you home, you know, unconscious as you were and stretched out across the carriage seat so that he was obliged to kneel on the dirty floor. It made a dreadful mark on his riding breeches. He has called almost every day to enquire about you. You really should thank him properly.' She had paused. 'Besides, I do believe he has another reason. . .'

'What other reason?' Georgie had asked, starting up in surprise, hope flaring for a moment, only to subside as soon as her aunt had spoken again.

'Why, to be sure, had you forgot he was going to offer for Felicity? He has come to ask for your blessing. There was no opportunity before and he is too nice in his manners to push himself forward when you were not well, but one can hardly blame him for being impatient. Does that not show how well-bred he is?'

'Yes, Aunt.'

'Then may I have him shown up?'

She could not say no, but she was trembling when he stood before her, taking her hand and enquiring how she did.

'I believe I am almost recovered,' she said, withdrawing her hand because he seemed reluctant to let go of it. 'I must thank you for finding me and bringing me home; I do not know what I would have done without your help.'

'It was my privilege, Miss Paget.'

'And thank you also for the flowers. Marguerites are my favourite.'

There was an awkward silence, when they simply looked into each other's eyes, unable to speak of what was in their hearts and yet unable to utter banalities.

'Major, may I offer some refreshment?' Mrs Bertram said into the silence. 'I do believe it is nearly time for the tea to be brought in.'

'That would be very acceptable, Mrs Bertram,' he said, dragging his eyes away from Georgie to answer her.

Unaccountably, instead of ringing for the maid, Mrs Betram went in search of her, leaving Richard and Georgie alone. 'I am truly grateful to you,' she told him. 'It was such a foolish thing to happen.' She smiled suddenly. 'It was such a poor beast that I could do little more than canter. I was certainly not trying to put it to the test or anything like that. . .'

'I should hope not!' He grinned at her, making her

feel so weak that she was glad she was seated. 'But why did you do it? Hyde Park is not Rowan Park, you know.'

'Riding clears my head. It always has done.' Then she completely threw him by asking abruptly, 'I collect the last time we spoke together you were going to approach my uncle. Have you done so?'

His heart sank; so much for his hope that he might change matters. She was obviously as set on the match as ever she had been. 'If you mean about your sister, no, I have not.'

'Why not?'

'It hardly seemed appropriate with you being ill. And I have seen so little of Miss Felicity this last week. . .'

'Whose fault is that? I am told you have been preoccupied with that ridiculous wager to ride to York. It is hardly a way to win a lady, is it?'

'Who told you that?'

'Felicity herself.'

'Then I ask pardon.'

'It is not my pardon you should request but that of my sister,' she said, her torment making her speak more sharply than she had intended.

'Then of course I will do it.'

Mrs Bertram returned, followed by a maid with the tea-tray, and the conversation returned to generalities, which surprised Georgie, for she had expected her aunt to push for an early announcement. It was only as Richard rose to take his leave that Georgie said, 'Major Baverstock tells me he is going to speak to Felicity very soon, Aunt.'

She was too cocooned in her own misery to notice

Richard's little start of surprise or her aunt's eyebrows shoot up almost into her hairline before she collected herself and turned to him with a smile. 'I am glad to hear it, Major. There has been too much speculation.'

He was astonished that Georgie should have mistaken his meaning in that fashion, but decided she had done it deliberately. He didn't like being pushed, but it told him one thing—she had no feelings for him or she would not be able to thrust him at someone else. Perhaps it was her way of telling him that she had not intended to respond to his kiss in the way that she had. He did not think she'd been so deeply unconscious that she had not known what was happening. She had dismissed him and what else was there for him to do but leave?

As soon as he had gone Georgie sank back into the cushions of her chair and picked up the rug she had discarded when he'd come into the room, putting it back over her knees. They were shaking so much that she thought her aunt could not fail to notice.

'So, he is going to do it after all,' her aunt said. 'I had begun to wonder.'

'Wonder what?'

'If I had been right to promote this match. He seemed not to be so sure as he had been.'

Georgie gave a hollow laugh. 'I cannot imagine anyone making him do something he does not want to, Aunt. The rest is up to Felicity. My only aim is for her happiness; nothing else matters and she must not feel she is being forced into a marriage she does not want.'

'Why do you say that?' her aunt asked, peering at her short-sightedly. 'Felicity has been in the Major's company any number of times and she has never given the slightest hint she does not want it, has she?'

'No.' She paused and drew a deep breath. 'Aunt, I would like to go home to Rowan Park as soon as possible.'

'But you must wait for the announcement. It must be soon because the Colonel and I leave for Paris at the end of next week.'

'I do not think it will be official until after that wretched race, Aunt. We can make the announcement from Rowan Park just as easily.'

'But Felicity will not want to go with you. She has promised to spend a few days with the Herewards at Richmond.'

'Then of course she must go. I can go home alone.'

'No, you cannot.'

'I have Fanny and Tom. It was how I arrived.'

'That was different. You were not getting over a serious accident. Also, you were not half promised to Lord Barbour and Felicity had not yet met Major Baverstock, all of which makes a great difference. I cannot allow it.'

'The doctor told me my recovery has not been as swift as he hoped and that the country air will do me good.'

This was perfectly true and the doctor confirmed it when asked by Mrs Bertram, but that didn't alter the fact that there was no one to accompany her home. And then the doctor himself stepped in.

'I have advised Viscount Dullingham to go home for his health's sake,' he said, returning later that same day. 'He says he will be pleased to escort you and your maid back to Rowan Park tomorrow. I believe the houses are only fifteen miles distant from each other.'

Georgie did not quite know what to make of this offer, but in view of her aunt's delight at her niece's good fortune in being taken up by so illustrious a personage, and because she had no reason to refuse, she accepted gratefully.

His lordship was a pleasant companion and Georgie found him easy to talk to, once they had settled themselves in his roomy carriage, with Wendens and Fanny, and with Tom on the box beside the driver. Georgie's own carriage had been left behind to be used by Felicity when she returned home. Fanny and Tom would return by stage to bring her back when her visit to Lady Hereward came to end. It seemed an ideal arrangement and allowed Mrs Bertram to supervise the closing of her house in Holles Street in peace. And Georgie managed to leave without encountering either Lord Barbour or Richard Baverstock again.

While they were in the coach in the presence of the servants the conversation was of general matters—the war just past, their hopes for lasting peace, the harvest to come and the price of grain, novels and music, horses and more horses. They passed through Islington Spa, a picturesque village with a pond on the green overhung with elms, then along the Holloway Road and up the hill to Highgate. East End was soon passed and then they were on Finchley Common and she was glad she had company for it was notorious for highway-men. Once past the turnpike at Whetstone she relaxed and very soon afterwards they drew up at the The

Swan in Stevenage where rooms had been booked for the night.

His lordship asked her to join him for supper in the dining-room and she gladly agreed. Before long she was telling him all about her father and her life at Rowan Park, even a few of her problems, and he told her of his son—not too much, for it would not have been appropriate to speak of personal matters with one so young, but it was enough for her to realise that he loved Richard very much and regretted the wasted years. 'I knew my wife was driving him away,' he said. 'And foolishly I did nothing to stop it.' He asked her about her plans for the stables and about Felicity. She answered as truthfully as she could and he listened and learned. And what he learned worried him. He said nothing, for what could he say? It was up to the young people themselves to come about, but he hoped most fervently that it would not take too long and no lasting harm would be done.

They were crossing Royston Heath the following afternoon when their coach was brought to a shuddering halt by the sudden arrival on the road of three horsemen with covered faces and pistols at the ready.

'High toby!' exclaimed Wendens. 'My lord, we are being held up!'

'So I see,' his lordship said drily as one of the highwaymen dismounted and flung open the door of the coach.

'Out, all of you.'

He had his pistol at the ready and one of his companions was watching them with deep boot-button eyes; the other was covering the driver and Tom. They thought it wisest not to argue.

Once they were all standing in the road, their coach was searched, all their luggage turned out and anything of value stowed in the robbers' saddle-bags. 'Make it look good,' one said to the others, a phrase which puzzled Georgie.

'You will be punished for this,' she said, incensed by the sight of all her clothes in a heap in the middle of the road and her trunk turned upside-down on top of them. 'Do you think it is worth losing your life for a few paltry jewels?'

'No, but that's not all we'll get, you can be sure.' He grabbed his lordship's watch and put it into his own waistcoat pocket.

'Oh, I see. You mean to hold us for ransom. Let me tell you there is no money for a ransom. . .'

The man put his head back and laughed. 'We ain't interested in Long Megs like you, miss, and we could wish you in Jericho, for what we are to do with you I don't know.'

'Then it is Lor——' She stopped and glanced at the Viscount. If they did not know who he was, she ought not to enlighten them.

'Oh, we know who he is right and tight,' said the one who seemed to be in charge. 'Now, my lord, if you was to be so good as to step over to the bushes here. We don't want to upset the lady, do we?' He took his lordship's arm and propelled him forward.

'What are you going to do with him?' Georgie demanded.

He was never to answer. From nowhere came the crack of a pistol and the robber dropped to his knees and rolled over, his head snapped back, revealing a thick black beard below the scarf he had tied about his face. His astonished companions turned as men appeared from the bushes, yelling and shouting and wielding clubs. The remaining highwaymen did not stop to count them or discover they had no other arms but the pistol which was now empty, but sprinted for their horses and disappeared over the heath in a cloud of dust.

Lord Dullingham, who had dropped to his knees when the man who held him fell, stood up, brushed himself down and turned to the men, who were only three in number. 'I am obliged,' he said, as calmly as if he were in a drawing-room.

'That's all right, sir, but obligations don't buy bread, do they?'

His lordship did not immediately answer for he had turned the dead man over with the toe of his boot and had bent to remove the scarf from his face. Now he was looking down at him in something like a dream. Georgie suspected he was more shaken than he liked to appear; she was certain the men had meant to kill him, though why they should do so she had no idea. His delay in answering seemed to anger one of their rescuers. 'Let's see what the varmints left behind,' he said, striding over to the coach. 'Where d'you keep the readies? Hidden, are they?'

Lord Dullingham stirred himself at last. 'What? Oh, of course I shall reward you.' He went to the coach and pulled at one of the squabs. It came away to reveal a little niche in which was a small box. Before he could open it, it was snatched from his hand.

'How dare you do that?' Georgie shouted. 'I know you. We saw you outside Bullock's Museum begging, didn't we? Major Baverstock spoke to you.'

'So he did, ma'am. Didn't see it was you, ma'am, but it don' make no difference. We need the money.'

'Is that how you repay kindness done to you? I am ashamed, truly ashamed, to think that any man who had been so generously treated could behave so. Do you not know who this gentleman is? He is Viscount Dullingham, the Major's father.'

They looked at first resentful and then shamefaced, but the man who held the box did not relinquish it. She took it from him. 'It was to Dullingham House the Major said you were to go, wasn't it? Dullingham House is the home of his lordship. Do you think you deserve to be helped now?'

They looked sheepishly at the angry young woman in front of them and then burst out laughing. 'We're bested by a skirt, lads,' their leader said.

The others grinned and reluctantly turned away, but were called back by Lord Dullingham. 'What are your names?'

'I'm Corporal Daniel Batson—leastways I was afore a grateful country decided to dispense with me services. This here's Josh.' He pointed to the taller of his companions, the one who had lost an arm. 'And that's Bill.'

'And what did my son say to you, Corporal?'

'Said if we was to go to Dullingham House we'd be given work. We was on our way there, but when we saw the coach stopped and the high tobies it seemed like our luck was in. I left fly the pop, didn't mean to kill the man, but I reckon if I hadn't he'd ha' done you in, m'lord.'

'Yes, I believe you are right,' his lordship said slowly, taking his box from Georgie, who was clutching it to her bosom as if about to defend it with her life. He extracted three coins. 'Here is a guinea each. Come to Dullingham House as my son suggested.'

'And him?' the Corporal asked, nodding towards the corpse.

'Give me your pistol. I will notify the watch in the next town we come to that I put paid to the man's life when he attacked us. I do not think there will be any questions asked.' He held out his hand and the pistol was placed in it, then he turned to Fanny, who had bundled Georgie's clothes back in her trunk. 'Help your mistress back into the coach. It is time we were on our way, if we are to reach Rowan Park before dark.'

Five minutes later they were moving again, a silent, thoughtful company, for everyone had realised that they had had a lucky escape—especially his lordship. But who, wondered Georgie, wanted him dead? And though she ruminated about it for some time she could find no answer.

It was late when they reached Rowan Park, but there was enough light for his lordship to see that it was a neat, well-run establishment. He allowed Georgie to give him a quick tour of the stables, where he picked out two almost matching horses which he said would do very nicely for his carriage, and then, declining refreshment, took his leave. 'I'll send someone over for the cattle,' he said and he waved her goodbye.

The next morning, clad once again in shirt and breeches, she rose early, ready to return to her usual routine. She was back at home, in the place she loved, doing what she most enjoyed doing—looking after her horses. Now she would settle down to become the old maid she had insisted she was and forget how she had loved and lost.

Bert Dawson was pleased to have her back and soon had Tom back at his work, while he escorted her on a round of inspection. She discovered that the gangling three-week-old foal was growing well and that Bright Star was making good progress. 'She's almost ready for her first gallop,' he told her, knowing she would want to be the one to give it to her. 'And Warrior has missed you.'

She laughed. 'How do you know?'

'He's been off his oats, miss, and acting up; won't let anyone near him without a lot of coaxing.'

She went to Grecian Warrior's box and stroked his nose. 'I'm back, Warrior, old fellow,' she said softly. 'No need to worry; no one else shall have you.' Dawson looked at her with one eyebrow raised in a question, but she did not tell him that she had been thinking of Lord Barbour. The horse nudged at her pocket and she produced the apple he knew she always had there and left him munching contentedly.

'Saddle Bright Star,' she said. 'I want to see what she's got in her.'

An hour later, reining the filly in at the furthermost part of the gallops, she knew she had a winner. The horse would need careful training but she had no qualms about being able to do it. With luck she might even be ready for the next two-year-old stakes at Newmarket.

Two days later, she was walking Bright Star quietly back to the stables after her second gallop, when she noticed a rider on the horizon. He was standing quite still, watching her. 'Have to watch our step,' she murmured, leaning forward to pat the filly's neck. 'Can't let everyone see how good you are.'

She turned to go back to the stables and the rider on the hill cantered towards her. She recognised the horse before she recognised him. There was no mistaking Pegasus. Her emotions, which she had thought she had under control, were once more thrown into confusion.

'Miss Paget.' He reined in beside her and touched his gloved hand to the brim of his hat.

'Major Baverstock.' Did she sound as confused as she felt? 'How nice to see you.'

CHAPTER SEVEN

WITHOUT waiting for an invitation, Richard turned to ride alongside her. 'I have come on an errand for my father. He tells me he has bought two of your horses. He wants me to take delivery of them.'

'You have come from Dullingham House? I thought you were still in London. You have not quarrelled with Felicity, have you?' She was acutely conscious of his tall figure beside her, his capable hands on the reins, hands which had carried her and held her. No, she told herself sternly, that must be forgotten as if it had never happened. She lifted her head and kept her eyes on the lane ahead of her.

He turned to look at her profile, the upturned nose, the jutting chin, both giving the impression of stubbornness, but the small rosebud mouth and the dimple in the cheek softened that. 'How could anyone quarrel with such a delightful young lady? You must know that your sister has gone to stay with Lady Hereward in Richmond, and as I had business in this area I took the opportunity to return home for a few days.'

'What business?' It was out before she could stop herself and she was forced to turn her head towards him. 'Oh, I am sorry. I should not have. . . Oh, dear, my foolish tongue.'

He laughed. 'Do not apologise, Miss Paget; it does not suit you. And there is no secret. I came to see how

Bright Star comes along.' He surveyed the filly carefully. 'She looks in peak condition.'

'Did you see her gallop?'

'Yes. She's a good goer, I think, but should you be
riding her yourself? After all, you have had a serious
fall.'

'I am fully recovered, Major. It was only a bump on
the head.'

'It was enough to keep you in bed a whole week.'

She blushed crimson at being caught out in the
deception, but recouped quickly. 'It suited me to keep
to my room, Major.'

'Oh.' It would not have been polite to ask her why
and he decided to change the subject. 'Tell me about
Bright Star.'

She felt easier when talking about horses and for the
next few minutes she went over Bright Star's training
programme with him in a relaxed and informed manner
and he was forced to the conclusion that she did know
what she was talking about and he changed his mind
about taking the filly's training away from her. If the
alternative to a prosperous stable was marriage to that
blackguard Barbour, then the more he helped her to
remain independent the better. 'I think she could have
her first outing at Newmarket next week,' she said.
'What do you think?'

'Yes, but only if you are sure she will be ready.'

'She will be ready.'

'I also came looking for mounts to ride. My father
has a few I can use, but I need more.'

'For that outrageous ride to York, I suppose.'

'Why outrageous?'

'Why?' she snapped. It was easier on her nerves to

be angry with him; friendship she could not cope with at all. 'Because you will ruin goodness knows how many horses and it cannot be good for you either, all those hours in the saddle. And all to salve your pride and score over a fat reprobate who puts one over on you.'

'Fat reprobate,' he repeated, grinning. 'Is that how you describe someone who hopes to become your husband?'

'He may hope,' she said flatly.

'You mean you have turned him down?' He was suddenly very cheerful, but then he remembered her sister and was sunk again into gloom.

'I have neither accepted nor rejected him, for he has never made the offer,' she said. 'Now, do you think we might change the subject?'

'Delighted to do so, my dear Miss Paget,' he said. 'How about coming to Newmarket with me tomorrow? I need to engage a good jockey for Bright Star if she is to race next week.'

She was about to refuse, but changed her mind. For Bright Star's sake she wanted to meet the jockey Richard chose for her and she really ought to keep up to date with what was going on. Moreover, it would not hurt to show herself as someone to be reckoned with in the racing business. Not for a moment would she admit that a day at the races with Richard Baverstock would be a pleasure she did not want to miss.

'Yes, I should like that,' she said.

'Good. I shall call for you with the curricle.'

She made no comment, though it crossed her mind that the vehicle would not be large enough to accommodate her maid. Their only chaperon would be his tiger, if he had such a thing in the country.

They returned to the stables and she handed Bright Star over to Dawson and asked Tom to lead out his lordship's horses.

'They're good,' Richard said, casting a critical eye over them. 'Almost a perfect match.'

'They are sisters.'

'And they will take postillions?'

'Of course, though Bess is more accustomed to being ridden than Silver.' She paused. 'Oh, you are not thinking what I think you are, are you?'

He gave her a disarming smile. 'Not unless it becomes necessary. I have to have thirty horses, Miss Paget, thirty horses with speed and stamina. What else can you offer me?'

'I do not know that I want to let you have any,' she said. 'You know how I feel about the whole mad escapade. In fact, I should like to buy Pegasus back.'

'He is not for sale. Besides, you cannot afford him; his value has gone up by leaps and bounds since I acquired him.'

'You are insufferable! I've a mind not to come to Newmarket with you after all.'

'Oh, that would be a pity,' he said. 'I need your help choosing a jockey and if I should make other purchases. . .'

She laughed suddenly. 'Are you saying, Major Baverstock, that you value my opinion?'

'Indeed I am,' he confirmed, doing his best to maintain a serious expression. 'Two heads are always better than one, are they not? Do say you'll come.'

'Oh, very well.' She tried to sound offhand but the

prospect was already exciting her. It had been like that the first time she had been taken there by her father. The noisy crowds, the betting, the beautiful horses, the jockeys in their colourful breeches and caps all served to create an atmosphere that was unique and heady.

'Do you think Dawson can spare Tom to ride up behind?' he asked. 'I am not such a coxcomb as to keep a tiger.'

He had realised the necessity for a chaperon, after all, and one of her own staff would be more acceptable than his. It was very thoughtful of him. She smiled mischievously. 'And would you wish him to dress in black and yellow stripes?'

'As he will be behind us and I shall not see what he is wearing, it is a matter of indifference to me.' He chuckled suddenly. 'Perhaps something a little less loud, perhaps? It would be best if we did not attract too much attention.'

Yes, she thought, because if they were seen by anyone of the *ton* it would be all round the capital in a couple of days, and though the outing was innocent enough and they had a legitimate reason for going and Tom was in attendance it might just be considered too daring of her. Not that she cared for herself, but Felicity must be protected from the least whisper of gossip.

He took his leave, leading the two new horses, and she went indoors to decide what she was going to wear the following day—certainly not a shirt and breeches.

It had taken Fanny, with the help of Mrs Thorogood, two days to clean and repair her clothes after their mistreatment by the highwaymen and being bundled willy-nilly back into her trunk but they had done their

best and most were still wearable. She picked out a
jacket in a soft blue jaconet which fitted her figure
closely, curving into her neat waist and then flaring out
a little over a flowing skirt of shot silk. The jacket had
a stand-up collar and was frogged in black across the
front. Her tall hat had a curling brim and an ostrich
feather which was fastened on one side and swept
across the brim to brush her cheek on the other side.
She offered up a little prayer of thanks to her aunt for
making her buy it. Now was not the time to worry
about what it had cost.

'You look a treat, Miss Georgie,' Fanny said as she
twirled before her the next morning. It was not for her
to criticise the actions of her beloved mistress, but she
fervently hoped that no one, not Miss Georgie or Miss
Felicity, or indeed that nice Major, would be hurt by
it. 'And the Major is waiting downstairs.'

Georgie went down to meet him, conscious of the
excitement which bubbled up in her and was making
her tremble and blush. What a ninny you are, she told
herself; you are only going to the races and he is only
a man. But what a man!

He had taken equal care with his appearance.
Although his mulberry-coloured coat was a civilian
one, it was cut in the military style and fitted him to
perfection. His plain waistcoat had silver buttons and
his cravat was a pristine white tied very simply and not
in the complicated fashion prevalent in London. He
wore buff-coloured nankeen breeches and hessians in
which it was possible to see your reflection, supposing
you were to stand close enough.

He looked up at her coming down the stairs towards
him and caught his breath. Not for the first time he

found himself comparing the strikingly beautiful woman she undoubtedly was with the ragamuffin urchin clad in breeches and voluminious shirt, pretending to be a man. She could never be a man, not in a thousand years, and he wished he could make her see that.

He realised suddenly that she had reached the bottom step and he was still staring at her as if mesmerised. He pulled himself together and went towards her, taking her outstretched hand and bowing over it. It was trembling a little, he noticed, and her cheeks were pale. 'Miss Paget, good morning,' he said. 'Are you quite well enough to go?'

'Of course I am. And I do not intend to miss a single race, so let us by on our way. Is Tom there?'

'Yes, and proud as a peacock in his Sunday go-to-church suit.'

They approached Newmarket across the heath and arrived at the course about noon. Race week attracted all manner of people from the highest to the lowest who rubbed shoulders together, often quite literally, to the detriment of expensive tailored coats and the pockets of the same, for pickpockets also abounded.

Everywhere people were making bets and shouting the odds. Young bloods, noisy and already half foxed, mixed with the more sober race-goers. In the paddock, the horses paraded restlessly, waiting to go to the start. Jockeys in light breeches in red, yellow, green and blue with caps to match were almost swallowed by the crowd as they made their way to be weighed in.

As Richard drove in among the huge variety of conveyances taking up their positions all round the railing, there was a concerted shout of, 'They're off!'

and six horses thundered round the track to the shouted encouragement of their backers.

Richard watched in amusement as Georgie stood up in the curricle in order to see better, jumping up and down in excitement. He looked at Tom and grinned; if she did not tip them all out it would be a wonder. 'Would you like to put a bet on the next race?' he asked her.

She had heard him but she was too absorbed in the race to answer until it had ended, when she sat down, almost too breathless to speak. 'Yes, let's go and have a closer look at the runners,' she said when she had composed herself.

Leaving Tom to look after the curricle, they made their way through the crowds to the paddock and after inspecting the horses she picked one out.

'Right,' he said. 'I'll back it too. You see how much faith I have in you?'

'Oh, dear,' she said. 'What if it loses?'

'Then we shall both have lost our money.'

'Then, I beg of you, risk only a modest sum.'

He laughed, almost carefree. 'As you say, a modest sum. A guinea perhaps? It is seven to one.'

They won on the next two races and lost on the third. After that, not being a true gambler, Georgie was reluctant to continue, but he laughed and said, 'You can't win them all, Georgie. Put on what you have won, then if you lose at least you won't be out of pocket.' He seemed not to have noticed that he had called her by her given name, and she had no intention of drawing his attention to the face.

'Very well. No more after this. And then I think we should think about finding a jockey for Bright Star. I have been watching them most carefully and there was one I thought might suit. He was in the third race.'

'The one you backed?'

'Yes.'

'He lost you your money.'

'So he did, but he did well to come second and I liked the way he rode.'

'Do I get a say in this? It is my horse, after all.'

She turned to him in surprise at the reminder. They had been having such a wonderful time and the note of censure dampened her spirits, but then she noticed the twinkle in his dark eyes and relaxed. 'I didn't mean to dictate, but I am sure he is the best. If you don't agree, we shall have to compromise. Tell me your choice.'

He laughed, a deep cheerful sound, in keeping with the man himself. 'Oh, my dear Miss Paget, I would not presume to disagree with you.'

'Now you are bamming me.'

He smiled and took her arm. 'Let us see if he is available, shall we? And after that we'll go to the sales ring.'

The jockey was engaged and, after some discussion, because Georgie was convinced that stamina rather than speed was required, Richard bought two good strong horses. 'Have them delivered to Rowan Park,' he told the auctioneer. 'Miss Paget will be training them.'

If there was a snigger on the man's face it was quickly wiped off when Richard glared at him. He shook hands on the deal and promised to have the animals at Rowan Park two days hence.

'I am overwhelmed, Major,' she said as they walked

away. 'Are you not afraid of being made a laughing-stock?'

'No,' he said promptly. 'Are you?'

'Most decidedly not. I shall prove myself, you see.'

'All alone?' His voice was soft, sensuous almost, and she gave a little shiver of apprehension. She had not minded the idea of managing alone until now. Today they had done things together, laughed together, won and lost together, and they had been surprisingly at one over their choice of horses. Even the hiring of the jockey and the purchase of the mounts had produced no more than a friendly exchange. There had been no discord. Togetherness was something she had tasted for the first time today and it looked like being the last. With him as her brother-in-law, she could ask his advice, but it wouldn't be the same.

'Yes,' she said firmly. 'Alone but for my family. I shall always look to them for support.'

He understood the implication of what she was saying without having to be told; he would be part of that family, her sister's husband. He had been deliberately prevaricating, not the behaviour of an honourable man, he knew, and the longer he allowed himself to drift, the worse it would get. Tomorrow he must return to London and set matters straight.

The sunny day suddenly became cool and the cheerful crowds seemed over-noisy and ill-mannered. He put a hand under her elbow to guide her back to the curricle, where Tom waited for them. They had almost reached it when she stopped suddenly.

'Look!' she exclaimed. 'Those men. . .'

He turned towards the group of bedraggled men she indicated. 'What about them?'

'They are the three who accosted us outside Bullock's Museum, don't you remember?'

'So they are.'

'And they rescued us when his lordship's coach was held up the other day. Did he not tell you about that?'

'Indeed he did.' He handed her up into the carriage. 'Pray stay here with Tom, Miss Paget; I must go and speak to them.'

He left her to push his way through to the three men, who were standing by the rails, though the last race had finished and the crowds were drifting away. Corporal Batson saw them and came swiftly to attention. He looked incongruous—ragged, unshaven, with the toe coming off his boot.

Richard smiled. 'At ease, man, you're not in the army now.'

The man relaxed. 'We were on the way to Dullingham House, Major, like you said, but we thought we'd 'ave a flutter first. You never know when your luck is in, do you?'

'I should say your luck was in when we met in London. Why did you not take advantage of my offer immediately?'

'We started out. Had to walk, you know. . . .'

'I gave you enough for a fare.'

'Food were more important, Major. And we sent most of the cash home.'

'Of course, I should have realised. But my father also gave you money; I suppose that is all gone too?'

'It is now,' one of the others said, smiling ruefully. 'The nags were all sheep.'

Richard smiled. 'Will you go to Dullingham House now? It is not above a dozen miles away.'

'Yes, sir. Thank you, sir.' This last as Richard handed him a few coins.

'And thank you for rescuing my father.'

'It were nothing,' the Corporal said. 'Did 'e tell you what 'appened?'

'He said the coach was held up but you drove off the attackers.'

'That all, sir?'

'Yes, why?'

'They meant to kill 'is lordship. He didn't resist nor anything like that, but one o' them took 'im to one side. He had a barkin' iron and he was goin' to use it, too. I let pop with mine and killed him dead.'

Richard did not ask how the soldier came to have a weapon; it was no doubt a souvenir from the war. 'He didn't tell me anything of this.'

'Just afore I let fly, I heard one on 'em say, "Make it look good." Now why should 'e say that, less'n he meant to make it look like a high toby job when it weren't that at all? Someone's got it in for the old fellow, that's what I says.'

Richard could not think who would wish his father dead; he had no enemies that he knew of. In fact, he was well-liked by everyone—friends, employees and tenants. 'Thank you for telling me,' he said.

'No thanks needed, Major. We 'ad our eye on the main chance, but your young lady soon put a stop to that. Brave young miss, she be, and not afraid to speak out.'

Richard smiled. 'Yes, indeed. But you may do me another small service.'

'Anything, Major.'

'Go to Dullingham House as soon as maybe and take

whatever situation his lordship offers you. I will double your wages if you keep an eye out for him. If anyone else tries to harm him, I want to know at once. Protect him, if you can.'

'Yes, sir!' Again that incongruous coming to attention, but this time Richard did not smile. He was still bemused by what he had heard. Had they been mistaken? He left them and returned to Georgie.

'We had better make a push to leave before the crowds make it impossible,' he said, climbing up beside her. It took all his attention to manoeuvre the curricle out of the course on to the highway, and he remained silent until they were bowling along the heath road towards Cambridge.

'Those men,' he said at last. 'They have just told me something so extraordinary I do not know whether to believe them or not.'

'Oh.' She waited to be enlightened.

'They say that the men who stopped Father's carriage intended to kill him, that they were not real highwaymen.'

'Did his lordship not tell you that?'

'No, he did not. He passed the incident off very lightly, though I must admit Wendens looked decidedly green about the gills when my father was telling me of it.'

'Perhaps he did not wish to worry you.'

'Perhaps, but if he is in some sort of danger, then I must know. Tell me what happened, Miss Paget, every last detail. What they did, what my father did. . .'

'He did nothing to provoke them, if that is what you mean. I remember thinking he was being so calm about it in order not to frighten me. But I did think it was strange when one of them took his lordship towards the bushes. I was quite sure he was going to be killed.'

'And you, what did you do?'

'What could I do? I was enraged, but very frightened too. They all had pistols.'

'The soldiers said you were very brave.'

She laughed. 'That was after it was all over and I had recognised them.' She paused, serious again. 'I can't really believe they meant to kill anyone. After all, they had taken all our jewellery and what little money we had on our persons, though Lord Dullingham had hidden the bulk of his money and they did not find that.'

'Can you describe any of the men?'

'Not really; they all wore scarves over their faces. One did have a black beard, but he was the one who was killed by the Corporal. And they all wore black suits. I might know the horses again.'

He laughed. 'Miss Paget, you are priceless.'

'Why, what have I said?'

'That someone in the circumstances in which you found yourself should have taken note of the robbers' mounts rather than the men themselves.'

'There was a bay-brown and a blue dun, both dishy, and a cob. It was a sturdy little animal and needed to be because its rider was a heavy man.'

'What happened about the dead man?'

'We left him there and went into Royston to report to the watch. I expect they dealt with him.'

'Thank you, Miss Paget,' he said quietly.

'If they did mean to. . .to kill your father, do you know why?'

'I have not the least idea, Miss Paget. Now, I beg of you, let us speak of more pleasant things.'

He seemed suddenly remote, once again the stiff, proud man, and their subsequent conversation mirrored that. It was not until after they had left Cambridge behind and were nearing Rowan Park that he mentioned the matter again. 'I have asked those three men to look after my father,' he said. 'If anything happens and they cannot find me, they will come to you. Do not be tempted into any heroics. If I cannot be contacted, simply report what they say to the appropriate authorities. Do you understand?'

'Yes, of course, but why will they come to me?'

He smiled. 'They think you are my young lady— their words. I did not disabuse them of the idea.'

'Why not?' she demanded.

'It is none of their business and besides, it would have been difficult to explain.'

'I don't see why,' she said. 'You are my prospective brother-in-law; it is simple enough.' She did not know why she had spoken so bluntly unless it was to make herself see the truth.'

'Your sister has not yet accepted me,' he said laconically. 'It would have been presumptuous of me to have pre-empted that.'

'Why do you delay asking her?'

'I intend to win the race to York first.'

'Why?'

He looked sideways at her and then decided she deserved the truth. 'Because it has been suggested that if you marry Barbour first he will be in control of Miss Felicity's dowry and that if I play my cards right I can regain possession of my horse in that way. That is not to my taste, Miss Paget.'

She began to laugh, almost hysterically, and he pulled the curricle up and turned towards her in alarm. 'What have I said that is so amusing? I am perfectly serious.'

'Control of my sister's dowry will not pass out of my hands, Major, I assure you.'

Did she mean she had decided to reject Lord Barbour? He dared not ask for fear that she would fly into anger and though anger made her more beautiful and desirable than ever he did not want to risk it. He might not be able to keep his hands off her. 'I do not see how you can be so sure, but if you are right, then it is even more imperative that I win this race.'

'And Felicity must wait, I suppose? What do you think the gossips will make of that?'

He did not know whether to tell her what had been happening in London since she left or not. Under Lady Hereward's easygoing hospitality the younger Miss Paget was enjoying herself no end, going to parties and routs, outings and picnics, surrounded by bevies of young gentlemen, all anxious for her favours. He had been present on two of those occasions and the last time, when he had said he was leaving town, she had accepted with equanimity. He doubted if she was even missing him. 'I am surprised at you being concerned about gabblegrinders,' he said, moving to the attack. 'You do not subscribe to convention yourself.'

'What I do in the country in the privacy of my own domain is my affair, Major. I did nothing in town to give Society reason to criticise and I would most certainly do nothing to harm my sister. Now, I suggest we continue before the poor horse cools down and catches a chill.'

He flicked the reins and they continued in silence until they were within sight of the buildings of Rowan Park. 'If you must win this wretched race,' she said slowly, 'tell me how I can help.'

'I need good horses,' he said, much relieved. 'I'll buy if I have to, but hiring will be better. I am riding north tomorrow to go over the route and arrange for mounts on the most distant part of the ride. I shall use those two I bought today on the early part of the race, so I am relying on you to bring them to a peak and get me in the lead early. I believe an early lead is imperative.'

'I can do that.'

'I should also like all the men you can spare.'

'Why?'

'To see fair play. Independent stewards have been appointed, but I don't trust Barbour. He cheated before and will do so again, given the chance. I intend to post my own men all along the route. Many of my friends have volunteered and I'll use as many men as can be spareed from Dullingham House and those three soldiers. And any you let me have.'

'It seems rather dire. Are you sure it's necessary?'

'The wager has attracted a certain notoriety,' he said, smiling ruefully. 'The side-bets on it are prodigious and there are some who might want one or other rider to come to grief, might even be prepared to help him to do that. I do not want to be held responsible.'

'Surely not.'

'I intend to be prepared. I know it is a lot to ask, but the men will not be gone above two or three days.'

'Very well, I will ask Dawson to let you know who can be spared.'

'Thank you.' He paused, wondering whether he dared make the next request. 'And there is one more thing you can do for me.'

The tone of his voice made her turn to look at him. If such a thing were possible she would have said he was looking almost sheepish. 'Go on, Major,' she said.

'Will you let me have Grecian Warrior for one stage?'

'What?' She was furious. 'You know what I think of the whole idea and I would not help you at all if it were not for Felicity's sake and because I can understand your reasons. But to ask for Warrior!' She laughed suddenly. 'He is very particular about whom he allows on his back.'

'Are you suggesting I cannot ride him, Miss Paget? I pride myself on the fact that there isn't a mount alive I cannot ride.'

'Now you are trying to goad me into making you prove it. Well, I will not give you the satisfaction, Major.'

Their beautiful day had been spoiled. She had been so happy, enjoying his company and pretending to herself that it was not the last time they would enjoy such a good rapport. But it was a hollow sham; he had been softening her up for the final *coup de grâce* and she had not seen it coming. Oh, what a fool she had been!

They had arrived at her front door; the day was at an end and she would never have another like it. She did not ask him to come in; it would not have been proper when there was only Fanny and the housekeeper on the premises, though if she had not been so angry she might have been tempted.

She stepped down from the curricle without waiting for him to help her down and, picking up her skirts, swept up the steps. At the top, she turned. 'Thank you for a pleasant day out, Major,' she said stiffly. 'You may rest assured your horses will be in good hands. And I will keep my promise to let you have the men. I suggest you go and see Dawson and make the arrangements.'

He stood on the gravel looking up at her, wishing with all his heart that he had not made that last request, but she had seemed so reasonable up until then and having Warrior for one section of the ride would have more than made up for Lord Barbour's use of Victor. It seemed he had misjudged her yet again. 'Bright Star's outing to Newmarket next week—I'll call for you, shall I?'

'No, Major, I shall travel with the horse. I am sure you cannot spare the time; after all, you have a much longer race to run, have you not?' Her smile was sugar and vinegar as she turned and went inside, too annoyed with herself and with him to notice that Mrs Thorogood was not there to open the door as she usually was when she heard carriage wheels on the gravel.

She did not hear him leave as she shut the door and leaned against it, letting her whole body go limp. After a few moments she pulled herself together and took off her hat and went towards the stairs, but changed her mind. She needed something to restore her nerves and a glass of wine would do no harm at all. She put her hat on a chair and went into the drawing-room to get it for herself.

She crossed the room, poured the wine, turned with the glass in her hand—and then she nearly died of shock. Ensconced in the wing-chair beside the hearth was Lord Barbour and he was smiling up at her in a way which turned her blood to ice.

'What are you doing here?' she demanded.

He rose and stepped towards her. 'As you seemed set on refusing to see me in London, I decided there was nothing for it but to beard the lioness in her den.' He sighed heavily. 'There was I dying for love and anxious because the object of my devotion had taken a tumble and no one would let me near her. Not well enough for visitors, I was told; must not be excited and a visit from me would surely excite you. I sent flowers every day, expensive blooms to match my passion and no one to thank me but the dragon who guarded you. Patiently I waited, only to be told you had fled to the country. What did you expect me to do? I followed.'

'How did you get in?'

'Your housekeeper was so good as to tell me I could wait for you.'

'But she had no idea how long I would be.'

'On the contrary, my dear Georgiana—I may call you that may I not?—the dear lady thinks you are lying injured in a hovel beside the road two miles from here, having fallen from the curricle in which you had been travelling. . .'

'And what is supposed to have happened to my companions?' she snapped.

'Do you know,' he said infuriatingly, 'she was in such a rush to render assistance she did not even stop to ask? But I had a tale of such treachery to tell, she would have been doubly incensed. You had been left stranded and forced to make your own way home.'

'And how are you supposed to have come by this information?'

'I found you, of course, and you were able to tell me before I carried you to a nearby cottage where a yokel in a smock is even now caring for you.'

'I never heard such a Banbury tale,' she said. 'And even if such a thing were true, why did you allow Mrs Thorogood to go to my aid and remain here yourself?

He smiled and his little dark eyes became almost lost in the flesh of his cheeks, though twin points of light remained, glittering malevolently. 'I should have thought the reason was obvious, my dear. I did not wish us to be disturbed.'

'Why?' He had moved very close and she backed away against a solid oak table which had stood in its place for half a century at least. 'What do you want?'

'Why, my dear Miss Paget, I want to marry you. I thought you knew that. Your uncle, the Colonel, has obligingly given his permission for me to ask you. I did not think you were averse to the idea.'

'No? Then you must have a singularly thick skin. I should have thought the fact that I came away without seeing you would have been enough to tell you I did not want you to speak of it.'

'Nerves, my dear, simply shyness and a little apprehension over the honour I confer upon you.'

'Honour! You bumptious, stiff-necked, rag-mannered clunch!'

'Dear, dear, such language!' He hooted with laughter, taking her glass from her fingers and putting it down on the table behind her. 'You are no great shakes either, but you've got plenty of ginger, I'll give you that.'

'I will give you a taste of it, too, if you do not leave my house,' she said, though the threat was an empty one. 'Mrs Thorogood will be back directly.'

'It will take her some time to find the cottage I described to her. In my haste I did not take proper note of its direction.'

'You fiend! Get out! Get out at once.'

'Not until I have my answer.'

She gave a cracked laugh. 'That's easy. It is no, no, a thousand times no.'

'Pity,' he said equably. 'I had hoped we could deal together in accord and I would not find it necessary to point out the bumblebath you are in.'

'I don't know what you mean. I am in no trouble.'

'Do you think we could sit down and discuss this?' he said. 'It would be so much more comfortable. I am sure that sitting on the edge of a table cannot be conducive to pleasant discourse.'

'I do not want to discourse with you at all,' she retorted, though when he moved back she took the opportunity to slip on to a chair, and glad she was of its support, for her knees were buckling. 'You should not be here. I am alone.'

'Precisely, my dear Miss Paget. May I be seated?' Without waiting for her reply, he flung up the tails of his coat and sat himself in a chair opposite her, leaning forward to look closely into her face. He meant to intimidate her and he succeeded. There was something about his manner which was frightening. He was more than the fat reprobate she had called him; he was evil. It exuded from his pores along with the perspiration which glistened on his forehead. 'You and I are alone in the house. That in itself is enough to condemn you . . .'

'Though not you, I suppose.'

'Well, it will not be considered good conduct on my part but I am consumed by passion, as everyone knows, and will be forgiven for it. And I am persuaded you too are a passionate being and not so particular about gossip.'

'My passion is one of anger. And so I shall tell the world.'

'Do you think they will believe you? I think not, especially after we have spent the whole night together.'

'The night?' If she had not been frightened before, she was terrified now. And yet in the core of it was the thought of Richard. Would he believe she was innocent? And leading from that was the certain knowledge that if there was a scandal Felicity would suffer.

'Why, yes, my dear. I have it in mind to cuckold the parson, just to be on the safe side and ensure your compliance.' His oily smile never wavered as he watched the changing expressions chase each other across her face.

'But why? If I say I do not wish to marry you, why do you persist?'

'Because I think we shall deal very well together. I do not ask for much. I already have my heir, so I am not particular as to that, though with such a body as you have I cannot promise to refrain altogether.'

'You are disgusting.'

'Oh, do you say so? Then you have not seen a really

depraved person, I assure you. An' I thought you a woman of the world.'

She must keep calm, she told herself. 'I would have thought you had better things to do than torment me, my lord. Have you not a race to win? Are all your arrangements complete?'

'They will be after tonight. It is of those I wish to speak.'

She gave a hollow laugh. 'And I thought you came a-courting.'

'So I did, but you force me to be less than the sensitive supplicant I would otherwise wish to be. You imagine yourself a businesswoman, though even you must realise that is nothing more than a silly chit's daydream. But if it is business you want, then we will deal in business terms.'

She attempted to laugh again but it stuck in her throat. When she tried to rise, he pushed her down again and held fast to her hand. 'You will hear me out, because my proposition is not so distasteful, as you shall see.'

He paused, but she could not bring herself to make any reply and he went on.

'Breeding is what I'm on about.' And as he heard her little gasp of shock his smile broadened. 'Not our breeding, though I ain't saying I'd be averse to that. No, I meant the horses. I'm being dunned left and right and what with this ride to York and all the expense of that I'm in a fair way to being dished up if I lose it, which I don't aim to do, by the way. So with your horses and mine we could win that little wager and let me tell you there is a great deal of money riding on it besides the wager itself. And afterwards the combined stables of Barbour and Paget could become a byword to rival Tattersall's.'

'They don't breed horses,' she felt constrained to point out, though why she should she did not know. She would never entertain him as a husband.

'All the better. Everyone will come to me for their cattle: young bloods, country squires, the army—Sir Henry had a contract for the army, did he not?'

'Yes, and I shall carry on where he left off. I do not need you and I certainly have no intention of allowing you to ruin my horses on that madcap wager.'

'You will have no choice after tonight, my dear. I have come here to ensure it.'

'If you think I will allow myself to be intimidated——' she began, but she did not finish because he rose to his feet and pulled her roughly into his arms. His mouth came down to hers and his brandy-laden breath filled her nostrils so that she felt sick.

'Come, my dear,' he said, grimacing because she was struggling and it was all he could do to hold her. 'Don't fight it, accept it. A great many marriages are based on less and are none the worse for it.'

'I am not interested in marriage to you or anyone. And if you touch me I shall scream.'

'We are quite alone; there is no one to hear you.'

'The men. . .'

'Too far away. Now, wench, we have talked long enough.' He started to drag her across the room. 'Come over to the sofa; it is a deal more comfortable.'

'No! No!' she shrieked, hoping Fanny would hear her, though if she was in her own room at the top of the house she probably would not. And, in any case, if her maid tried to intervene, she would probably be knocked down; the man was in no mood to allow an elderly retainer to stand in his way.

'Now,' he said, pulling her down on the sofa beside him and pulling open her jacket to kiss her throat. 'A few minutes of pleasure, just to make sure you do not change your mind, followed by the announcement all the world is expecting to hear, and then I will trouble you no more. At least, not until after the wedding.' He laughed suddenly. 'Just to show you how generous I can be, we will give Victor as part of your sister's dowry when she marries that scapegrace Baverstock. It will diminish him to have to accept it from me. What do you say to that?'

She had gone very quiet and he relaxed his hold slightly, believing she was becoming compliant, but her brain was working and the mention of the horse was the last straw. Never, never would she give in. He would have to kill her first. She forced herself out of his grasp and made for the door.

Moving surprisingly swiftly, he darted to cut off her escape and dragged her back into the room, so infuriated that he could not contain himself. He ripped her jacket from her, tore at her blouse and chemise, exposing her breasts. The sight of them inflamed him further and he bent down to kiss them, fumbling behind her for the ties of her skirt. She bit the lobe of his ear as hard as she could.

'Bitch!' he screeched, slapping her face with the back of his hand and making her head rock.

She opened her mouth and screamed as loudly as she could. He put a hand over her mouth and dragged her back to the sofa. 'You want a fight, miss, then you shall have it.' He tossed her on to the sofa and threw himself on top of her, struggling to lift her skirts. He was heavy, too heavy. She squirmed beneath him, crying and begging. All pride had gone now; there was nothing left but to appeal to his mercy. But he had none. His mouth was roaming all over her neck and breasts, his hands were kneading her thighs, forcing them apart. There was nothing she could do. She managed to free one hand and thrust it upwards, but there was nothing to get hold of; she grasped the empty air. It was the end for her and she wished sincerely that she might die.

CHAPTER EIGHT

RICHARD had driven the curricle round the house to the stables in order to talk to Dawson about the arrangements for the race and was pleased to see the groom's craggy features break into a broad smile at the prospect of being involved. It was a capital rig and he assured the Major that he knew Miss Georgie very well and though she might grumble she was not really a crosspatch and when the time came would enter into the spirit of the thing and be as keen as anyone on it. He'd lay odds she'd come round about Warrior too and the Major would be able to count on having the stallion. 'She knows it won't do her stables a ha'porth of harm to put up the horses for the winner,' he said. 'And you will win, won't you, sir?'

Richard smiled. 'Naturally I will. There are two horses coming from Newmarket the day after tomorrow. Miss Paget has agreed to bring them up to scratch. You'll watch out for them?'

'Yes, sir.'

They spoke for several minutes about the training of the horses and the positioning of the men and as Richard turned to leave Dawson asked, 'What did you think of Bright Star, Major? Do you think she's a goer?'

'Undoubtedly. We've entered her for a race at Newmarket next week with Manfred up. She should get through the first heats, at least.' He climbed into

the curricle and picked up the reins. 'I must be going if
I am to get home before it is too dark to see. Goodnight
to you, Mr Dawson.' He flicked the reins to turn the
vehicle in the yard.

'Did it to a whisker,' Tom said, watching in
admiration.

The curricle was just about to leave the yard when
Fanny came running from the house in great distress.
'Help her!' she cried. 'Help her! Miss Georgie, she's in
trouble. . .'

Richard had scrambled down at the first sight of the
distraught maid and without waiting for explanations
rushed into the house and through the kitchen. He
paused in the hall, wondering which way to go, and
then he heard the pitiful cries. In a second he had
crossed the floor and thrown open the drawing-room
door. It crashed back against the wall, startling the
man who lay sprawled on the sofa. In two strides
Richard was upon him. With one hand he pulled him
upright by the collar of his coat and with the other
crashed a fist into his face. The man sank to his knees
on the floor, bleeding from the nose, just as Dawson
arrived.

'Throw him out,' Richard commanded, and turned
his attention to Georgie, sitting down beside her on the
sofa and taking her in his arms. 'Hush, my love,' he
said, stroking the hair gently from her face as she
sobbed in his arms. 'Hush now. He won't trouble you
again.' Gently he pulled her torn blouse across to try
and cover her and held her close to him, shielding her
nakedness from the two men.

Dawson strode across the room, so incensed that he
would have attacked Lord Barbour, peer of the realm

or not, if Richard had not looked over Georgie's head and seen his fury in his eyes. 'I said, throw him out, man, no more.'

'Not until he gets what he deserves.' The stable-master raised a fist but surprisingly Lord Barbour stood his ground, watching Richard and Georgie.

'What a pretty picture,' he sneered, taking a hand-kerchief from his sleeve and wiping blood from his nose. 'I see it now. That is why she was so stiff-rumped with me; the wench had other irons in the fire. Does your sister know about it, my dear Georgiana?'

Richard started up, intending he knew not what, but Georgie pulled on his sleeve. 'No, Richard, he is not worth it. Let him go. He can't harm us.'

'Can't I? Zounds! We shall see about that.' Dawson was tugging on his arm, but he was resisting strenuously. 'All London shall know of your duplicity. I came here, with the permission of your uncle, to propose to you, and find you not alone in the house, chaperoned by servants, as everyone supposed you to be, but in the arms of a lover. Everyone says what a prodigious good sister you are, always putting Felicity before yourself; what will they say when they learn that, far from that, you have been deceiving her, entertaining this. . .this thatchgallows? No one will want to know either of you, least of all your families. Not only you but your sister, Miss Paget, will be ruined by the scandal.'

He looked Richard up and down with contempt. 'As for you, I collect the Viscount turned you out of his house. . . Something to do with your stepmother, wasn't it?'

Richard scrambled to his feet and dealt his lordship a blow to the chin that sent him sprawling against

Dawson, who stepped back, allowing him to slide to the ground.

'Get up!' Richard commanded. 'Get up and put up your guard.'

The man rose to his knees and Richard stood with feet apart and fists clenched, ready to knock him down again, but Lord Barbour, knowing that pugilism was one of Richard's sports, was so slow in taking up the challenge that Georgie was able to run between them.

'No, Richard, you'll kill him!' She grabbed his upraised arm, forgetting her chemise was torn. It fell open and she hurriedly pulled it together again. 'Please don't make matters worse.'

The red rage subsided and he turned to put his arm about her shoulders. 'No, you are right—he is not worth it.' To Lord Barbour he said, 'Go now, before I change my mind.'

His lordship scrambled to his feet and made his way to the door, where Fanny stood with mouth agape. She moved aside to allow the two men through. On the threshold Lord Barbour turned. 'I shall see you at Tyburn in two weeks, Major. If you are not there, your wager will be lost along with your reputation. I advise you to take very good care of yourself until then.' Then he was gone to find the horse he had hidden in the lane, closely followed by Dawson to make sure he went.

Richard ordered Fanny to make up a soothing draught for her mistress, then shut the door and went back to Georgie, who was standing in the middle of the room clutching her torn clothing.

The whole incident had passed in a matter of minutes, but it had taken so much out of her—the physical

struggle, the mental anguish, the emotion and relief
when Richard had rescued her—that she felt drained.
The room seemed to spin and her knees buckled. He
was across the floor in seconds, picking her up and
carrying her back to the sofa, where he put her down
very gently. He did not take his eyes off her face and
for a long time they looked at each other, their
emotions too heightened for them to speak. He tried
to smile, to reassure her, but found he could not.

Bending his head, he kissed her very gently on the
lips. It was a butterfly touch, undemanding and all the
sweeter for that, and she found herself weeping. He
moved his head back so that he could look at her and
was overwhelmed with love and tenderness. He lifted
a finger and stroked the tears from her pale cheek. She
shivered at his touch, wanting him so desperately.

'What are we going to do?' she whispered.

'I think we should call Fanny to put you to bed.' His
voice was a croak.

She smiled weakly but he did not move. 'I meant
about. . .' She stopped. What did she mean? That she
loved him and his kiss had told her that he was not
entirely indifferent to her? Or was he simply trying to
comfort her? She gulped. 'About that devil. Can he
ruin us?'

'Only if we let him.'

'No one will believe the truth, will they?'

'Of course they will.' But he did not sound at all
convinced.

'I have ruined everything for Felicity.'

'You have done nothing wrong, my dear. It is that
blackguard. . .' His jaw tightened and his fists clenched

involuntarily when he thought of what might have happened.

'If he goes back to London and spreads his evil, we are done for.'

'You don't want to marry him, do you?'

'It is the last thing I want.' She shuddered. 'It was because I refused that he tried to. . . But he might just as well have done, for that is how Society will view it. And now you and I are alone. . .'

'Then marry me.'

She scrambled into a sitting position and stared at him in astonishment. 'I beg your pardon?'

'Marry me. It would answer the gossips.'

'Indeed it would not,' she said so quickly that he was taken aback. Just because he had rescued her from a terrible fate, and she had lain in his arms, that was no reason to take advantage of her. She had been weak, but that was all over; now she felt surprisingly strong and abrasive. 'And I am surprised at you, Major Baverstock, for suggesting such a thing. Have you no feelings for my sister? Or any consideration for me either?'

'It was consideration for you which made me speak. And I doubt your sister will have me, after all.'

'Nonsense!' she said, entirely misunderstanding him. 'My sister will not believe his lordship's evil gossip; she is far too sensible. If you go to her, explain exactly what happened here, she will understand.'

'Go to her?' His hopes, so high a moment before, were dashed. 'As if nothing had changed?'

'Nothing has changed, Major.' She swallowed hard. 'I am indebted to you for your help, but you must go now.'

It was in his mind to protest that it was dark outside
and a journey of some fifteen miles across somewhat
rough country in a curricle would be hazardous, but he
hurriedly decided against that; such ploys would put
him on a par with Lord Barbour in her eyes. And he
must have been mistaken in his reading of the
expression in her eyes a few moments ago. It was
gratitude, not love, and he had been a blind fool,
blinded by his own feelings for her, and clumsy too.
Instead of extricating himself he had thrown himself
even deeper into the mire.

He rose stiffly and, taking her hand, bowed over it.
'Goodnight, Miss Paget.' And with that he strode to
the door and flung it open.

Out in the hall Fanny was holding a glass containing
some thick dark liquid and relating her version of
events to Mrs Thorogood, who had only just returned,
in a fine stew at not being able to find her beloved
mistress, and who now, knowing she was safe, was
leading forth at great length at having been sent on a
wild-goose chase. They both turned towards him as he
came out of the room.

'Go to your mistress,' he said. 'She has had more
than one great shock today.' Then he left by the front
door without another word and climbed into his
curricle.

Georgie heard the carriage wheels on the gravel
growing fainter and fainter and knew he had gone. She
had half risen from her seat, perhaps to go after him,
but now she sank back and, putting her head in her
hands, sobbed as of her heart were cleft in two.

'There, there, Miss Georgie,' Fanny said, offering
her the glass containing some horrible concoction she

had made up. 'Drink this up and you'll feel better. That horrible Lord Barbour has gone; he won't trouble you again. It was a good thing the Major was still here.'

'Yes,' Georgie agreed, taking the glass and looking up at her maid with red-rimmed eyes. 'But how did it come about?'

'I didn't know his lordship was in the house, truly I didn't. To be sure I heard the doorbell but I knew Mrs Thorogood would answer it and I was busy in your room, sorting your clothes. I took a torn skirt up to my room to mend and didn't hear a thing more until I finished it and was bringing it back to hang in the wardrobe. I thought I heard voices in the drawing-room and I wondered who was there; I hadn't heard you come back, you see. I saw your hat on the chair in the hall and went down to fetch it and put it away. Then I heard you shouting and a man answering. I knew something was wrong and ran out to the stables to find Mr Dawson. The Major was just leaving. Oh, how glad I am he was there. I dread to think. . .'

'Then we will not think,' Georgie said crisply, once more in command of herself. 'I think I shall go up to bed.'

She stood up and was surprised to find that she could walk quite steadily. Fanny rushed to her aid, but she waved her away. 'You see what a tough old bird I am, Fanny.'

Fanny did not believe her and continued to hover behind her as she made her way upstairs, following her into her room and helping her undress. 'Now there's more mending and pressing,' she grumbled, but it was only meant to cheer her mistress. 'I've only just finished setting all to rights after the last little adventure. Seems to me, Miss Georgie, you attract adventure like a magnet.'

'I do, don't I? But burn those clothes; I shall never wear them again.'

'But there's nothing wrong with them that can't be repaired.'

'Do as I say. I cannot bear to touch them after. . .'

'Yes, Miss Georgie, of course.' Fanny did not think her mistress was as tough as she pretended to be. And she must be worried by his lordship's threats as he left. 'Don't you worry, my pretty,' she said softly, using an endearment she had used when Georgie was a child, as she tucked her between the sheets. 'That man can't hurt you, not when me and Mrs Thorogood are ready to swear you were never alone with him. Nor with the Major neither.'

'You mustn't perjure yourself for me,' Georgie murmured, drowsy now that the sleeping-draught was taking effect.

Fanny smiled as she bundled up the discarded clothes, ready to obey Georgie's orders to burn them. Her servants would lie for her, of course they would, and they would kill for her if they had to. 'Go to sleep,' she said, creeping from the room.

Georgie slept but as soon as she opened her eyes the following morning she relived the whole incident, every detail, every gesture, every word that had been said. In the cool light of a summer morning, with the sun shining and the birds twittering outside her window, it seemed as though it must have been a terrible nightmare. Had Lord Barbour really come here and tried to rape her? Had Richard really rescued her? Had she lain in his arms half naked and not even cared because it was so comforting to be held by him? Had she cried his name? Had he really suggested she should marry him to avert a scandal over her good name at the expense of Felicity's?

That was the hardest to bear, because in any other circumstances she would have been overjoyed at the prospect of having him for a husband, but not like this. She was beginning to wonder whether he was a suitable spouse for her sister if his affections could so easily change direction. But what to do about it she did not know. If only there were someone to ask. She could write to her aunt, of course, but what could she say? I don't think Felicity should marry Richard Baverstock, after all? What reason could she give that sounded reasonable enough for her aunt not to think she had taken leave of her senses? Besides, Mrs Bertram was due to leave the country any day now and it would be unfair to trouble her. She had to cope alone.

Coping, to Georgie, meant work and as soon as this decision was reached she jumped out of bed and dressed in her old comfortable shirt and breeches and went down to the kitchen. Mrs Thorogood bade her good morning but made no other comment as her mistress sat at the kitchen table to eat toast and drink chocolate. She watched her eat and cleared away after she had gone out to the yard. 'She's got over it remarkable well,' she told Fanny when the maid came down searching for her mistress. 'Gone out riding, I'll be bound. And after that she'll get back to work. To be sure there's nothing like it for curing a broken heart.'

'You reckon her heart is broken?'

'Yes, don't you?'

'Maybe, but I think we should keep our thoughts to ourselves.'

'Well, I'm sure I'm not one to prattle,' Mrs Thorogood said stiffly. 'I mind me own business.'

Georgie herself would have agreed with her servants; her heart was broken, but no one but those two would have known it as she settled down into her old routine, caring for her beloved horses. She was the same practical down-to-earth woman she had been before her trip to London, but her problems had not gone away. There were too few customers and her overheads were overwhelming.

Lord Barbour had known that, of course. With a man in control, the customers would come, for there was nothing wrong with the stock. Perhaps she ought to have made a greater push to find a husband as soon as possible after her father died, but it was too late now. Lord Barbour would spread his evil gossip and those few customers she did have would cease to patronise her. She would be obliged to sell, and sell at a ridiculously low price.

But it had not come to that yet. She was a fighter and she would go on fighting. She had the money from the two horses she had sold to Lord Dullingham and that would help pay wages for a few weeks more. And there was that race. It was going to cost quite a bit in extra hay, oats and wages, for she needed extra men to look after them. The race was becoming as important to her as it was to Major Bavestock, though for different reasons.

Next time he came, she would tell him he could have Warrior. But would there be a next time? Would he simply send her curt messages about what he wanted done? Would he assume his horses were ready without coming to check for himself? She knew him too well to believe that; he would want to oversee every detail himself. She would have to meet him, talk to him, and pretend nothing was wrong between them.

What had he said to Felicity? Were they already betrothed? Each day she looked for a letter from her sister but none came. She did not know what to make of that but there was so much to do, she was able to push it from her mind. Richard's two new horses had arrived and were being fed and put to work to strengthen their stamina, and there was Bright Star, whose training was coming along nicely according to plan. She had been walked out every morning, followed by trotting on the open land at the top of the hill, and every afternoon the filly had a rest in her box, looking out over the door with intelligent interest in what was going on around her. Feeding and grooming and inspection filled the rest of her day. Tomorrow morning, she was due for another gallop. Georgie became almost cheerful.

One of the men whom she had taken on was a real find. His name was Jem Brown and he had come with excellent references from a titled gentleman in the Shires and was hard-working and knowledgeable. He was a very big man, forty or thereabouts, neatly dressed in fustian breeches and gaiters, with a clean stock and a striped waistcoat, in the pocket of which he kept a very fine timepiece. She felt she had seen it before, but when she commented on it he said it had been a parting gift from his previous employer. He had, he told her, only left there because his sister had been recently widowed and needed him to live with her. Dawson, for some reason she could not fathom, didn't take to him, though he was careful not to let it show. She concluded that her old friend and retainer was jealous and took particular care not to do anything to exacerbate it.

It was Jem who came to her one day with the news that Bright Star had been injured.

'I only left her a minute, missus,' he said. 'She backed herself into the wall and there was a hay-rake there. . .'

'What was a hay-rake doing in her box to start with?' she demanded, running to the filly's stable and throwing open the door. Bright Star was standing in her box with a wild look in her eye which frightened Georgie. Her rump was streaming with blood from a very deep cut.

'Shouldn't go near if I was you,' Jem said. 'She'll kick as soon as look at you.'

'Nonsense. Go and fetch my bag; we'll have to dress that.'

He returned in less than a minute with the bag in which she kept salve and liniment, followed by Dawson. The two men held the filly while Georgie tended to the cut. It was very deep and she was afraid it had touched the muscle, in which case there was no question of racing her. Not until the animal was comfortable did Georgie begin questioning the lads to find out how the rake had come to be left in the box. It was Tom's task to clean the stable out, but he tearfully maintained that he had not left the rake there. 'Soon as I finished I put it in the tack-room,' he insisted. 'You gotta believe me.'

'I found it in the box,' Jem said belligerently. 'Are you calling me a liar?'

'No, of course he is not,' Georgie said, and then to Tom, 'Are you quite sure? Perhaps you had to do something else and just put it down and forgot it.'

'No, and whatever I had to do I wouldn't be such a ninny as to leave a rake in a box with a horse, would I? I don't ever put the animal back after her exercise until I'm sure everything's right and tight. It's what I ha' bin taught and it's what I do.' His face was bright red with resentment; he couldn't understand why Miss Georgie should believe he'd do anything so dreadful.

'I am sure you are right,' she said, but it did not answer the original question. How had the rake got there? Had it been a deliberate attempt to harm the filly? In that case, she could discount Tom and, come to that, all her old hands. That left the new ones. She was tempted to dismiss them all, but she knew she could not manage without them and it would be palpably unfair to punish them all for the wrongdoing of one.

She ordered a watch to be kept twenty-four hours a day and worked out a rota for those entrusted with the task. It made them tired and irritable because they still had their ordinary work to do and it did not stop the troubles. One of Richard's new mounts developed colic, which necessitated throwing out a large part of Georgie's valuable store of feed which had become contaminated. And another went lame, although fortunately not seriously.

Georgie began to think she was either very unlucky or the victim of a calculated attempt to ruin her. She knew she ought to send word to the Major, tell him what was happening, because loss of horses would affect his chances in the race to York, but she had no idea how to reach him. And he would think her a poor sort of trainer if she could not protect her own animals. She resolved to be even more vigilant.

Bright Star did not heal as quickly as she had hoped and she was forced to withdraw her from the race, but with all the care she was receiving the filly did begin to mend. However, the nursing and the patrolling of the stables half the night, besides riding out and schooling the younger horses, took their toll of Georgie's health and she began to look and feel haggard, weighed down by her responsibilities. Perhaps everyone was right; perhaps managing a busy stables was no job for a woman. She scolded herself severely whenever such a traitorous thought entered her head and bent to her work with added determination.

She was crossing the stable-yard one morning with a bucket of water, slopping it about because it was heavy and she was too tired to carry it properly, when the sound of a rider coming into the yard made her look up. It was Richard on Pegasus, as tall and handsome and lordly as ever.

He dismounted and stood and watched her as she set the bucket to one side and came to meet him. She looked deathly pale and moved as if her shoes had lead weights in them.

'What's wrong?' he demanded when she drew nearer and he could see the dark circles under her eyes.

'Nothing I cannot handle.'

He smiled; she had become no less stubborn since he had seen her last. 'Don't gammon me, Miss Paget. Have you been ill?'

'No, it's the horses. Come, I want to show you something.'

He handed his reins to Tom and followed her to Bright Star's box. She opened the door. 'See.'

He whistled. 'How did that happen?'

'My negligence,' she said. 'Fine trainer I turned out to be, didn't I? I have failed you.'

He made no attempt to contradict her; in her present mood she would not have listened. 'Tell me what happened.'

She did, as briefly as possible. 'I had hoped it was only superficial, but as you see the cut is quite deep. She won't be able to make the start next Tuesday.'

'No, of course not. But I am sure of one thing; that wound was not made by falling against anything. If it was a rake, it was quite deliberately drawn down her flanks, and hard, too.'

'That's what I thought. But I cannot think who could have done it. I have questioned everyone and got nowhere. Someone does not want you to win, but it is only a minor race and I cannot think who could be so cruel to a defenceless animal.'

'You have obviously done all you can,' he said, giving the filly a sugar lump and leaving the box. 'She is recovering but I am not so sure about you.'

She did not want to talk about herself. 'There have been other incidents. Only small ones, but they have mounted up. I have to have eyes in the back of my head.'

'You must rest. Never mind the horses; Dawson is quite capable and trustworthy.'

'But they are my responsibility. I am trying to prove my worth, or were you not aware of that?'

'I am only too aware of it, Miss Paget. It is taking over your life and if you go on in this way you will be burned to the socket. Come indoors; I wish to talk to you.'

She led the way inside, ordered Mrs Thorogood to make tea and called to Fanny to come and sit with her, then she preceded him into the drawing-room and invited him, as formally as she could, to be seated. He obeyed, knowing that this was going to be a strictly business meeting and she was protecting herself from any chance of intimacy. Neither spoke until the tea-tray was set before her and Fanny had stationed herself in the window-seat with some embroidery.

She poured the tea and handed him a cup with hands that shook. 'I must give you a report on the horses you bought,' she said. 'And also those which Dawson had set aside for you to hire. Bright Star you have seen. I shall allow her only gentle exercise on a lunge until that cut is healed; she cannot be ridden.'

'Do not blame yourself,' he said softly, wishing he could take the worried look from her face. 'There will be other races, many of them.'

She gave him a quick look of gratitude and then dropped her gaze to her teacup. 'The horses for the York ride are all ready and we await only your final instructions.'

'I have been over every inch of the route in the last week,' he said. 'Ostlers will be at the ready at every stage to bring forward a new mount and care for the one I leave behind. Refreshment for me will be waiting as well, though I doubt I shall need much. I have hired the horses for the last half of the run locally and arranged for them to be taken to the various posthouses. I'll take Pegasus for the first stretch and ride him as hard as I dare, then the two I bought in Newmarket, followed by four from Dullingham House. The grooms there will see that they are in place. That will bring me to the Barley Mow near Baldock. Then if you can have yours ready for the middle stages that covers them all.'

'Do you still want Warrior?' she asked.

He looked up with a smile and their glances met and held for a long second, then he smiled. 'He would make all the difference.'

'Then you may have him. Where do you want him stationed?'

'The Barley Mow will be ideal. If one of your men could bring him there for midnight?'

'He will be there.' She indicated his empty cup. 'More tea?'

'No, thank you. I must get myself to London if I am to be there in good time to rest Pegasus before the start.' He rose to go and she accompanied him to the door.

'Did you see Felicity when you were in town?' she asked as soon as they were out of earshot of Fanny.

'No; I called on Lady Hereward but the young ladies were out on a boat trip up the river and were not expected back until late. I could not wait.'

'So she still does not know what happened?'

'Not from my lips.'

'Oh, Richard, how could you not make a greater push to see her? If Lord Barbour has already started to spread his lies, she will have heard all about it from others and it is not the way I wished her to learn of it.'

He felt constrained to defend himself, though her

use of his given name cheered him. 'Dammit, I hung about for hours and all to no purpose. Why didn't you write and tell her yourself, if you were so worried about it?'

'Writing is not the same as saying something face to face, is it? Besides, I have not had a minute to myself to compose such a difficult letter.'

'Difficult?' he queried, a half-smile playing about his lips. 'Yes, I suppose it would be.'

'You will go and see her the minute you arrive in town, won't you? I fear what Lord Barbour will do.'

'He is far too busy making his own arrangements to win the race to have time for spreading rumours,' he said, hoping to reassure her, though he was not so sure himself; his lordship had a knack of getting others to do his dirty work for him. 'And in any case he will want to do it when it has maximum impact and that is not now, when everyone is talking about the race and wondering if in two days' time they are going to be very rich or plucked clean.' That much was probably true. 'But if it pleases you I will go and see her as soon as I arrive.'

'Thank you.'

She stood on the front steps and watched him go down and mount Pegasus, whom Tom had brought to the door for him. Then he was gone again with no more than a, 'Good-day to you, Miss Paget.'

She went back indoors and returned to her now cold tea. There was to be no more intimacy with him and that was as it should be. Their relationship was a business one and looked at like that the next few days would be the turning point as far as the stables were concerned. They would stand or fall with Major

Baverstock and the irony of it was not lost on her. She suddenly felt so weary that she knew she could not go on without a rest. 'I'm going to lie down for half an hour,' she told Fanny. Perhaps when she had rested she would be able to view the prospect of Richard as a brother-in-law with more equanimity.

Richard himself, riding at a leisurely pace towards London in order not to overtire Pegasus, could not think of her as a sister, would never be able to. He made up his mind to see Felicity as she had asked, as he had tried to do before he had gone to York, but only to throw himself on her mercy. He might not have offered for her formally, but everyone expected it and it would be difficult to back out of the interview without humiliating her. He could not refuse to marry her; his only hope was that she would reject him. She did not want to marry him, he was fairly sure of that, but was she strong enough to defy her aunt and disappoint her sister? And even if she did, would he be able to win Georgie? He did not think so.

All Miss Paget thought about was her horses and keeping the stables running, an impossible task for a woman and the state she was in proved it. Looking at her today, he could hardly believe she was the same delightfully feminine woman who had danced the night away in London and galloped in the park; she had looked exhausted, careless of her clothes and hair. He had longed to take the strain from her, to tell her he would undertake everything and she was not to worry, but he knew her well enough to realise that that would only have served to infuriate her. She would have taken it as a direct criticism of her ability to manage;

she had to be allowed to realise her limitations for herself.

He smiled wryly as he walked Pegasus into the inn yard of the Swan at Stevenage; she had not reached her limit yet; there was more strength in her, more pluck than in many a man, and he loved her all the more for it. But at the end, what then? How could he help her? Marrying her seemed to be the obvious answer, but if she thought for a single minute that it was pity for her situation or a desire to control Sir Henry's stables which prompted him to ask she would turn him down flat. And neither was true. He wanted her for what she was, the woman he loved, the woman he could not be happy without. His love for Maria had faded into the mists of the past; he could not go on living in the past.

He smiled, imagining a future full of bright happiness, surrounded by a loving family, wife, sister, father and children. Yes, Georgie's children would be tall and beautiful. But it was only a dream. Felicity might not turn him down, however he phrased his proposal, and that mischievous baronet might do untold damage.

And there was that race. If he won, then Rowan Park would be given as much credit as he could manage, but, if he lost, the reputation of the stables, which had been on a down slope ever since Sir Henry died, would slide even further down to extinction. It was no longer a race between two men over a single horse, it was life and death to Georgie and his own hopes for the future. He rode into London next morning with two things foremost in his mind: to see Miss Felicity Paget and to win the race to York. He would look no further than that.

He had not been back at Baverstock House above half an hour when John Melford called on him.

'Good to see you back, old fellow,' he said on being shown into the library where Richard was sitting at his desk poring over a well-used map with a glass of Madeira at his elbow. 'Been watching out for you.'

'Come on in. Sit down and have a glass of wine. I was just going over the route for the last time.'

John poured himself a glass of Madeira and sat in a chair, though he seemed somewhat on edge. 'You've been over it?'

'Every step. Timing is all-important.'

'And, of course, Rowan Park is not on the way at all.'

Richard gave no indication of surprise or puzzlement, other than a slight lifting of one eyebrow. 'Not precisely on the route, no, but it is only a dozen or so miles off it. Why do you ask?'

'Thought you might have called there.'

'I did. You must know Miss Paget is looking after some of my horses and lending me others.' He paused and looked hard at his friend. 'Why are you quizzing me in this fashion?'

'Didn't know I was.'

'Yes, you are. Out with it.'

'There is talk. . .' He stopped, knowing Richard's temper could sometimes be volcanic. 'Talk that you have spent time there. . .'

'I just said I did, didn't I? If you are insinuating any impropriety, then I shall have to ask you to leave.' His voice was dangerously calm.

'Oh, stow it, Richard, I was just warning you to expect squalls, that's all.'

'From Miss Felicity Paget, I suppose.'

'No, I should hope it ain't yet reached her ears. And she wouldn't judge you anyhow; she's far too sensible. But I shouldn't like to think you were doing the dirty on her. If you were, friend or no, I should be constrained to call you out for it.' He looked so thunderous, Richard laughed.

'I am trembling in my boots, John.'

'It is no laughing matter.'

'Oh, I agree whole-heartedly. But who can possibly be spreading these malicious rumours, I wonder? Could it be a certain aristocratic gentleman who has more than a little to gain if I lose this race?' He tapped the map in front of him. 'Let's concentrate on that, shall we?'

'Very well. What can I do to help?'

'Go to York, be in at the finish. I'd appreciate a friend to greet me when I arrive. Take the Baverstock coach post-chaise, so we can return in comfort; somehow I don't think I shall want to ride back. You'll have to leave tonight if you're to be there on time.' John's hesitation was only momentary but it was enough for Richard to raise his eyebrow once again. 'Does that not suit?'

'Yes, yes, of course. Delighted, my dear fellow. I'll take my leave—got to cancel an engagement.' He threw the remains of his wine down his throat, set the glass down and stood up, all in one movement. 'See you in York for breakfast the day after tomorrow.'

Richard rose to see him to the door. 'I take it you have seen something of Felicity Paget this last week?'

'I have been privileged to be in her company on one or two occasions,' he said stiffly. Then, realising that

Richard had not asked out of idle curiosity, he added, 'I hope you are not implying that there is anything improper in that. We have always been in other company and besides, I would not. . .' His voice faded and colour suffused his face as he realised he was giving himself away. 'You absented yourself, after all.'

'I am not implying anything, my dear friend,' Richard said, smiling so cheerfully that John began to wonder what had come over him. 'I shall see you in York.' A footman came forward with John's hat and gloves and opened the front door for him. Richard watched him go down the steps and get into a curricle which stood in the drive, smiling as the vehicle lurched away, narrowly missing the gates as it turned on to the road.

Richard went back into the library where he sat musing on the strange conversation he had just had with his friend. Could it be? And if it was, would it be better to delay, once again, his approach to Felicity, or precipitate matters? But he had promised Georgie that he would speak to her sister and so that afternoon, dressing carefully in a buff coat of superfine and biscuit pantaloons, he ordered the Baverstock barouche and was driven to Richmond. . .

All the horses except Warrior had been taken to their stations, those who had only a few miles to go being ridden gently to their places, the furthest being transported in carts, to the huge amusement of any who saw them on the road. The men who took them were to patrol their particular section and see fair play. Georgie had waved them off, calling, 'Good luck!' as they trundled out of the gates.

Rowan Park seemed strangely empty and silent after they had gone, although there were still a few horses left to be looked after—mares and their foals, one or two yearlings and Bright Star, now well on the way to recovery. Two elderly grooms had been left behind to see to them, besides Jem who was to take Warrior to the Barley Mow, and there was little for Georgie to do except wander about looking into empty boxes and watch Royal Lady cavorting in the paddock with her sturdy little filly. It was too soon to say if the filly would make a racehorse, but she was beautiful. Would Rowan Park still be in existence as a breeding stable when she grew old enough to ride? Would there still be a Paget in residence then? So much depended on that wager to York and she wished it did not.

She strongly disapproved of deep gambling; a flutter at a race was one thing, but this! She was as bad as those young bloods who spent whole nights in gambling hells and lost fortunes. How had she allowed it to happen? Could she have prevented it? No, she told herself; it was all tied up with her ambitions for Rowan Park and her love for Richard Baverstock. He had had faith in her and she must have faith in him. If anything could bring him victory it must be the knowledge that she believed in him.

The race had attracted a great deal of publicity and she could imagine the crowds standing in the gathering dusk at the start, waving the colours of the riders— Richard had chosen deep blue and white stripes, Lord Barbour, purple laced with gold. There would be betting and side-shows; flares and torches would be brought out to illuminate the scene as darkness deepened. There would be a platform built for the starter, and grooms and attendants surrounding the horses as they came to the line. And then they would be off, riding into the night. Some people might try to follow on horses or in swift phaetons, but they would drop back to be replaced by others who had stationed themselves along the route.

How she would have liked to be part of that, caught up in the excitement, instead of sitting at home waiting, waiting. It would be at least a day and a half before news of the final result could reach her. She might as well go to bed and catch up on her lost sleep. But she could not. She dashed indoors, calling for Fanny to lay out her habit.

The contestants had hardly left London, so she had plenty of time, but that was good; she could walk Warrior gently along and rest him when she arrived at the station. According to Richard's calculations, he should be there a few minutes before midnight, with a third of the journey behind him.

Fanny thoroughly disapproved and she made no attempt to hide it. 'You can't ride alone, Miss Georgie; it'll be dark soon. And what are you putting them breeches on for? You're never going to be seen out in them?'

'I'm going to wear them under my habit.'

'You're riding astride. Oh, no, Miss Georgie, what will people think of you?'

'I can't take a side-saddle, now can I?' she said, reasonably. 'Major Baverstock will most likely put his own saddle on him, but one of the men will have to ride the horse back. Besides, it will be dark; no one will notice.'

'I don't see why you have to go at all. Why can't you wait here?'

'Oh, Fanny, I can't. I'll go mad.'

Half an hour later, with her habit pulled up to allow her to ride astride, she set off on Warrior to ride to the Barley Mow, leaving Jem in charge of the stables, much to his chagrin. She rode slowly and carefully but it looked like being a moonlight night and Warrior was footsure enough; she had no qualms. At the head of the lane she drew rein, debating whether to take the road or ride across the heath. The road was only a narrow one and full of potholes and it might also be busy with spectators converging from miles around. She decided on the solitude of the heath and thereby missed her aunt whose chaise was approaching Rowan Park in a frenzy of galloping hooves.

CHAPTER NINE

MRS BERTRAM'S state of mind was not improved when she discovered that the only people at Rowan Park were servants, and precious few of those.

'Where are my nieces?' she demanded of Mrs Thorogood who had answered her imperious rap on the door.

'Nieces?' queried the good lady. 'Why, Miss Paget has gone to the Great North Road, taking a horse. . .'

'I did not meet her.'

'I reckon she went by way of the heath. It'd be quicker. She was taking the Major one of his mounts.'

'That pestilential race! Do you know I had the devil's own job to find anyone to let me have horses? I was offered such sorry-looking nags as you wouldn't believe and have been hours on the road.' The race was not the only reason she was miffed, but she had no intention of divulging her more important errand.

'You must be fatigued, ma'am,' Mrs Thorogood said, trying to be helpful. 'May I offer you refreshment? Fanny will make up a bed for you.'

'Bed! I do not want a bed, not when my nieces are goodness knows where. Am I to assume Miss Felicity is with her sister?'

'No, ma'am, I haven't seen Miss Felicity since she left here to go to London with you.'

Harriet sat down hurriedly before her legs gave way beneath her. 'She's not here?'

'No, ma'am. Is anything wrong?' The question was
superfluous; there was obviously a great deal wrong.
'Here ma'am, you'd best take a glass of brandy to
restore you.' She took a decanter from a side-table,
poured a generous bumper and handed it to Mrs
Bertram, then stood over her waiting to be
enlightened.

Harriet Bertram took the glass and sat sipping it,
more to give herself time to think than because she felt
she needed it. All the way from London she had been
trying to convince herself that Felicity would have
come home. Where else would she go when in trouble
but to her sister? That she was in trouble her aunt did
not for one minute doubt. How were they going to live
down the scandal? She looked up at the woman,
standing with the decanter in her hand as if intending
to refill her glass the minute it was emptied. Or was
she just curious? It was a curiosity she did not mean to
satisfy. 'Tell me exactly where Miss Paget has gone.'

'Miss Georgie?'

'Georgiana, yes.'

'She was riding that great black stallion, going to the
Barley Mow just north of Baldock.'

'I have just come from there. The place is in a fair
old mull, what with horses and conveyances of every
kind and people filling the streets. It's impossible to
move. Has my niece really gone there?'

'Yes, it is one of the stages for the race.'

'Has everyone run mad? She will be trampled
underfoot.'

Mrs Thorogood thought it prudent not to comment
on this, though to some extent she was in agreement.

'When are you expecting her back?'

'Can't say, Mrs Bertram; she'll likely stay until the morning.'

'All night!' She grabbed the decanter from the woman's hand and refilled her glass, spilling it in her haste. 'And I suppose it is too much to expect that Fanny has gone with her?'

'No, Fanny is up in her room.'

'Did no one try to stop her?'

'Ma'am, there ain't any stopping Miss Georgie when she gets an idea in her head. Fanny tried. . .'

Mrs Bertram was only too well aware of that. 'What are we to do?'

It was a purely rhetorical question, but Mrs Thorogood took it at its face value. 'Shall I make you some supper, ma'am?' she asked.

'No.' Mrs Bertram stood up pulled herself up to her full height, diminutive though that was. 'I am persuaded that if I want to speak to my niece tonight I shall have to chase after her. Ask my driver to bring the carriage round to the door again, if you please.'

'But it's dark now.'

'So it is.' Not for a minute would Harriet Bertram admit that the prospect of riding through unfamiliar country at night daunted her. She was a soldier's wife, used to travelling under difficulties. 'My driver knows the road and the moon is full. Now go on, do.'

Before the housekeeper could obey, they heard the sound of a horse on the gravel and Harriet flew most indecorously for the door. 'She's back; thank the good Lord for that.'

But when she flung the front door open and stood on the top step looking down at the rider who was dismounting her heart fell into her boots. It was not Georgie but Viscount Dullingham.

He looked up at her, smiling. 'Why, this is an unexpected pleasure, ma'am. I had not thought to see you here.'

'I came to visit my niece before leaving for France, my lord.' She stood aside to allow him to enter, trying to calm her nerves. Of all the people in the world to witness her humiliation she would rather it were not Viscount Dullingham. Why, he was to be Felicity's father-in-law. That was, if Richard Baverstock would have her after this. Oh, what a fix she was in! 'You find us at sixes and sevens,' she said, leading the way into the drawing-room and wondering if he had heard the sound of her carriage being brought to the door. How was she to get rid of him without being rude? 'That foolish wager, you know. . .'

'Yes, indeed. Forgive me for arriving so unexpectedly and so late, but I had been sitting at home thinking about that race and wishing I were nearer to the action. And then I thought, Why not hack to the Great North Road and see them riding by? I reckon if my son has the lead by the halfway stage he may very well keep it. Barbour is too fat and out of condition to maintain an early pace.'

'Let us hope so,' she said politely.

'I came to ask Miss Paget if she would care to ride along with me. Where is she, by the way?'

'I believe you have missed her, my lord. She left a little while ago.' There was no mistaking the sound of her chaise now, and her driver whistling; he at any rate seemed to be happy about their swift return. 'I was about to set off back to town myself. No doubt I shall encounter my niece at Baldock, where I intend to change my horses.'

'Will there be any?' he enquired mildly.

'If there aren't I shall stay there overnight and proceed in the morning.' She hoped that would be possible; she hoped that Georgie would be able to allay her fears and she could post back to London in time to leave for Dover the following day with the Colonel.

'Forgive me, ma'am, but you seem a little out of sorts. Is anything wrong?'

'Nothing, nothing at all, my lord, except disappointment at finding Georgiana not at home and me not able to spare the time to wait for her here.'

'Then may I accompany you in your carriage? You see, Richard has left only the poorest of nags in the stables and the mount I used to ride here belongs to my nephew. It is the most uncomfortable I have ever encountered. William never did have an eye for a good horse.'

How could she refuse him? And if she was honest with herself she would have to admit that she was glad of his company. It would be another matter when they reached Baldock but she didn't suppose she would have any trouble losing him then. All she hoped was that Georgiana would be there and would have the answer to her dilemma. But it was a forlorn hope.

His lordship's hack was put in one of the empty stables and one of the remaining grooms instructed to look after him, and they climbed into the carriage.

'Go as fast as you can,' Mrs Bertram instructed her driver as his lordship handed her up and got in beside her.

He raised an eyebrow; there was no doubt the lady

was in a high state of agitation, probably something one of her nieces had done or neglected to do, but he thought it wise not to enquire. If she wanted him to know, she would tell him in her own good time. But he hoped the old carriage would stand the strain of being jolted over the rutted road.

The heath was bathed in moonlight and there was very little cover except for a few stunted trees, but Georgie could not help thinking about the hold-up she and Viscount Dullingham had suffered here, and in broad daylight, too. The body had been removed, hadn't it? It wasn't still lying there, half consumed by grubs and flies. Where had it been exactly? She could not tell but managed to resist the temptation to hurry; she did not want to tire Warrior. A nice easy pace would warm him up ready for the gallop ahead of him.

All the same, she was glad when she came out on to the narrow lane which would lead her to the back of the Barley Mow. For two or three miles it ran through a triangle of wood, which she knew extended from the lane she was on to the Great North Road itself and was quite dense in places. Here she lost the benefit of the moon and found herself riding in pitch-darkness.

It would be catastrophic if Warrior were injured now. She dismounted to lead him, treading carefully, using every bit of meagre moonlight which filtered down through the branches of the overhanging trees. She was glad she did, for she almost stumbled over an overturned cart. A young lad was standing beside it, looking distraught. She stopped to ask him what had happened, although it seemed obvious that the vehicle

had hit a tree root or something of the sort in the dark
and overturned. Seeing her, he grabbed her arm. 'Miss,
you gotta help. Me ma. . .' He pointed to the cart.

'She's trapped under there? Oh, my goodness.' She
stooped to try and see the woman and something very
heavy struck her on the back of the head.

She recovered her senses to find herself lying on a
truckle-bed in a tiny room lit by a single candle which
stood on a small table in the middle of the floor. She
turned her head and found that it hurt, even more than
it had after her fall in the park. She lay back and shut
her eyes again in order to think. But her thoughts took
her nowhere except to the conclusion that someone
wanted to prevent her taking Warrior to Richard.

Where was she? What had happened to the horse?
Who had hit her? The answer which first came to mind
was that it was Lord Barbour, but he must surely be in
the middle of the race and being carefully watched.
She felt sure that whoever was responsible had also
been the perpetrator of the accidents at the stables.
Richard had said there might be some skulduggery but
she had hardly believed him. Now she was paying for
her carelessness.

After a few minutes her headache eased a little and
she pulled herself into a sitting position. There was no
one else in the room; whoever had put her there did
not think she could escape. Leaving the bed and
picking up the candle, she took it to explore the room.
It did not take long; it was only about ten feet square,
furnished with the table, a cupboard, a couple of
rickety chairs and the truckle-bed.

There was a window, but the shutters to that were
fastened on the outside, and there was only one door.

She moved over to it and discovered it was very ill-fitting; she could see light through a crack. Putting her eye to it, she was able to see a little of the next room. It was similar to the one she was in except that it was lit by an oil lamp and had a stove on which there was a pan. She could hear voices and held her breath as someone moved across her line of vision towards the stove. It was the boy who had stopped her. He put something from the pan on to a plate and took it to the table. 'Here, eat this. It's all we've got.'

She had been expecting the broad accent of a country child, for that was how he had spoken before and how he was dressed, but his voice now was cultured and she noticed that his hands were clean. This was no working child. She wished she could see more, but the crack in the door was so narrow, her field of vision was severely restricted. Of one thing she was sure. The only way out was through that room.

What would Richard do when he arrived at the Barley Mow expecting to find Jem with Warrior, warmed up, ready for him? Would he hang about hoping a man and horse would soon arrive or would he carry on to the next stage on the same horse? Either way his chances of winning the race would be quite spoiled and he would be decidedly angry with her for letting him down. If she could free herself and find Warrior, she might find her way through the wood to the road and intercept him.

She heard the scraping of a chair on the flags and a shadow blocked her view of the room. She just had time to return the candle to the table and fling herself back on the bed, when the door was opened and a man came in carrying a plate and a mug. But it was not the plate and mug which took her attention, but the man himself. It was Jem!

He grinned at her. 'Awake, I see.'

She sat up. 'How did you get here?'

'On a horse, of course.' He put the food down on the bed beside her. 'Best eat that; I know you've had no supper.'

'What horse?' she demanded. 'And how did you get in front of me?'

'On one of the spares. Had to gallop it a fair distance and circle round you, but you weren't going at any great pace.'

'If you've harmed it. . .'

'Don't expect it to be fit for anything for a few days, but it'll recover.'

'But why?'

'Why, Miss Paget? Now, if you were meaning why did I take a horse from your stables and go hell for leather to get ahead of you, that's simple. According to the Major's plan and yours too, I was supposed to ride Warrior to the inn. That suited me fine, but you had to go and change everything, didn't you? You had to bring the stallion yourself, so you've only yourself to blame for the fix you're in.' He paused and favoured her with a tigerish smile and she wondered how she had ever come to trust him. 'On the other hand, if you mean why was I intending to take possession of Warrior and hide him up until after the race, then that's another story.'

'Where have you put him?'

'He's safe enough. You have to admit, Miss Paget, whatever I am, I know how to look after a horse.'

'And after the race is over? I assume you did it to prevent the Major winning?'

'True.'

'And from that I infer you have been paid by Lord Barbour.'

'Oh, he's only part of the lay. It goes a great deal deeper than that, Miss Paget, a very great deal.'

'What do you mean?'

He tapped the side of his nose. 'There's some, closer to home than Lord Barbour, as wouldn't be averse to seeing Richard Baverstock come a cropper.'

'I do not understand.'

'You do not need to, not if you're a good girl and keep out of it. Settle down here and it'll soon be over.'

'I will pay you generously to let me go on with Warrior as if nothing had happened and I won't deliver you up to the law, provided you leave the district.'

'Very tempting, Miss Paget, but I know how strapped you are; you could not afford to match his lordship's offer. Besides, I've put a monkey on the outcome of the race at fifteen to one and that's not to be sneezed at.'

'Where did you find that much money?'

'Now that would be telling, would it not?' He took out his watch and noted the time. 'The contestants will be at the Barley Mow very soon. Who do you think will be the first away?'

Furiously she picked up the plate of hot food, threw it in his face and made a dash for the door. He yelled at his accomplice to warn him and sprang after her. The boy stood in front of her and blocked her path. She tried to push past him, but Jem had her by the arms and pulled her back into the room. He slapped her face hard with the flat of his hand, first one way then the other, then he threw her on to the bed. 'Now, Miss Paget, you have cooked your own goose. Matt, bring me a rope; we'll have to tie her up.'

'No,' she shrieked.

'Yes. I have to go out and I can't be sure you'll not find some way of hoaxing Matt, here, into letting you go.' He took the rope from the boy and tied her up very thoroughly, finishing by knotting the end around the bedhead. Then he and the boy left the room and the door was bolted on the other side.

'I'm off on to the high road to meet your pa,' she heard Jem say. 'Just you make sure she don't get away. Don't open the door to anyone but me or Charlie, do you hear?' She heard a door slam and after that there was silence.

Richard had made good time, though he had often been hampered by the spectators who would keep running out into the road to get a closer look and by young bloods on horses trying to ride alongside him. The stewards were doing their best, but they couldn't be everywhere.

But there was one big advantage to having the route lined with people; many of them carried lamps and torches and the road in many places was well-illuminated. He could see the lights of Baldock ahead and risked a look over his shoulder. There was no sign of Lord Barbour, but he knew he was not far behind. He really ought to increase his lead. He dug his spurs into the mare and raised her speed a fraction. The next section would be done on Warrior and that should give him a great advantage.

The Barley Mow loomed up, emblazoned with light and as crowded as if it were broad day. He pulled up and slid from his horse's back. Already his thighs and buttocks were crying out for a rest and he was hardly a third of the way. Someone ran forward to take his horse, someone else thrust a tankard and a leg of chicken into his hands. He drank the ale in one or two strong pulls and nibbled at the food. 'Where's my next mount?'

'Not arrived yet,' an ostler told him. 'We sent out to see if it was coming but there was no sign of it.'

Richard swore comprehensively and looked about him. His lordship's next mount was already saddled and was being walked slowly about the yard to keep it warm. It seemed to be the only animal in the yard except for the one Richard had just brought in. 'Have you got a spare mount?' he asked.

'No, sir.'

'Anything will do. An old hack, a carriage horse. . .'

'Not a one, sir. Everything that can take a saddle and some what can't have been let out. People want to see the race from the best vantage point, you know.'

Richard strode out to the crossroads and looked along the lane in the direction of Rowan Park. The moonlight flooded down on to trees and bushes and the ruts in the road, making them look deeper than they really were, but of Warrior and his groom there was no sign.

He could not believe that Georgie would let him down like that. She must have mistaken the time or misinterpreted his instructions, or the groom had. He tried to remember which man had been given the task of bringing the horse. It was that new chap—Jem, he thought his name was. Wasn't he the one who had found Bright Star injured in her stall? It was no good standing about in the road; the horse was not there and there was nothing else he could do.

He hurried back to the inn and ordered his previous mount to be re-saddled. He was waiting for it to be brought out when Lord Barbour rode up and dismounted. Ignoring Richard, he called for ale, limping about the yard to ease his stiff limbs. 'Blister me, but it's saddle-sore I am.' Then, seeing his adversary, he smiled. 'Well, well, no mount, Major?'

'Of course I have a mount.'

'But not the one you were expecting, eh? I wonder what can have become of it? Let you down, did she? I could have told you she would.'

'What do you mean by that?'

'Why, that stiff-rumped, horse-dealing ape-leader, she promises one thing, does another.' He was grinning from ear to ear, but Richard, conscious that everyone within earshot was listening, would not allow himself to be goaded, though it took all his self-control.

'I expect there has been a delay; the horse will be here directly.'

'But too late, eh?' He took a look at the mare being led forward for Richard; someone had made a start on rubbing her down, but had not finished, and her coat still gleamed with sweat. 'That one is spent. Are you ready to concede defeat? I must admit I should be glad of it, for I can hardly stand upright.'

'No, my lord, I ride on.'

'Pity,' his lordship said, handing back his ale pot and taking the reins of his new mount from a groom, motioning the man to hold his hands for him to mount, for he was in no condition to spring into the saddle. 'I wonder how many other problems you will have to encounter before the night is out? I am persuaded Lady Luck is not with you.'

Richard watched him ride out of the yard, reluctant to follow if there was any chance of Warrior turning up. His lordship was right; those last few yards of hard galloping had as good as finished the mare and he was reminded of his promise to Georgie that he would not ruin any of the horses. But what else could he do? Give up?

One of the official referees appointed for each stage approached him. 'You must go on, Major, or concede defeat.'

Reluctantly he got back in the saddle and walked his horse slowly out of the yard. He would have to nurse her carefully for the next stage and he didn't see how he could ever overtake his opponent, unless he too had a stroke of bad luck. The lights of Baldock faded behind him and the road became darker than ever as he entered a wood. There were a few spectators on this particular stretch and he was alone with his thoughts.

As far as Richard could remember, no one had told Lord Barbour that Warrior had not arrived, so how had he known? And he had been gleeful about it. Had he been responsible? Had the stallion never left Rowan Park? It was a logical step from there to wonder if anything had happened to Georgie. He remembered all the so-called accidents that had happened at the stables and how distressed and exhausted she had been.

Walking his horse steadily along the Great North Road in the dark, he could not shake off the feeling that Georgie was in danger. He was reminded of Maria, who had died because she had tried to help him. He had always blamed himself for that and if anything had happened to Georgie he would feel ten times worse. His passion for Maria had faded to nothing but a fond memory, but Georgie was here and alive and he loved her. Maria had known the dangers, but Georgie. . . She was more important to him than anything else in the world, including a race. He reined in and turned back.

Corporal Daniel Batson was patrolling the stretch of road alongside the wood, eyes and ears alert, just as he had done many and many a time in the Peninsula, musing on the turn his life had taken and looking forward to a pot of ale and a good meal in the Barley Mow when he had finished, when Lord Barbour rode towards him, not galloping as he had expected, not even cantering. He was walking his horse as if he had all the time in the world. Daniel could have sworn the Major would reach him first, so where was he?

His service had made him a cautious man; he darted nimbly behind a tree and watched. Not fifty yards away, a man stepped out from the bushes and approached the rider, who dismounted to speak to him. There was definitely something smoky going on. The watcher moved, silent as the grave, from tree to tree, and was soon within listening range.

'Well, man?' Lord Barbour stood slapping his crop against his boot, impatient to be off again. 'Why d'you stop me? You got it, didn't you?'

'Yes, my lord, though it didn't go exactly according to plan.'

'What do you mean?'

'I didn't have the bringing of the animal. Had to set up a bit of a diversion, so to speak.'

'Who did bring it and what have you done with him?'

'It ain't a him, it's the Long Meg herself. She's our guest. I took her to the woodman's cottage; she's tied up right and tight with your boy on guard.'

'Where's your partner?'

'Charlie? He's keepin' watch up the road aways. What do you want me to do with the article?'

His lordship did not speak again for a minute and Daniel, who could see very little, thought he might have gone away. He was about to risk a look, when Lord Barbour went on. 'It's no tragedy. We'll just have to change our plans, that's all.'

'Well, I tell you now, I ain't in the business of topping women.'

'You don't have to, but she'll make capital bait; he'll take it hook, line and sinker. Just arrange one of your little diversions for him. Stop him, tell him she's had an accident—you know the sort of thing.'

'Where is he?'

'Back at the Barley Mow, but if I know him he'll find himself a new mount or ride the old one; either way he'll be along directly. If he isn't, you'll find him at the inn.' He paused. 'Where's the old fellow?'

'Tucked up in his bed. He's out of it.'

'Good.' There was another slight pause. 'I'm glad about that, you know; didn't fancy putting his light out; we used to be friends in our younger days.'

'You could ha' fooled me.'

'Needs must when the devil drives, but the son is another matter. I shall enjoy that. Now, I've got a race to win.'

The man laughed. 'Race with only one runner?'

'I'm not to know that the other contestant has met with an unfortunate accident, am I? Now, get back and do as you're told if you want the blunt at the end of it.'

'And the woman?'

'Bring her on to Melton Mowbray with you.'

'How? We can't put her on a stage trussed up like a chicken and she won't go no other way.'

'You can persuade her, can't you? Tell her the Major's had a fall and needs her; she'll come easy enough then.'

Daniel waited until the sound of the horse's hooves faded and cautiously peered out from his hiding place. Lord Barbour had gone, as he'd expected, but he could just make out the outline of the other man walking away from him in the other direction. But there was a third man and he didn't know exactly where he was. Apart from the soughing of the wind in the trees and the distant call of an owl, there was no sound, and no light either. But the Corporal was used to moving about stealthily in the dark, as many a French bluecoat had learned to his cost, and he was not going to wait until the Major rode into the ambush.

Darting silently from tree to tree along the edge of the road, he made his way back in the direction of Baldock, two miles distant. Once clear of the wood, he stepped out into the road and walked smartly along it, expecting to meet Richard at every turn.

But there was no sign of the Major and he arrived back at the inn without having set eyes on him, only to find him in the yard, impatiently questioning the ostlers and anyone else who might be able to throw some light on the stallion's disappearance. The Corporal lost no

time in recounting his tale. 'They're lying in wait for
you about two miles up the road,' he finished.

'Are they, by God? Then I think we'll have to turn
the tables on them.' He turned back to the ostler. 'Find
me another mount. I don't care where you get it from,
just get one.' And as the man went to obey, muttering
to himself that he weren't no magician, Richard turned
again to Daniel. 'If he's hurt a hair of her head, by
God, he'll pay.'

'What are you going to do? Walk into the trap?'

'No, let them sweat a bit. I mean to find Miss Paget
first.' Then he said to the ostler, who was leading a
very small cob with a well-worn saddle, 'I want to find
the woodman's cottage; do you know where it is?'

'In the wood,' the man said, making Richard fume
with impatience.

'I know that, man. How can I find it?'

'Go down the back road; it's easier to find from
there, and quicker. There's a track, just wide enough
for his cart. It leads straight to it.'

Richard looked at the cob and could hardly suppress
a smile. 'Is that all you could find?'

'Yes, it belongs to the landlord's daughter.'

'I can't ride that; I'll break it's back. Corporal, you
ride him; you're a deal lighter than me. I'll take my
mare again.' And so the mare was once more pressed
into service and the two men rode out of the yard.

Richard was silent as they rode. There was something very sinister going on; this was no simple race to
win a wager; the stakes were higher than that. Someone
had wanted him dead. Why? And why involve Georgie,
brave, resourceful, vulnerable Georgie? Just what was
going on?

They found the track they were looking for and dismounted to lead their mounts, walking cautiously. In a very few minutes they discovered a clearing and in the middle of it, bathed in moonlight, was a dilapidated cottage with smoke coming from its chimney. 'That's it,' Richard whispered, tying his mount to a tree. 'Leave the horses here.'

Daniel was tethering the cob, when Richard put a hand on his arm and he froze. Coming towards the cottage from the opposite direction was a man Richard recognised. 'Jem,' he whispered. 'Is that the man you saw?'

'I reckon so, though I didn't get a good look. He must ha' got tired of waiting for you.'

'He maybe thinks I've given up. He'll be going to the Barley Mow to look for me and lure me out here with some Banbury tale.' He grinned in the darkness as the man disappeared inside the building. 'Wonder how many of them there are?'

'If they're the same ones as held up his lordship's coach, there were three to start with and I slipped the wind of one o' them. And maybe this Charlie he talked of is another. He's likely left him on the road to watch out for you.'

'He's got a long wait, then,' Richard said grimly. 'But we won't take any chances. I'll take a look first.'

There was a shack near by which was probably used for storing logs, for there was a pile of them next to it and an axe stuck in a chopping-block. They crept forward and, once they were out of the shelter of the trees, darted for the cover of the logs. Behind them, in the shack, they heard the restless chomping of a horse. Richard left their hiding place to take a look. 'It's

Warrior,' he said, returning. 'You keep under cover while I go and take a look around.'

He looked about him, then quickly crossed the open ground until he was in the shelter of the wall of the cottage. Bending low, he moved along and peered in the window. Jem and Lord Barbour's son were sitting at a table, deep in conversation. There was no one else to be seen.

He ducked down and went round to the back. The window there was shuttered. He peered through a crack and could just make out the figure of someone sitting on a bed, someone in a woman's riding habit. He was just about to pull it open when he saw Jem come into the room and untie her from the bed. Then, with her hands still bound behind her, he pulled her roughly into the other room. Richard returned to the Corporal.

'She's there. One man and the boy. You let Warrior out. Make as much noise as you can to draw them out. Lead them away; give me a bit of time.'

'Yes, sir.' Daniel was once more the soldier, obeying orders; he felt comfortable with that.

'Wait for me to get into place. I'll throw a stone as a signal.' Then he was gone again, scampering to the cover of the cottage wall.

'Sit down,' Jem commanded Georgie, pushing her into a chair at the table. 'He ain't come; seems he couldn't get another mount after all, so we'll just have to invite him here.'

'Who?' She had recovered from the shock of her capture but she was still very frightened because she had suddenly remembered where she had seen his watch before. It had been taken from Lord Dullingham by the highwaymen!

She had thought at the time that there was something strange about that hold-up. The men had strewn their belongings about the road and taken the jewellery they had been wearing and the money on their persons, but they had made a poor job of searching the coach. Experienced high tobies would have realised that his lordship would have hidden his money and anything of real value and they would have made him tell them where it was. And they had said something about making it look good.

She looked up at Jem; the servile look he had adopted while working at Rowan Park had gone and now he was scowling. 'What are you talking about?' she asked.

'Who do you think? Your lover, of course.'

'I have no lover.'

'No?' he sneered. 'That ain't what the tattlers are saying.'

So, Lord Barbour had spread that malicious lie after all. For a moment she forgot her own predicament in her concern for Felicity. Poor girl! But would she believe such duplicity of the sister who loved her so much that she would sacrifice anything for her? But she did not know that, did not know Georgie had given up all hope of happiness for herself. 'What care I for gossip?'

'I reckon you'll care afore another day passes. It will get worse.' He seemed delighted by the prospect. 'Now you are going to write a letter. A love letter.' He put a sheet of paper, an ink-well and a quill on the table in front of her and untied her wrists. 'Write what I say and no funny business.'

She made no move to obey and he picked up the quill and put it in her hand. 'Write, unless you want to taste the back of my hand.'

She looked up at him, frantically searching her brain for some way of including a secret message which Richard would understand. It was to the Major she was writing, she was sure.

'Let me see; how shall we begin?' He turned to her. 'Now, how would you begin a letter to him? My darling, or dearest, or dear heart—which is it to be?'

'It might help if I knew to whom I was writing,' she said coldly.

'Major the Honourable Richard Baverstock, heir to Viscount Dullingham, who else? Mind you, he's only lately become the heir and that's his misfortune. Before that it was. . .' He shrugged. 'Enough of that. Address the letter to him.'

She wrote 'Dear Major Baverstock' and looked up at him for further instructions.

'I am in a little trouble,' he dictated, then laughed. 'You might as well tell the truth. It will serve. Tell him you are being held hostage and if he wants to see you again he is to accompany the bearer, who will bring him to you.'

'He might not come.'

'And pigs might fly. He'll come, especially when he sees it is Lord Barbour's son who brings him the message. They are old adversaries.' He nodded to the boy who was sitting in a rocking-chair by the fire, rocking himself back and forth in a kind of contained glee.

'Supposing the Major has continued with the race? He might be long gone.'

'He hasn't got a mount, not one that'll carry him far. Besides, I've got someone on watch on the road. He'll stop him if need be. Now write.'

'And if I refuse?' She didn't really want to know the answer, but she needed time to think.

But she was not to have that time and neither was he. There was a great commotion outside, a heavy rumbling followed by the snorting of a horse and then hoofbeats. Warrior had got loose and was creating mayhem! Jem threw open the door and went chasing after the stallion, falling over the logs which had tumbled from their pile and were rolling all over the place. The boy looked at the man, who was swearing and trying to get to his feet, then back at Georgie, obviously wondering what he should do, but before he could make up his mind Jem straightened up and found himself face to face with Daniel Batson. A couple of swift punches, one to the head and one to the belly, were enough. He sank back among the logs. The boy abandoned Georgie and tore off through the woods.

'Let the boy go, man,' commanded a familiar voice. 'Go and get the other villain while I tie this one up.'

Georgie, who had been sitting at the table half mesmerised by the action taking place in the yard, scrambled to her feet just as Richard came in the door, grabbed the rope which had been used to tie her and went outside again to truss Jem up. That done, he returned to Georgie. She flung herself into his arms.

'Hush, my love, it's all over,' he said, holding her close against him, stroking her hair from her face, feeling the wild beating of her heart against his chest. 'No harm's done.'

'How did you find me? Oh, Richard, they were going to kill you. I couldn't have borne it.' She shuddered. 'My blood runs cold to think of it.'

He leaned back to lift her chin with his finger so that he could look into her eyes. 'You do care, don't you?'

'Of course I care.'

'Weren't you worried about what they would do to you?'

She smiled weakly. 'Terrified. But I don't understand what it was all about. It wasn't just the race, was it?'

'No, I don't think so. Oh, my darling, I am so sorry you had to be mixed up in it. Why did you bring Warrior instead of sending him?'

'I just wanted to see a little of the race.' She smiled again, feeling stronger with his arms so comfortably about her and his face, so full of concern, looking down at her. 'The boy stopped me, pretended he was in trouble, then someone hit me on the back of the head. The next thing I knew I was here. Where are we?'

'In the wood not three miles from Baldock. The Corporal overheard Jem talking to Lord Barbour. He came back to tell me.'

'Back? Do you mean you abandoned the race?'

'Yes. When no one turned up with Warrior, I knew you must be in some sort of trouble and you are far more important to me than any race. You are——'

'But you must go on.' She was almost desperate to stop him saying any more. It could not be; it just could not. 'We'll find Warrior; he won't have gone far.'

'No. We have to talk. I must know.'

'No, no. You must go on.'

He stepped back to take her shoulders in his hands and look down at her. 'Georgie, look at me.'

Slowly she raised her eyes.

'I love you.' He bent his head to kiss her. She shivered as the kiss deepened from a simple meeting of lips to something that held the fire and passion they both felt. Her whole body cried out for him and she clung to him, returning his kiss, abandoning herself to the delightful sensations his touch aroused. It was some time before he gathered his self-control and lifted his head, though his arms remained around her. 'Oh, my dear. You do feel it too.'

If it was meant to be a question she did not answer and he did not repeat it. Instead, he said, 'We can't go on like this.'

'Like what?' Her voice was flat with the effort of trying to control her overflowing emotions. To have been abducted and threatened then rescued by the man she loved so much, to be kissed and know that he loved her too, and then to have to spurn him, was too much. But spurn him she must.

'I need to know if you love me,' he said.

Unable to look into his eyes and lie, she lowered her gaze. 'You are betrothed to my sister.'

'I am not. I haven't seen her. I tried, believe me, but she seems not to want my advances.'

He had hoped to be able to go to Georgie after the race and tell her he was free to ask her to marry him, but he had been unable to see Felicity. She was a little out of curl, he had been told, a slight indisposition, nothing to worry about, but she was staying in bed for a day or two. He suspected she was doing to him

exactly what Georgie had done to Lord Barbour—
avoiding him in order not to have to receive his offer.
He could not dangle there while she made a recovery;
he had left to start the race, knowing his failure would
annoy Georgie.

He gave a strangled laugh. 'All I wanted was to give
her the opportunity to turn me down.'

'She wouldn't do that. She knows what a good match
it will be for her and. . .'

'And how much you have sacrificed to bring it about?
I am not blind, Georgie, even if you are.'

'Don't you have any regard for her at all?'

'Of course I do, because she is your sister. I admit
when my father and your aunt began pushing me
towards her I complied like a dutiful son, but it did not
take me long to realise it just would not do. It is you I
love.'

She felt drained of energy and there were no tears
left in her to shed; they had evaporated, leaving her
like a dried-up shell, devoid of feeling. 'So, you want
to defy your father again,' she said, moving away from
him to put enough distance between them for her to be
able to control her turbulent emotions. 'You would
break Felicity's heart and make us all the subject of the
most horrible gossip?'

'Do you really think she will be heartbroken?'

'You can't mean to back out. She will be mortified
with shame.'

He looked miserable, cursing the strict code of
etiquette which forbade him to withdraw with any
honour, even though he had not actually made an offer
of marriage. ' I know I can't, but if she were to refuse

me. . .' He paused and said softly, 'Georgie, you must tell her. . .'

'I can't possibly do that.'

'You are the most infuriating woman I have ever come across, do you know that? You will make three people miserable for the rest of their lives, perhaps four. . .'

'Four?'

'There may be someone who loves your sister very much and she might love him. . .'

'Do you know that for a fact?'

'No.'

'Then I suggest you find Warrior and carry on with the race. I need you to win, Major Baverstock, for the sake of Rowan Park. It is all that matters to me.'

'It's too late. I've lost an hour at least.'

'No, it isn't. There is still a long way to go and anything could happen. Lord Barbour might be thrown; his horse might go lame halfway between one post and the next and he'd have to walk a few miles, wouldn't he? He might even miss the way or slow down, believing you have been taken care of.'

'I can't leave you.'

'The Corporal will escort me back to the Barley Mow. Come on.'

Taking a deep breath to steady herself, she walked away from him towards the track which continued past the cottage and on through the trees towards the Great North Road. The Corporal had gone that way to take care of the second conspirator. Because there was little else he could do, Richard untied the mare and the cob and followed. They had almost reached the road when they found Daniel sitting with his back to a tree waiting for them. He had Charlie tied to another tree and Warrior tethered near by.

'There you are,' he said, getting to his feet. 'All nabbed, right and tight, and no harm done to the beast.'

'Good man,' Richard said.

'Corporal, I have been trying to persuade the Major that it is not too late to go on,' Georgie said. 'He can easily catch his lordship, can't he?'

'Course he can,' Daniel confirmed. 'I'll look after the lady, sir, and them two Jeremy Diddlers, don't you worry none.' He fetched the stallion and brought him alongside Richard. 'Come on, let me give you a leg-up. I got money on this here race and so have a good many others.'

Richard, realising that he was going to make no progress with Georgie that night, or indeed ever, reluctantly allowed himself to be persuaded. He held his fidgeting mount to look down at her. She was standing very still, making no move to go to him or bid him goodbye. There was nothing more to be said; he dug his heels in and cantered away.

'Oh, miss,' Daniel said, turning to her and seeing the tears streaming down her face. 'There ain't no reason for you to cry now, is there? It's all over.'

She forced a watering smile. 'Yes,' she said 'it's all over.'

CHAPTER TEN

MRS BERTRAM was at her wits' end. To have had no choice but to invite the Viscount to accompany her back to Baldock was bad enough, but then to be proved wrong about the route over the heath was even worse. She had been in so much of a ferment over not finding Felicity and wanting to see Georgiana as soon as possible that taking a short-cut had seemed to be the only thing to do. His lordship had demurred about the possible state of the road, but in the end had given way to her, and though she had been triumphant at the time she was more than sorry for it now. For they had not gone far when a wheel had fallen into a deep rut and thrown them both on to the floor in a great heap of legs and petticoats. She felt mortified even now, when she thought of the way his lordship had extricated himself from under her skirts and helped her out of the coach.

They had stood looking at the sorry state of it, while James, her driver, had struggled to calm the horses. It had looked as though the axle had broken, and when James had examined it he'd said it was split but with a little ingenuity he might be able to mend it well enough to get them to the Barley Mow. He had vouchsafed the opinion that the inn would be able to effect a more permanent repair. Mrs Bertram's response had been to urge him to get on with it.

Even so, it had taken some time because it had

necessitated finding a piece of wood strong enough and straight enough to strap round the axle, but after a diligent search one had been found and, with the help of a few tools James kept in the boot and some odd leather straps, the axle had been bound up and they had been able to resume their journey at a snail's pace.

It was no good suggesting that they go faster; they were lucky they were able to move at all and Harriet was obliged to contain her impatience behind a flurry of small talk, which became more breathless and inconsequential as time passed. His lordship was unfailingly calm and cheerful and had even helped the driver with the repair, getting his lovely riding coat covered in axle grease in the process.

By the time they turned into the yard of the inn, well past midnight, Mrs Bertram was aching in every joint and glad to descend and make her way into the parlour, leaving Lord Dullingham and her driver in the yard to give instructions about the repair of the coach. The room was empty except for a lone waiter, collecting up dirty glasses. 'I had expected to find my niece here,' she said, looking round the untidy room; they had obviously been very busy earlier in the evening. 'Miss Paget, you know. Has she been here?'

'There've been a good few young ladies, one way and another, ma'am, seeing's everyone wanted to see the riders go through. None here now, though.'

She turned as the Viscount came into the room. 'We missed them,' he said.

'And so I have discovered, but where is my niece?'

'I am afraid she never arrived,' he said. 'Nor the horse either. Richard went on without it.'

Mrs Bertram's reaction to this was to fall on him in

a faint and as she was no lightweight she almost took him down with her. He managed to haul her to a chair and shout at the waiter to fetch a feather and soon the stench of burning feathers being waved back and forth beneath her nose revived her. Almost at once she began to cry.

'Dear lady,' his lordship said, helping her to sit up so that she could fish her handkerchief from her reticule. 'You have had a most upsetting time. I have bespoken a private room for you and the landlord's daughter will help you to bed.' He beckoned to the waiter. 'Bring a bumper of brandy.' And as the man obeyed he said, 'Drink this down and then go and rest. Things will look much better after you have had some sleep. In the meantime I shall endeavour to find out what has happened to Miss Paget.'

'Where, oh, where can she have got to? Oh, I shall never live it down. Never. Never.'

'Compose yourself, ma'am, I beg you. No doubt she is safe and sound and so we shall discover in the morning.' He looked up as the inkeeper's daughter entered the room. 'There you are. Would you help Mrs Bertram up to her room? I am afraid she has had a shock.' To the lady herself he said, 'Go now. I shall see you in the morning.'

'You do not think I shall sleep, do you? Oh, what is to become of us all?' She carried on in like vein for several minutes, but as she allowed the young woman to conduct her from the room at the same time she was soon lost to his lordship's hearing.

He went out to the yard to hire a mount, but learned, as his son had done before him, that there was nothing to be had. Unable to proceed very far, his lordship contented himself with walking down the road a little way, looking in the hedgerows as he went, just in case Georgie had been thrown, though if Richard's account of how she could ride were to be believed that was highly unlikely. And where was the horse?

He began to suspect foul play. He sincerely hoped nothing had happened to her for he had become very fond of her. She was a spirited thing, practical and forthright. He had been amused and impressed by the way she had spoken to those soldiers after the hold-up, as if she were defending him! It was a funny thing about them. They had been no ordinary highwaymen and the fellow who had been shot had once been one of his grooms. He had dismissed him for ill-treating a horse. Had it been done for revenge? It was rather excessive, if it had.

The road he was walking along went through a wood and was dark as pitch. Geogie might have been lying at his feet and he would not have been able to see her; he should have brought a lantern, but where there were no trees the moon was very bright and he had not thought about it. He turned to go back.

Georgie pulled the mare up in surprise. Surely that was her aunt's chaise in the inn yard? What was it doing here? Mrs Bertram should be on her way to Dover by now to catch the packet to Calais. She slipped from the horse, leaving the Corporal to deal with the horses and hand the prisoners over to the town watch, and hurried inside. The landlord, who was dozing in the chimney corner, roused himself at her entrance and tried to look alert, but he had been at work for nearly twenty-four hours and it was an effort.

'Mrs Bertram,' Georgie began. 'My aunt.'

He nodded wearily. 'First room at the top of the stairs.'

It was all Georgie could do to make herself walk and not run up the stairs and knock on the door. A weak voice bade her to enter.

Her aunt was propped up in the bed, fully clothed. Her face was ashen and her hair all awry. As soon as she caught sight of Georgie, she burst into fresh tears.

'Aunt, whatever is the matter?' Georgie ran to comfort her but it was some time before the lady could speak coherently.

'I did not know what to do,' she said, between sniffs and dabs with her handkerchief. 'And then his lordship came and I simply could not tell him, and he insisted on riding with me, and then we broke down and you were missing. Oh, Georgiana, such a day as I have had, I never wish to endure another like it.'

'Aunt, do please compose yourself and tell me why you are here. Were you on the way to Rowan Park?'

'I went there, but your housekeeper said you had left on that great horse of yours, so what could I do but come after you? And then who should come along but Lord Dullingham, asking if he might ride with me, and how could I refuse him? But if he finds out the truth we are done for.'

'His lordship is here?'

'Yes. Did you not see him?'

'No.'

'I believe he might have gone searching for you.'

And come to some harm. They had arrested two conspirators but how could they be sure there were no more? Had they finished off the job they had started when they had held up the coach? Oh, had they not had enough troubles for one night? If only Richard were here! She forced herself to pay attention to one thing at a time. 'Aunt, please tell me what has happened. Why did you abandon your plans to go to France?'

'This!' Her aunt fumbled about in her reticule and produced a piece of much folded paper. 'This is what Lady Hereward found on Felicity's pillow yesterday morning—well, the maid found it but it amounts to the same thing. She—her ladyship, I mean—brought it round to me just as I had all my packing done and was about to leave. The chit meant me to be gone before it was found, I'll wager.'

'Found on her pillow?' Georgie's heart sank. What had her foolish sister been up to? She opened the note and read it swiftly. Felicity had written:

Dear Lady Hereward

I am indeed sorry for the inconvenience and embarrassment I must surely cause you, but I am in desperate straits. I know that as soon as this race to York is done Major Baverstock will return to speak to me and I cannot put off seeing him again. I am leaving to be with the man I love. We will be married as soon as possible. I thank you most sincerely for looking after me so comfortably.

She had signed it simply, 'Felicity.'

Georgie's reaction was so mixed up she did not know whether to shout for joy or join her aunt in tears for the mull Felicity had got herself into.

'Why are you smiling?' Mrs Bertram asked. 'It is no laughing matter, I can tell you. Poor Lady Hereward is prostrate with guilt that it should have happened under her roof, though to be honest she always was more relaxed over discipline than I ever was. And now she is paying for that folly and us with her.'

'I hope you did not tell her so.'

'No, she feels badly enough about it without me ringing a peal over her. And I am partly to blame for allowing the chit to go to her.'

'It was very thoughtless of Felicity not to think of that. But where can she have gone?'

'I thought she might have come home to you, that she had heard something. . .'

'Heard what?'

'Of course I denied it, denied it absolutely, said you wouldn't be such a scapegrace, but it is gaining ground. . .'

'What is gaining ground?'

'Thought she had come home to see you to face you out, tell you to your face that she did not want to marry the Major. I had to let the Colonel go to Dover without me. I came post haste to fetch the pair of you back to London. We must announce both your engagements at once, before there is any more scandal. . .'

'Please, Aunt, what have you heard?' But she knew the answer and it sickened her.

'That you have been entertaining Major Baverstock at Rowan Park and none there but you and a couple of cork-brained servants.'

'They are not cork-brained and if it were not for them. . .' Georgie paused. 'It was Lord Barbour who put that rumour about, Aunt. It was he who came to Rowan Park and tried to rape me. Now, don't go into a spasm, please, or you will not hear the end. Major

Baverstock was in the stables at the time, talking to Dawson about his horses. Fanny ran and fetched him and he sent his lordship packing.'

'It is beyond comprehension.'

'It is the truth. Now, having got that out of the way, what about Felicity? Where do you think she may have gone?'

'As she has not come home, as I hoped, I am forced to the conclusion that she must have gone to Gretna Green. Oh, how will we ever live it down?' She heaved a huge sigh. 'I have done my best for you both, you cannot deny it, and to be put to the blush by Lord Dullingham was the last straw.' And once more she resorted to her sodden handkerchief.

'You must be right about Gretna Green, but who is the man?'

'I have no idea.'

'Come, we must put our heads together. Who has been paying her more attention than usual?'

'How can I know that, when she had been staying with the Herewards? The Major, of course, to start with, but after he had left to make his arrangements for the race I don't know. She went out and about with Juliette and the young people of her set. According to Lady Hereward, they were always well-chaperoned.'

Suddenly Georgie understood. She remembered blushes and how one young man seemed to bring Felicity out of her shell more than any other, and the use of a given name, quickly corrected. 'Including Captain Melford?' she asked.

'Yes, I suppose so, but surely not? Isn't Juliette. . .?'

'What's that to the point? Do you know where Captain Melford is at this moment? He is in York, waiting for Major Baverstock to arrive. And York is well on the way to Gretna Green, is it not?'

'Yes, but if Felicity has gone there the Major will see her and he will be embarrassed and angry and——'

'I don't think he will, Aunt.'

'Why are you smiling like that? It is not the least bit amusing. Major Baverstock will withdraw his offer. . .'

Georgie made herself look suitably grave. 'He hasn't actually made it yet, Aunt.'

'Well, he never will now.' She brightened suddenly. 'Unless we can persuade him that Felicity went north to see him win the race.'

'Certainly not; there has been too much pretence already, which is why we are in this bumblebath. But I agree we must try and find her. If she wants to marry Captain Melford, she must do it properly.'

'If you are right and it is Captain Melford and not some scapegrace or tulip, it would not be so bad. But how are we to go? My coach is broken and the horses spent and whatever shall we do about Lord Dullingham? He mustn't know. Is it too much to hope he has washed his hands of us and gone home by some other means?'

'He would not be so ungallant.'

'We must pretend to be going back to London and then turn round and go north. But the coach!'

'Aunt, there is nothing we can do until daylight. Now, you try and sleep and I will see what is being done about the coach. If it cannot be repaired we must hire another and a driver too. Poor James must be as exhausted as you are.'

Mrs Bertram lay back on her pillows and closed her eyes. Georgie bent to kiss her cheek and left her, smiling a little. It had not occurred to Mrs Bertram to ask her niece where she had been and what she had been doing, which was just as well; she had had enough to contend with for one night.

Strangely Georgie did not feel tired; she felt elated and so buoyed up with hope, she wanted to laugh aloud. Felicity did not want to marry Richard! How blind they had all been and how very stupid! But that did not alter the fact that Felicity must be rescued from her own folly. An elopement would give the tattlemongers something to get their teeth into for weeks to come.

She returned downstairs and went out to the yard to make enquiries about the coach, but at the back of her mind was another worry. What had become of Viscount Dullingham?

She discovered, when she went out into the yard, that the coach had been taken into a workshop at the back of the premises and men were already working on it by the light of several lanterns. His lordship must have been truly silver-tongued, not to mention open-handed, to have worked such a miracle.

There were more people in the yard now as the spectators began to drift back to return the mounts they had hired, to change their carriage horses or to order an early breakfast. Grooms and ostlers, rubbing sleep from their eyes, hurried about, calling to each other and commenting on the best twenty-four hours of business they had ever done. Those few who had been on duty earlier had taken to their beds and there was no one who had seen the carriage and its two occupants arrive. Georgie was beginning to think Mrs Bertram's wish had been granted and the Viscount had returned home by other means, when he strolled into the yard.

She was so relieved to see him, she dashed up to him and, without even waiting for him to greet her, said, 'Oh, my lord, how pleased I am to see you safe,' which was such an extraordinary thing to say that he looked completely nonplussed for a moment.

Then he smiled slowly and tipped his hat. 'And, my dear Miss Paget, I must say how pleased I am to see *you* safe. Now we have our mutual relief out of the way, do you mind telling me why you think I might have been in any danger?'

'Those men. Oh, dear, I really do not know where to begin.'

'I always find the beginning the most effectual, my dear. Shall we go inside and find a comfortable seat? I have a feeling this might take some time.' He took her arm and guided her indoors to the parlour where he found them seats in a quiet corner away from all the young bloods who were going over every minute of the race and forming their own opinions as to why the Major should have lost his lead on Lord Barbour.

'Now,' he said, when they were seated with two steaming cups of coffee before them, 'I take it you have seen your aunt?'

'Yes, and what a tale she had to tell. I am very thankful, my lord, that you were with her.'

'I do not think she is quite of the same mind, Miss Paget. Indeed, I'd go so far as to say that some of the time she wished me in purgatory. There is something troubling her, but whenever I opened my mouth to ask if I could be of any assistance she started talking a great deal of trivial nonsense to prevent me speaking.'

'Yes, I know, she told me. I am sorry she did not feel able to confide in you.'

He smiled. 'But you are going to.'

'Yes.' She was surprised how perfectly at ease she felt in his company. 'It's all on account of my sister, Felicity. I am afraid she has been rather foolish, but it is not entirely her fault.'

'The beginning, if you please, Miss Paget.'

She took a deep breath and told him the whole story.

'Then we must go to York,' he said when she had finished. 'The race must be nearly over, but we will learn the result all the sooner, don't you think? Is that not reason enough to go?'

'Yes, my lord, but we cannot allow you to inconvenience yourself. . .'

'Nonsense, it is quite an adventure, is it not?' He was suddenly serious. 'I must take my share of the blame for what has happened and the sooner all is put to rights the better. Now, you must not worry about a thing.'

'Thank you, my lord. But there is something else I ought to tell you. While you and my aunt were having your adventure, I was having one of my own.'

'Go on.'

He listened intently without comment while she related it and when she had finished he patted her hand and smiled. 'You were wonderfully brave, Miss Paget, and I am sure my son would agree with me.'

'I knew those men were no ordinary highwaymen,' she said. 'Can you think why anyone should want to harm you?'

'No, but it's of no consequence.'

She was not sure if he was telling the truth or not,

but she could hardly call a man of his calibre to account, and if he chose to keep his thoughts to himself, then that was his affair. She had not been completely honest either; she had not told him of her love for Richard. She dared not, not until the business with Felicity had been sorted out and Richard himself had confirmed his love for her; he might even want to wash his hands of the whole Paget family. But oh, how she hoped not. He had given her a taste of paradise and she wanted to feast on it.

'I do not trust Lord Barbour not to try something else to detain Rich——Major Baverstock.' She corrected her slip very quickly but she was sure he had noticed.

'We are a match for him, are we not? Now, it is nearly daylight. I shall go and see how the coach repairs are coming along and order breakfast for us all, while you go and wake your aunt and tell her that I have taken over the arrangements for the whole journey. You had better find one of your men and give him a message for your housekeeper. We can't have a hue and cry because she thinks you are missing, can we? I am afraid there will be no sleep for you.'

'Oh, I do not mind in the least.'

An hour later, with a good breakfast inside them and a new axle on the coach, they were standing in the yard wondering if it would be safe to entrust the driving to Mrs Bertram's exhausted driver, when Bert Dawson came in on the night mail with another of the Rowan Park men. They had been patrolling the early part of the race and had been able to snooze on the coach bringing them home. Dawson, Georgie knew, would be discretion itself and readily agreed to drive them.

One of the grooms from the inn was given an exorbitant sum to ride ahead and arrange for fresh horses to be ready at the posting houses and in no time at all they were on the road again, hoping to snatch some sleep on the way.

It was a forlorn hope. The coach was old and uncomfortable and the road in many places so full of potholes that they were thrown about like sacks of grain, and Mrs Bertram, remembering what had happened the evening before, was in a paroxysm of fear that fate would repeat itself. She would have liked to insist on going slowly, but she was as anxious as everyone else to reach their destination as speedily as possible.

Late in the afternoon, when they were still several miles short of Grantham, his lordship suddenly broke the silence. 'We'll go to my shooting box. It's only a mile or two out of our way and we will be sure of a comfortable bed and a good meal.'

'But we won't be expected, my lord,' Georgie demurred.

'My staff are used to unexpected comings and goings, my dear. They will rise to the occasion and find something, even if it not a banquet. And we will be able to set off again tomorrow much refreshed.'

'But ought we to delay, my lord? Felicity has two days' start on us.'

'Yes, but she will have travelled by public coach, the mail at best, and I doubt she will leave York again immediately. My son will undoubtedly remain in York another day to rest and perhaps to celebrate, and Captain Melford is bound to want to join him in that.' He smiled. 'And to settle his wagers, one way or another. Add to that your sister's undoubted fatigue and you have pressing reasons for remaining another day.'

He sounded so calm, she felt reassured. 'Do you really think so?'

'Yes. Now, what do you say?'

Georgie turned to look at her aunt who was sound asleep in the corner with her bonnet fallen over her face. Poor thing, she had tried to keep awake because she'd felt she ought to converse, but had given up the struggle a few miles back. She needed a good night's sleep; they all did. 'If you are sure it will not be too much trouble.'

He put his head out of the window and called up to Dawson. 'Take the turn to Melton Mowbray, driver. You'll find a gate on the right-hand side about five miles up the road. Missen House, it's called.' He turned to smile at Georgie. 'The house was my mother's childhood home, but since I inherited it has been used by the family as a shooting box, though truthfully it is a trifle larger than one would expect.'

Georgie smiled at his understatement when she saw the house, standing at the end of a long straight drive; it was a substantial country mansion. And what was even more surprising was the fact that it was not shut up as she had expected. The curtains were drawn back and some of the upper windows were open. The minute the coach drew up, the front door was opened by a man in a black tailcoat who stood on the step peering at them as if unsure whether to welcome them. But, of course, they were in Mrs Bertram's old coach, not the spanking new Dullingham carriage. As soon as the

vehicle stopped, Lord Dullingham stepped down and
turned to help Mrs Bertram down.

She was still half asleep, having been shaken awake
by Georgie when they'd turned in at the gates. Now
she looked about her, unsure where she was. The
Viscount smiled. 'Welcome to Missen House, ma'am.'
He went to hand Georgie down but she had already
climbed out and was shaking the creases out of her
riding habit. It was when he turned to escort them up
the steps that he saw the servant. Georgie noticed the
slight pursing of his lips and the drawing down of his
brows; it was an expression she had seen on Richard
when he was displeased. 'Who are you?' he demanded.

'Jenkins.' There was something about his lordship's
bearing that made him add a belated, 'Sir.'

'Where's Gordon?'

'Gordon is no longer with us. If you give me your
name I will announce you.'

Georgie thought his lordship was about to explode.
'I do not need to be announced in my own house, man.
Someone should have told you.' He walked past the
astonished man and into the oak-panelled hall. 'Where
is my nephew? I assume it is he who gives you your
orders?'

The man looked blank and Georgie, passing him,
whispered, 'That is Viscount Dullingham. Did you not
know?'

'Don't care who he is. My orders are to admit no
one but. . .' He stopped and turned as if to detain the
irate Viscount but changed his mind and shrugged.

There was a gust of laughter from one of the rooms.
His lordship strode towards it, but before he reached it
the door was opened and a maidservant came out

carrying a tray. Georgie, who had followed, could just see a long polished table at which two men were seated over the remains of a meal. The one who faced the door was, she assumed, William Baverstock. There was a slight resemblance to Richard in the shape of the head and the well-defined brows, but there it ended. This man was thin and his features pasty, as if he never saw the sun. The other occupant of the room had his back to the door, but Georgie recognised his staccato way of speaking. 'Heard a carriage. Must be my man and the wench.'

'Twelve hours late. I sincerely hope, for your sake, he has done his job well.' Mr Baverstock was clearly displeased and then he looked up and his expression changed to shocked incredulity.

His companion, noticing this, swivelled round to see Viscount Dullingham framed in the doorway and, behind him, the furious figure of Georgie. His mouth dropped open, but he recovered himself swiftly. 'My lord, this is indeed a pleasure. When William invited me, I had no idea you were to be present too. And goodness me, Miss Paget, how delightful!'

Lord Dullingham turned to look at Georgie. She was trembling with fear—or was it rage? Knowing something of what had happened between them, he could understand if it was both. 'My dear,' he said softly, 'I will deal with this.' He looked past her to where the servant who had opened the door was hovering. 'Show the ladies to the drawing-room,' he said. 'Then have rooms prepared for them.'

The servant loooked at William Baverstock, who said, 'Go on, man, you heard his lordship.' He smiled at his uncle. 'Sir, if you had let me know, we could have been in a fit state to receive you.'

Georgie heard his lordship growl, 'What have you done with Gordon?' before he closed the door.

She turned to take her aunt's arm and together they followed the servant into a well-furnished though untidy drawing-room. There was a tray containing a teapot and a single used cup and a discarded *Lady's Magazine* on one of the tables, but she decided it would be imprudent to ask the servant who the lady might be.

Half an hour later, tea and a light meal having been consumed, Jenkins reappeared to show them to their rooms. After locking her door, Georgie took off her dress and petticoat and lay down in her underclothes. Ten minutes later, despite her determination to the contrary, sheer exhaustion sent her to sleep.

She awoke very early; it was barely light enough to see; something had disturbed her, though what it was she could not have said. Everywhere was quiet, but there was no question of going back to sleep. Her thoughts were in a tumult. What was Lord Barbour doing here? Had he come as soon as the race was over or had he not completed it? If that were so, had Richard won it by default? She could not imagine Lord Barbour conceding it so easily, especially when he had had such a lead over his opponent after the incident at Baldock. Had something happened to prevent Richard finishing? If so, where was he? Where was Captain Melford? And where, oh, where was Felicity?

She got up and went to the window. Somewhere out there were the two people she loved most in the world and she wished she had second sight and could pinpoint their whereabouts exactly. Her room looked down on a very extensive stable-block, which was not surprising considering the house was used as a hunting base. Her aunt's dilapidated coach stood next to a spanking curricle—Mr Baverstock's presumably. But it was growing light and she was anxious to be on the road; she dressed and went to wake Mrs Bertram.

Ten minutes later they went downstairs, to find Lord Dullingham already at breakfast. His riding coat had been cleaned and he looked calm and refreshed. He rose to greet them. 'Good morning, ladies. I am afraid the new butler took to his heels last night, but please help yourself to some breakfast while I go and order the carriage, then we can be on our way. I have sent a man ahead to make sure there are fresh horses for us.'

Georgie longed to ask him what had happened the previous night, but judged that it might be considered an impertinence, and besides, everything seemed so normal. The sun was shining and the birds singing in the eaves and there was no sign of Mr Baverstock and Lord Barbour. She began to wonder if she had dreamed them.

Half an hour later they were back in the coach. Georgie, glancing up at the house as her aunt settled herself, saw a girl's face pressed against a window on the upper floor. She looked as though she was trying to open it, but a hand appeared from behind her and pulled her back into the room.

'I saw something—someone,' she said to Lord Dullingham, who was giving last-minute instructions to Dawson. 'At that window.' She pointed. 'A young woman.'

He stopped with his hand on the door. 'A servant perhaps?'

'I don't think so. I knew there was someone else here last night—there was a tea-tray in the drawing-room—and knowing Lord Barbour as I do. . . Oh, my lord, supposing he has someone else here, keeping her against her will? I only caught a very quick glimpse, but. . .'

'Wait here.'

He strode back into the house, but she could not sit still and wait for whatever was to come; ignoring her aunt's protests, she hurried after him.

He bounded up the stairs, stopped outside a door and knocked. There was a little cry from inside, quickly silenced. He tried the door but it was locked. He turned and ran downstairs again, returning with a pistol in each hand. The noise as he shot the lock off the door almost deafened Georgie. The broken door swung open. A woman screamed, a man growled and sprang forward, toppling his lordship to the ground, where they struggled for possession of the second gun. But Georgie had no eyes for them; she was looking at Felicity, sitting on the bed, tears streaming down her face, a paper-white face blotched with weeping.

She ran to put her arms around her. 'It's all right, love. You are safe now.' But this only made her sister cry the more. It was no good asking her what had happened; the poor girl was too distraught to speak coherently; all Georgie could do was hold her and murmur soothing words of comfort. But she did not feel as tranquil as she sounded; there was a red rage inside her which threatened to explode. Lord Barbour! And her darling sister. And they had nearly ridden away and left her there. It was too horrible to contemplate.

He was still struggling with Lord Dullingham, trading blow for blow. The bed-hangings were ripped, ornaments sent crashing, a tray which must have contained Felicity's breakfast was overturned and broken crockery added to the hazards. William Baverstock, hearing the commotion, had arrived on the scene and stood in the doorway looking down at the men with an expression of superior disdain. Behind him, panting for breath, was her aunt.

'Do something!' Georgie shouted at him. 'Do something before someone is killed.'

He smiled and picked up the unfired pistol, then touched Lord Barbour with the toe of his boot. 'Get up, man.'

His lordship obeyed, pulling his torn jacket about him. 'You never said he was a pugilist,' he said, rubbing his bruised chin.

Georgie was furious. 'Lord Barbour attacked Viscount Dullingham. Lock him up and send for a constable.'

'Why should I do that? As I see it, my uncle fired at him without the least provocation; Lord Barbour was only defending himself.' The man's cruel smile sent shivers down her spine. Could he really be related to Richard? 'And your honour.'

'My honour?' She was mystified.

'Lord Barbour is your salvation, didn't you know that? If you want to hold your head up in Society, that is.'

She looked at Felicity, who had stopped crying and was staring at him with wide, frightened eyes. 'He promised he would take me to York. . .' The thought of who was waiting for her in that city reduced her to tears again.

'Oh, for pity's sake dry your eyes, girl,' William said impatiently as Mrs Bertram went to help his lordship. 'I cannot abide watering-pots and you've got nothing to cry for. No one has hurt you, have they?' And when she did not answer he repeated, 'Have they? No one touched you. Tell this suspicious sister of yours your virtue is intact.' He smiled suddenly. 'Or as intact as it can be, all things considered.'

Felicity looked up at her sister and smiled weakly. 'They didn't touch me, truly they didn't. But what am I to do? No one will believe it and there's John. . .' She stopped suddenly and her pale face became suffused with colour.

'You are right—no one will believe it,' Lord Barbour said. 'But your dear sister knows the remedy.'

Georgie stared at him for several seconds while her mind whirled. That odious man had not given up his quest for her, or more accurately his quest for Rowan Park. And because his first attempt to have his way had failed he was making use of Felicity. But how had she come into his clutches? And why bring her here? He could not have anticipated Lord Dullingham's arrival.

He must have known what she was thinking because he grinned. 'Jem was supposed to bring you here after he had disposed of a certain encumbrance. . .'

'That's enough!' commanded William Baverstock sharply. 'I think you should go. You have outstayed your welcome.'

Lord Barbour looked at him as if he had gone mad. 'What did you say?'

'I said, take yourself off. I wonder why I ever trusted such a bumbling fool as you are. Go, while you can.'

They looked at each other for several seconds, but the pistol in Mr Baverstock's hand decided his lordship. Uttering oaths which put all three women to the blush, he flung himself out of the room.

William looked at the two girls, the injured Viscount and Mrs Bertram, who was hovering uncertainly in the doorway, and laughed. 'I'll leave you all to sort yourselves out, but don't try to leave.' Then he too left the room.

Mrs Bertram ran to the girls, who were sitting white-faced and silent on the edge of the bed, while Lord Dullingham hauled himself to his feet and sank into a chair. He was breathing heavily and knew the struggle had not helped his heart condition. He fumbled in his pocket for the pills his doctor had given him and took one.

Georgie turned to Felicity. 'Do you think you can tell us what happened now?'

'I am so ashamed. I thought. . . I couldn't. . .'

'Lord Barbour, of all people!' Mrs Bertram put in. 'How could you? You knew he was dangling after your sister.'

'Aunt Harriet!' Georgie was shocked. 'You surely did not think Felicity came here of her own free will?'

'Oh, but I did!' Felicity said. 'He said he would make all right with you and would take me to York, but he didn't. . .' She began to weep again.

Georgie handed her a handkerchief. 'Please, dearest, calm yourself and tell us exactly what happened, right from the beginning. You were going to elope with Captain Melford, isn't that so?'

'Yes, but how did you know?'

'I guessed. Now, what was the plan? You must have had one. You did not go to Lord Barbour for help, did you?'

'No, of course not.' She shuddered. 'Juliette helped me. She told her mother I had the headache so I could leave while they were all having dinner. It was the night before the race.'

'I thought Juliette and Captain Melford. . .'

'No, she looks on him as a childhood playmate. She hopes to persuade her mother to let her marry Freddie Forsythe.'

'So you left during dinner and then what?'

'Juliette said not to go by way of the Great North Road because it would be all at sixes and sevens with people taking their stations to watch the race and someone might recognise me. In any case all the seats were taken. I took a coach to Bedford. The coachman assured me I should still be in York by the time the race ended.'

'All by yourself? Weren't you frightened?'

'Oh, yes, but once I'd left I had to go through with it and I kept thinking of John at the other end.'

'Captain Melford was going to wait for you in York?'

'Oh, no, he did not know I was coming. I thought once he knew I was prepared to face danger to join him he would see the right of it.'

'You mean he did not want to marry you?' Georgie asked incredulously.

'Oh, yes, he wants to very much. It is simply that he thought I ought to receive Major Baverstock and reject him and then he would feel free to offer for me.'

'Quite right too,' their aunt put in.

'But I couldn't,' she said, addressing her aunt. 'You had told me so often I should not disappoint Georgie and I knew that once the Major stood in front of me I should go into a quake and not be able to stand against him.'

'Oh, you foolish, foolish, girl,' Georgie said, hugging her. 'He is not such an ogre; he would have accepted your decision like the gentleman he is. And why could you not tell me all this?'

'You had a fall, you remember, and I could not worry you. And then you went home to Rowan Park and I went to Richmond and it all seemed so hopeless.'

'How did you meet Lord Barbour? He was supposed to be riding in that race.' How long ago that seemed now, but it was only the night before last.

'I had to change coaches in Bedford and take another one for Grantham to bring me back on to the Great North Road. It set me down at the Angel. Oh, Georgie, the town was so crowded; the race had caught everyone's attention and there were so many people, and they had nearly all taken drink. The inn was full and they would not let me have a room. I walked down the road to the George, but that was even worse.

'It was then I saw Lord Barbour, talking to Mr Baverstock, only I did not know it was Mr Baverstock then. I thought his lordship was going to marry you and I could trust him. I told him the whole and he asked me if I minded him confiding in his friend, Mr Baverstock. I didn't know what to do but as he was a relative of the Major I agreed. Mr Baverstock said I could stay at his house for the night. It was not far away and there would be other guests. He said he would take me to York the next morning.

'Only there were no other guests. They made me come up to my room, said it would be best because there would be bound to gossip if anyone saw me.' She turned to his lordship who had been sitting quietly, listening to what was being said and trying to shake off the most appalling headache. 'I am sorry to speak uncivilly of Mr Baverstock, my lord,' she said. 'But they are hand in glove in whatever it is.'

'I know.'

'The highwaymen,' Georgie said suddenly. 'Lord Barbour was expecting Jem. . .' She stopped suddenly. 'And your nephew?'

'I believe so.'

'But why?'

He smiled. 'I believe he had a yearning to be Viscount Dullingham, or, to be exact, his wife decided she wanted to be a viscountess. It was her mother, my second wife, who put the idea into her head and as she could not have Richard she settled for the next in line. While my son and I were estranged, she knew she was on safe ground, but when Richard came home and William told her that I had hinted I might change my will back to what it was she urged William to do something about it before it was too late. Hence the highwaymen. When they learned that I had seen my lawyer and it was already too late, Richard became the target. A fatal accident during the race seemed to be the ideal opportunity.'

He smiled again, though his lip had been split and it was a painful thing to do. 'You foiled that, my dear. Lord Barbour thought he did not have to complete the race because his opponent was out of it and he had won by default. He hinted as much last night.'

'But how did he persuade Lord Barbour to agree to such a thing?'

'He didn't need much persuading. He is in debt up to his ears at Baverstock's bank and he needed more money to finance the race to York. My guess is that William offered to write off the debt and stand buff for the expenses.'

'Will he try again?' She could not sit still and got up to pace the room. 'Perhaps he has already done so. I must find out what has happened.'

She did not care that they all looked very strangely at her. She did not care about anything except finding the man she loved before Lord Barbour did. William Baverstock had sent him away because it had been expedient at the time to do so, but she did not believe he had really given up. And, judging by the look in Lord Dullingham's eyes, he didn't think so either. If Lord Barbour did William's dirty work for him, no blame would attach to him, especially as he had witnesses to prove he had been at Missen House, with none other than Viscount Dullingham himself.

'Will Mr Baverstock let us go?' she asked him. 'He won't try and keep us here, will he?'

But he did, telling them that although he had sent Lord Barbour packing he had to give him time to show a clean pair of heels. He was, or had been, a friend, and he was a peer of the realm. He required them, very politely, to have patience for a couple of hours. Two hours! And in that time Richard could die!

'We'll have to stop and change the horses soon,' John said, looking down at his friend, who lay slumped across the opposite seat, trying to sleep.

The race was won, though it had taken all of twelve hours and not the nine Richard had anticipated, and it had proved too much for his opponent, who had failed to arrive at all. There had been a day of celebration and catching up on lost sleep, but now they were on the way home. John, however, who was supposed to be responsible for the arrangements for the return journey, had neglected to send on ahead for horses to be ready and, though they had managed the first few changes, when they'd arrived at Grantham there had been none to be had, either at the Angel or the George.

'Can't imagine why you are in such haste,' Richard grumbled, without opening his eyes.

'I should have thought you would be anxious to get back yourself.' John paused, impatient to know. 'Have you spoken to Felicity?'

'No.' Richard opened his eyes and looked at his friend, guessing what had prompted the question. 'I have not been given the opportunity.'

'Then you must do so the minute you return.'

'I intend to. But is it any of your business?'

John took a deep breath. 'Indeed it is.'

Richard sat up; now he would hear the truth. 'You? And Felicity?'

'Yes. I'm sorry.' He could not understand why Richard was grinning from ear to ear.

'Why be sorry? I am delighted. My felicitations. You have saved my life.' He looked out of the window, suddenly impatient with their progress; he longed to go to Rowan Park and tell Georgie, to take her in his arms again. . . The pleasure of anticipation filled him. 'Where are we?'

'I believe the Melton Mowbray turn is just coming up.'

'Then that's where we'll go.' He put his head out of the window and shouted instructions to the driver. Then, withdrawing his head, he added, 'My father has a shooting box not five miles from here. There are bound to be horses there.'

The driver checked the horses and the carriage began to turn, but it never completed the manoeuvre. The driver shouted, the horses shrieked and the coach rolled over with an ear-splitting rending sound. 'Damnation!' Richard said, extricating himself from the wreckage. 'Are you all right, John?'

'Yes.'

Richard hauled himself out of the door, which was above his head, and pushed it open. Their horses were lying in a heap, neighing and struggling to free themselves. The driver had been thrown clear and was sitting in the ditch, shaking his head in a daze, but apparently unhurt. The two men scrambled out and it was then that they discovered the curricle. They had collided with it on the corner and it now lay in a mangled heap of splintered wood and broken wheels. Its horse had broken free and was cantering back the way it had come, reins trailing.

'The driver!' Richard said, and began pulling at the wrecked curricle. 'He's here. My God, it's Barbour!'

They hauled him out, but without the protection of a hood his skull had taken the full force of the crash. There was no doubt he was dead.

'Now what?' John said.

It was while they were laying the body on the grass verge that they heard the sound of horses and looked up to see a dilapidated old coach bearing down on them. It drew to a stop as it reached them and Richard was astonished to see Bert Dawson sitting on the box. Before he could ask him what he was doing there, the carriage door opened and Georgie jumped down and flung herself into his arms. He was vaguely aware that there were other people getting out of the coach, but he took no notice as he held her close and kissed her tenderly.

At last, realising they had an audience, they drew apart. 'I was afraid,' she said. 'Lord Barbour meant to kill you.'

'He's dead,' he told her, jerking his head at the body.

She shivered at the sight of it. 'Mr Baverstock would not let us come after him; he was in the plot, you know, but Lord Dullingham has said he will give no more trouble because his bank won't stand the scandal. He didn't mean to let us go until Lord Barbour had got clean away, but Dawson thought there was something amiss when we didn't go back to the coach and he rushed in to rescue us and what with his lordship telling Mr Baverstock just what he thought of him and Dawson getting his gun. . .'

Richard laughed, though he still held her very tightly, as if afraid to let her go. 'Hold on, you're going too fast.' Then he caught sight of his father and Mrs Bertram and Felicity, who was standing with John's arm about her, which didn't seem to surprise him at all. 'My goodness, is the whole family here?'

'Yes, and such a long story it is.'

'I think we had better return to Missen House,' said his lordship, eyes twinkling. 'We shall all be more comfortable going over what has happened there. And we can decide what explanation we are going to give to the world about how we all came to be here.' He turned to speak to Dawson, who was helping Richard's driver to extricate the horses. 'Any damage there?'

'Nothing serious, my lord.' He led one of them on to the road, while the driver brought the other. 'We'll walk them back.'

'Good.' His lordship decided to take control because his son and the young captain both seemed reluctant to let go of the Misses Paget. He ordered Lord Barbour's body to be put over one of loose horses and everyone else into the coach. 'I'll drive,' he said, making Richard smile, but he did not argue.

It was a dreadful squeeze and the two loving couples were constrained by the presence of Mrs Bertram, though that dear lady seemed to be in a daze. She kept shaking her head from side to side and saying, 'Oh, dear, oh, dear. Whoever would have thought it?'

Georgie was quiet; there would be time for explanations later, but now it was enough that she had Richard beside her and he would be beside her for the rest of her life. She reached for his hand and smiled up at him. He bent his head and whispered in her ear, 'I love you, Georgie Paget. Will you marry me?'

'Shh. . .' She indicated the other occupants of the coach but John and Felicity were whispering with their heads together and her aunt was nodding off again. She smiled. 'Yes, oh, yes, please.' Her beloved Rowan Park was safe, her horses were safe and, best of all, she was safe and Richard loved her. What more could a girl ask?

LEGACY *of* LOVE

Coming next month

A KNIGHT IN WAITING
Juliet Landon

North Yorkshire 1350s

Lady Aletta Markenfield relished the freedom of
widowhood, and found she was good at running her estate.
It was a grief to her that she had proved to be barren, but
otherwise she could not regret the death of her brutal
husband.

The arrival of new neighbour Sir Geraunt de Paine
overturned all her pleasure—the laxity in the wake of the
Black Death meant that some of Sir Geraunt's serfs had
moved to her estate, and Geraunt had no hesitation about
using blackmail! Aletta was faced with equally upsetting
choices—disrupt the fledgling families or become
Geraunt's mistress. Disguising the fact with a betrothal ring
was small comfort…

ADORING ISADORA
Elizabeth Bailey

Regency

Grieving for her father, Isadora Alvescot faced the prospect
of losing her home to Viscount Roborough, a distant family
connection who had become her father's heir. The most she
and her mother, plus assorted dependants, could hope for
was to be allowed to continue to live at Pusay, even though
money would be short.

But the Viscount who arrived was the son, Titus, and he had
some hard decisions to make, whatever he might feel about
Isadora. *Her* madcap scheme to save the family by
becoming an actress, and so avoid *any* obligation to Titus—
despite being so drawn to him—was surely the answer!

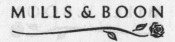

MILLS & BOON

are proud to present...

A set of warm, involving romances in which you can meet some fascinating members of our heroes' and heroines' families. Published each month in the Romance series.

Look out for "A Bittersweet Promise" by Grace Green in October 1995.

Family Ties: Romances that take the family to heart.